THE PRINCESS
AND THE PRIX

By Nell Stark

Running With the Wind

Homecoming

The Princess Affair

All In

The Princess and the Prix

By Nell Stark and Trinity Tam
the everafter series

everafter

nevermore

nightrise

sunfall

Visit us at www.boldstrokesbooks.com

THE PRINCESS
AND THE PRIX

by
Nell Stark

2015

THE PRINCESS AND THE PRIX

ISBN 13: 978-1-62639-474-2

This Trade Paperback Original Is Published By
Bold Strokes Books, Inc.
P.O. Box 249
Valley Falls, NY 12185

First Edition: November 2015

CREDITS
Editor: Cindy Cresap
Production Design: Stacia Seaman
Cover Design by Sheri (graphicartist2020@hotmail.com)

Acknowledgments

Like my Monegasque Princess Alix, I didn't initially have much of an appreciation for Formula One—that is, until I began to research this novel. But the more I watched and read, the more respect I gained for a sport that combines athleticism with technology in a celebration of the limits of human endurance and engineering. Several sources were especially useful during my investigative process: the documentary *1*, about the history of Formula One; the documentary *Senna*, about the life and tragic death of famed Brazilian driver Ayrton Senna; and the book *Rush to Glory*, which chronicles the epic rivalry of drivers James Hunt and Niki Lauda.

Like Formula One, my writing process is unpredictable: sometimes it feels like flying, and sometimes I'm stuck revving on the starting grid. I remain indebted to my wife, Jane, for her inspiration, encouragement, and patience. Our life together brings me so much joy, and our love makes all things possible.

I am also privileged to be a member of the best team in LGBT publishing. My enduring thanks go to Radclyffe for giving me the opportunity to publish with Bold Strokes Books, and I would like to thank all of the hardworking people at BSB—Lee, Sandy, Connie, Lori, Paula, Sheri, and others—for helping to market and release quality product year after year. My fellow BSB authors are a nurturing and inspirational community. I learn so much from you, and am proud to count you in my extended family.

Special thanks go to my editor, Cindy Cresap, who continues to teach me so much about the craft of storytelling. Her helpful and always-witty feedback has been instrumental in my growth as a writer.

Finally, thank you to the many readers who have supported my work throughout the years. This book is for you!

For Jane. Love conquers all.

CHAPTER ONE

Thalia d'Angelis knew she was going to win. She also knew it wouldn't matter. But as she guided her car around the first corner of her penultimate lap, she couldn't afford to indulge in self-pity about her exclusion from yet another season of Formula One. She had to catch and then overtake the man in front of her—some young hotshot whose name she couldn't remember, but who would doubtless be promoted at the end of the year while she languished here.

Swerving through the chicane, she steadily gained on him. He had either misjudged his pit stop or was driving inefficiently, because his tires were wearing out while hers were in good shape. She followed him closely down the straight and watched how he handled the left-handed curve. The best place to pass him was coming soon—a hairpin turn he wouldn't be able to handle as quickly as she could.

As they barreled closer, she watched him hug the inside line. Sensible, since the inside of the track was now filmed over with the rubber laid down by twenty-two cars over the course of almost two hours. It would have more grip, and the closer to bald his tires became, the more grip he needed. She would have to overtake him on the outside, where the track was slipperier.

Anticipating the pain of gravity, Thalia sucked in a quick breath and grit her teeth as she slammed her left foot onto the brake pedal and turned hard into the corner. Lateral force lashed out, battering at her shoulders and neck. The effort of keeping her throbbing head raised caused Thalia's vision to tunnel. Her throat burned in sympathy with her muscles, reminding her of just how long it had been since the pump for her drink bottle had malfunctioned.

But that didn't matter. Nothing did, except making it through this turn on the higher line. Trusting in her tires, and guided by instinct combined with long hours on the simulator, Thalia took her foot off the brake and tapped the accelerator at the apex of the turn. Now, gravity pushed against her chest like a vise, arresting her breath. Her peripheral vision caught sight of the brightly painted exterior of the other car mere inches from her own, before she shot off down the straightaway.

When the vise loosened its grip, she gasped for air. As her peripheral vision returned, so did her urgency. She had to maintain her lead now, and the best way to do so was to stake out the fastest racing line as soon as possible. She didn't think her opponent—what *was* his name?—had a snowball's chance in hell of overtaking her, but to discount the possibility would have been folly.

"Great work there, Thalia." The calm cadence of Dolf's voice over her headset played a sharp counterpoint to the hammering of her heart. "Just keep it clean and you'll be popping the champagne before you know it."

She flicked the button that opened her radio channel. "Will do."

The remainder of the race was satisfyingly dull, as Thalia pulled away from the rest of the field and was shown the checkered flag almost ten whole seconds before anyone else. At the end of her victory lap, she fired up the crowd by doing a few donuts. That kind of stunt would never have been acceptable in Formula One, but since she wasn't there, she didn't care.

After pulling into the first place spot, Thalia robotically followed the post-race protocol. She exited her car, patted it, and then waved to her fans. She entered the stewards' booth and hopped onto the scale that would verify that her weight (coupled with that of her fuel-spent car) had never fallen below the minimum. She wiped her sweaty face with a towel and combed her fingers through her hair in an effort to look less like a drenched weasel and more like the glamorous racecar driver she was supposed to be. The most glamorous driver in the minor leagues.

As she stepped out on the podium, she tried to shrug off her bitterness. It was going to be a long season if she couldn't manage to find any joy in winning the opening race. Thalia knew she wasn't supposed to feel this way: that conventional—and therefore misogynist—wisdom demanded she maintain a positive attitude and keep on keeping on. She had at first believed, and then catered to, that wisdom for years. By now, she was sick and tired of it. No one told men to suck it up and be patient. They were tacitly and explicitly encouraged to be downright aggressive in pursuit of their goals. To suffer no fools and show no mercy and take no prisoners. Why should she behave any differently, just because one key chromosome had an extra leg?

Thalia plastered a smile on her face and half embraced her teammate Martin, who had taken third. Still blanking on the second-place finisher's name, she was relieved when someone called him Didier, and she made an effort at good sportsmanship by shaking his hand. They were joined by the political officials who would distribute the trophies, and by the grid girls who were there to ornament the track. But no matter how many people wished her congratulations, Thalia couldn't shake the uncanny feeling that she was watching herself go through the motions.

When "The Star Spangled Banner" began to play, she sang along. While she could claim dual citizenship with the United Kingdom, Thalia didn't care to see the Union Jack behind her or hear "God Save the Queen." England might be her chosen home now, but she was a product of the American Wild West, born and raised by a mother as beautiful and demanding as the desert. The product of a one-night stand at the U.S. Grand Prix twenty-six years ago, racing was in her blood. Looking back now on the terrible fights she'd had with her mother as an adolescent, Thalia couldn't blame her for trying to steer her toward another course. Instead, she had fought her own War of Independence at sixteen, entering her father's custody. He had promptly shipped her off to boarding school, but he had also allowed her to begin Karting in the summers.

Had he thought it would be a phase? Or was he proud of her accomplishments? Sometimes she believed he didn't think of her at all, unless she was in front of him. He had never seen her as a person, but as a dependent who had to be cared for. Certainly, he had done his duty to the letter of the law, and beyond. But did he care that she had followed in his footsteps?

The anthem ended. The trophies were presented, but the silver cup felt too light as she hoisted it above her head. When the master of ceremonies directed their attention to the magnums of champagne at their feet, she took a long drink before halfheartedly shaking it and spraying the drivers who had come in behind her. They turned to spray the grid girls, but she refrained. Having slept with more than a few of them throughout her career, she knew they only grudgingly accepted a champagne shower as part of the job. It was hell on the eyes.

While Formula One always grabbed someone famous to conduct the post-race interviews—movie stars, models, politicians—GP2 always turned to Eric Fox, the top F1 reporter. As he stepped out onto the stage, Thalia indulged in a few more sips of champagne. He began with Martin, asking him about his strategy in the overtaking move he had pulled off on the last lap to claim third. He then moved to Didier and grilled him about his team's decision to pit earlier than may have been advisable for his tires. Thalia almost felt sorry for him.

And then Fox turned to her. "Thalia d'Angelis! What a way to begin this new season: with a decisive showing on the track that will return to Formula One next year as the French Grand Prix. How do you feel about your performance today?"

"My engineers did a great job of setting up the car," Thalia said, wanting her team to have some slice of the glory. "And we had a solid game plan going in that I managed to execute."

"Indeed you did," said Fox. "Flawlessly." He leaned in closer. "Do you consider this drive a response to the Ferrari bosses for promoting Terrence Delamar above you, despite his inferior record?"

In the weeks leading up to the beginning of the season, Thalia had fielded other questions almost identical to this one. Despite her role as a member of the Ferrari Driving Academy, and despite having won the GP2 driver's championship last season, she had been passed over by the bosses at Marinello—of whom her own father was one—in favor of Terrence, her teammate and the second-place driver. Ever since the decision, she had been seething on the inside while making every effort to remain outwardly supportive of the Tifosi cause. In a one-on-one interview just last week, she had even commended Terrence's driving and wished him luck.

No longer. Fatigued by her first racing effort of the season, and emotionally exhausted by maintaining a friendly and supportive stance despite having been the clear target of chauvinism, Thalia finally lost her cool. The sensation, as she registered it dimly in the back of her burning brain, was oddly refreshing.

"Can I just tell you how sick and tired I am of that goddamn question, Eric?" she asked. "Can't you come up with anything original? I've answered it at least ten times since Ferrari's announcement last month."

When Fox, whom she had clearly caught off guard, began to stammer something in response, she rolled her eyes. "Look. Terrence Delamar is not a better driver than me. He's not even close. His instincts are all wrong—he's too loose when he should be running tight and too tight when he should be loose. Ferrari hired him for what's between his legs, not what's between his shoulders."

The gasps from the audience were audible, but Thalia didn't care. She really didn't. Maybe she would care tomorrow when they fired her—if they even waited that long. But she was going to take a stand, damn it. Right here and now.

Fox was clutching his microphone for dear life, but he managed to recover quickly. "Are you suggesting that Ferrari is a chauvinist organization?"

"Suggesting?" Thalia laughed into her mic without humor. "No. Asserting, yes." She stared out over the murmuring crowd. "I'll probably lose my job over this, but it's true. And it's not just Ferrari, either. The glass ceiling is alive and well in Formula One. Women have the ability to drive at the highest level. We're not there because the owners and team managers—and even some of the other drivers— don't want us to be."

"How can that culture be changed?" Fox pressed. Thalia had to give him credit. He was doggedly persistent and capable of thinking on his feet.

"Honestly, I have no idea. I appreciate the chance to race here in GP2, but that isn't enough anymore. It hasn't been for a while. I've proven myself to be more than capable of racing at the highest level, and I deserve that opportunity." She saluted the crowd with her bottle. "Cheers."

And with one final sip, she ducked inside to meet her fate.

❖

Thalia went straight from the train to Heaven. The underground club, set below the Charing Cross railway station in the heart of

London, was the perfect place to get lost, get drunk, get laid, and start the process of getting on with her life.

Thalia knew the owner and the bouncers, and she could always count on getting in immediately. Better still, because the club held almost two thousand people, she generally managed to maintain her anonymity. Tonight, as she slipped through the massive doors, the groans of the plebians who had been waiting in the lengthy queue followed her inside. She felt guilty for all of five seconds before the thunder of the electronic music drowned out her discomfort.

First stop: the bar. She found a narrow sliver of space at the far corner and caught her favorite bartender's eye. Billy might have looked like he had just come from a boring desk job had his Oxford shirt not been cut off at the shoulders to reveal the perfect musculature of his tattooed arms.

He ducked in close to her. "Hey, T." He never used her full name in an effort to help her fly below the radar, and she loved him for it. "You were a stupendous badass yesterday. They're bloody imbeciles."

"Thanks." She pointed to a spot on his forearm that hadn't been filled in the last time she'd been here. "The new ink looks good."

"Smooth talker." He threaded a fresh towel through one low-slung belt buckle. "One Flaming Gaytini, I presume?"

"You know me well."

"Art imitates life," he said with a wink before swaggering off to mix the drink.

Thalia looked down the length of the bar. As usual, it was populated mostly by men, but the occasional pair or small group of women had staked out space for themselves. Thalia had no intention of spending the night alone, but neither was she in a hurry. Despite the first place trophy having been shipped to her flat to join its place with the rest of her meaningless mementos, she had descended from the train feeling more defeated and disillusioned than ever.

The drink arrived, and Billy carefully floated Bacardi 151 on top before setting the liquid afire with his lighter. "Always reminds me of a phoenix." He shot her a crooked smile. "Will life imitate art?"

The phoenix: a legendary bird that, when it died, was consumed in self-immolation only to hatch again and rise from its own ashes. Billy was trying to inspire her, but all Thalia could think of was how exhausting it must be for the poor, mythical avian to cobble itself back together out of cinders. Still, he was always kind to her. She couldn't let him down.

"Sure," she said and raised her glass. "Cheers."

The blue flames flickering from its mouth had attracted the attention of a group of passers-by who wanted to know what the concoction was called and how to order one. A few decided to be so bold, and for several minutes, Billy had his work cut out for him. But one woman kept looking over her shoulder at Thalia, and then just as quickly looking away when their eyes met. Thalia continued sipping calmly but feared she had been recognized.

Sure enough, once the woman had her drink in hand, she approached. Strawberry blond and freckled, wearing a stretchy white T-shirt that clung to her torso and clearly revealed her lack of a bra, she managed to seem at once sexy and wholesome.

"You're Thalia d'Angelis," she said.

"I am." Intrigued that someone not a regular at the club would be able to recognize her from one brief encounter, Thalia made just enough room at the bar for them to stand side by side, shoulders touching. "And you are?"

"Danielle Collins. You can call me Dani." Her words had a subtle Australian accent to them. Less subtle was the way she leaned her shoulder against Thalia's—not that she minded. "The video of your post-race speech is viral, did you know?"

Thalia nodded. Her agent had called to break the news while she was on the train. He had been so upset with her that she had fired him on the spot. Why not? She wasn't going to get another job in GP2, and Formula One might as well be the moon. Her future was about as bright as its dark side. Blackballed from motorsport, what could she do? Racing had always been her life. She was a one-trick pony.

"You're a fucking hero."

Dani's adulation roused her from the spiral of pity into which she had allowed herself to descend. She was now the second person to praise Thalia, presumably for her courage in standing up to "the man," as embodied by Ferrari. Racing might no longer be an option, but perhaps she could do advocacy work?

Thalia almost snorted into her martini. Advocacy work? She didn't want to be some pretty, quasi-famous chess piece in the struggle for civil rights. She wanted to push the boundaries of speed. She wanted to stand on the top step of an F1 podium and force the world to admit they'd been wrong about her place in it. Now, all of those dreams were out of reach.

The warmth of Dani's forearm pressed against hers reminded Thalia that not *everything* was out of reach. "I'm glad you think so," she said.

For the rest of the night, she wanted to forget all about the chauvinist bullshit and focus on enjoying the company of another woman. And unless she was completely misreading Dani's touchy-feelyness, she was interested in the same thing.

As a test case, Thalia leaned into Dani's space, positioning her mouth a fraction of an inch away from Dani's ear. The light shiver that greeted her movements was an excellent sign. "I think we need some flaming shots to complement our flaming martinis. You?"

"Oh, yes."

She signaled to Billy, who approached them within seconds. "What can I do for you, ladies?"

"We need a round of shots that are on fire."

He laughed. "I know just the thing."

Within minutes, Billy had them licking sugar off each other's wrists and knocking back a concoction that tasted like butterscotch. As soon as Thalia triumphantly slammed her glass onto the bar, Dani flung her arms around Thalia's neck and kissed her. Thalia responded automatically, kissing her with equal force and turning Dani so her back was pressed against the bar. Better friction that way. When the onlookers nearby erupted into hollers and catcalls, Thalia gave them the finger with one hand while cupping Dani's butt with the other.

When Dani's hand snaked between their bodies to tweak Thalia's nipple, Thalia pulled back with a laugh. "Feisty, aren't you?"

"Don't tell me you're complaining," Dani said, licking her lips.

"Not by a long shot." Thalia tilted her head toward the bar. "Another?"

After their second round, Thalia managed to claim a barstool for Dani, and in between bouts of kissing and fondling, they finished their drinks. As much as Thalia wanted to get utterly shit-faced, she was here alone and couldn't afford to be that vulnerable. Besides, she had ulterior motives for the evening that involved remaining semi-functional. So when Billy asked if she wanted a refill of her Gaytini, she forced herself to say no and to close out her tab instead.

When she returned from signing the receipt, Thalia rested both hands on the chair on either side of Dani's thighs and leaned in close. "Do you have a bedroom of your own?"

Dani's eyes widened and she nodded. "My flat's in Fulham and my roommate's going home with her boyfriend tonight."

"Perfect. Once you've finished with that"—Thalia indicated Dani's drink—"why don't you take me home with you."

Dani raised the glass to her mouth and downed it in three long swallows. Thalia, beguiled by the inviting expanse of her neck, trailed a series of kisses up to her ear and flicked lightly at the freckled lobe.

"Ready?"

"God, yes."

As Dani hopped down, Thalia tossed a fifty-pound note onto the bar. She might end up poor as a church mouse now that she would be blackballed from motorsport, but tonight she wanted to live generously.

The half-hour odyssey to Dani's flat was spent scandalizing the other Tube riders. Dani spent the ride curled up against Thalia's side, provocatively stroking up and down the inner seams of her jeans while Thalia kissed her languorously. Three separate times, people entered the train and rode one stop with them, only to switch to another car as soon as possible. Thalia couldn't understand why they didn't stay and watch, but that was their business.

By the time they reached Dani's stop, Thalia's desire had been honed to a razor's edge. After so much teasing, all she could think about was getting Dani naked and then reciprocating. She planned to make her wait, no matter how much begging she might resort to.

The lift in Dani's building was old and narrow, featuring one of those metal accordion doors. As soon as Thalia pulled it shut, Dani was pressing her to the wall, hands on her shoulders and mouth on her neck. Automatically, Thalia's arms circled her waist.

"You're so fucking hot."

This was a sentiment Thalia had heard before, and she never knew how to reply. Instead, she ran her fingers through Dani's hair and pulled her closer, hoping her actions would speak louder than words. When Dani groaned softly and circled her hips, Thalia knew her tactic had worked. She let her hands trail down Dani's spine and then beneath the hem of her shirt, sighing in pleasure when her fingertips found soft, warm skin. Touching another woman was always such a lovely and gratifying odyssey of discovery.

The lift lurched to a halt and Dani grabbed her hand, pulling her into the hallway. As soon as they were inside, Thalia backed her up against the wall. Panting with need, she forced herself to slow down temporarily.

"This okay?" She always made it a point to ask, though she would have bet all her savings on Dani's affirmative answer.

"Yes," Dani breathed.

Thalia smiled. "Good. Then let's get rid of this." She tugged at the hem of Dani's shirt and was gratified by how quickly she divested herself of it. Her breasts were full and firm and tipped with nipples the color of dusky rose petals that hardened as Thalia feasted her eyes. "You're beautiful."

"I want to see you." But when Dani began to undress her, Thalia took one step back. She wanted to be firmly in control of this situation.

"I'll let you. But only if you stand there with your palms against the wall and don't move."

"Oh fuck," Dani murmured, and Thalia knew she had judged correctly that Dani didn't want to be the aggressor in this encounter.

Thalia took her time ridding herself of her shirt, but her own need incited her to shed her bra quickly. When she stepped forward again, Dani's arms began to extend until she apparently remembered the rules. She slapped her palm against the wall in clear frustration, but moaned loudly when Thalia captured both nipples between her fingers.

"How about this? Okay?"

"Better than o—*oh*." Dani's hips bucked as Thalia pinched lightly. "Yes, fuck yes."

Thalia played with them gently, thrilling to the sounds of Dani's labored breaths and truncated moans. When she slid her thigh between Dani's legs, she moaned again.

"Harder," Dani whispered without opening her eyes. "You can— oh!"

Completely intoxicated by the sounds of Dani's passion, Thalia lowered her head to swallow the rest of her exclamation in a kiss. She alternated the pressure of her fingers—teasing, always teasing—until Dani was writhing against her in a desperate effort to get some relief.

Thalia dropped to one knee and stroked up and down Dani's fly. "May I?"

Dani nodded frantically. "Yours too."

Thalia peeled the pants down Dani's legs and then shucked off her own jeans, throwing both across the room where they landed on the sofa. She turned back to the sight of Dani, clad only in her black bikini underwear, a beautiful flush spreading down her neck and across her freckled chest.

"Gorgeous," Thalia breathed, and leaned in to kiss her stomach.

And then her phone rang, chirping out the ringtone that meant she didn't have the number on file. It was after midnight on a Saturday. Who could be calling her now that she didn't know?

"Is that you?" Dani asked breathlessly.

"Forget it. Don't worry about it." Thalia nipped at the skin below Dani's navel, cursing herself for not turning the damn thing off earlier. Once it stopped making noise, she gripped Dani's restless hips and held her in place, tormenting her with sucking kisses along her rib cage and on her thighs.

As she began to edge Dani's underwear down her abdomen, her phone rang again. After a moment's hesitation, Thalia decided to pretend it didn't exist. Still on one knee, she looked up to meet Dani's eyes. "I want to take these off."

"Please," was all Dani said.

Grinning, Thalia gripped the hem with her teeth and tugged, enjoying the sound of Dani's giggles. Sex was supposed to be fun, and finding a partner who felt the same was always a treat. Once she had divested Dani of the scrap of fabric, Thalia leaned in, parting her folds with both thumbs and massaging lightly. Dani's labored breaths and hitching moans were music to her ears. Who cared what the rest of the world thought of her? Right now, she was a goddess.

The phone rang a third time, shattering the moment. Unease blossomed in Thalia's chest, and she sat back on her heels. Had something happened to a family member, or at her apartment?

"You should probably get that." Dani breathlessly vocalized her thoughts. "It sounds like it might be an emergency."

"Yeah. I'm so sorry." Cursing under her breath, Thalia pulled away and stumbled across the room. She fished her phone out of her pants pocket and stared at the unfamiliar number on the display before stabbing at it with her thumb.

"Hello?"

"I'm calling for Alistair Campbell," said a female voice with an Irish accent. "Please hold."

Alistair Campbell. The name was familiar, but Thalia's fuzzy brain couldn't immediately place it. He must be someone important, though, because the woman was clearly his assistant.

"Who is it?" Dani called. She was now sitting on the floor, her back against the slice of wall to which Thalia had pinned her.

"Not a clue. Just hang on for a few minutes. Promise I'll make it up to you."

Dani lowered one hand to her inner thigh and began to stroke herself provocatively. "I want you to drive me hard and fast and—"

Drive. The pieces flew together, and Thalia's brain exploded when she realized that Alistair Campbell was none other than the manager for Petrol Macedonia, the newest Formula One team. An upstart organization owned and bankrolled by a British earl, they had defied all expectations last year by coming in third in points in the Constructors' Championship. And when Aiglon Motors had stupidly decided to let Peter Taggart go, Petrol Macedonia had snapped him up in a heartbeat. Now, with Peter and another former world champion, Luiz Serra, as their drivers, they had a shot at making a legitimate run for the title this year.

But why would Alistair be calling her, especially after she had opened her big mouth in France? The only logical assumption was that he needed a test driver, but surely there were many other contenders.

"Thalia, hello," he said, his syllables clipped and his tone brooking no nonsense.

"It's a pleasure to be speaking with you, Mr. Campbell." Thalia prayed she sounded sober.

He didn't apologize for the lateness of the hour, or for instructing his assistant to blow up her phone until she answered it. All he said was, "I'd like you to consider joining Petrol Macedonia as our number two driver, behind Peter Taggart."

Thalia sat down hard in the chair over which she had thrown her pants. She suddenly couldn't catch her breath, and tiny spots of darkness darted across the field of her vision like minnows across the surface of a pond.

Alistair Campbell was offering her a job in Formula One.

Thirty seconds ago, she had believed she would never be welcome at another Grand Prix circuit. Now, she was being offered her dream job—and not by a team at the bottom of the table, but by a team with the potential to legitimately contest the championship. But Campbell had said she would be joining Peter, not Serra. What had happened to him?

"I'm very interested in your offer," she managed to say. "But last I heard, Luiz Serra was your second driver. Has something changed?"

There was a brief moment of silence. "We've not yet made this information available to the public, but he has decided to pursue Indy Car racing in America this season. We would prefer to have his replacement decided upon before the press release."

Thalia had so many questions, but most of them boiled down to *Why me?* and that wasn't particularly productive when you didn't want the person offering you your dream job to second-guess his decision.

"I see," she said, pressing one palm over her heart in an effort to calm its galloping. "I'm very interested, but of course I'll need to see all the details of the offer."

"Of course. Are you free tomorrow? If so, I'd like to bring you out to headquarters so you can meet Sir Alexander, Peter, and our engineers."

"I'm free."

After hammering out the logistical details of their meeting, he signed off rather brusquely and hung up. Thalia leaned forward in the chair, clutching her phone for dear life. What on earth had just happened? Was she dreaming? Surreptitiously, she pinched the skin above her wrist. It stung.

This was real.

"What's going on, baby?" Dani called from across the room. "Are you okay?"

The unwelcome term of endearment melted the haze from Thalia's thoughts. Immediately, one thing became clear: there was no way she could stay here tonight. She had to return to her own flat and do as much research as possible into Petrol Macedonia before trying to get at least a few hours' sleep.

For the first time in her life, she didn't have time for sex.

"I'm fine. But I can't stay. I'm sorry."

"Not even for just a few more minutes?" Dani's voice was breathy, and her hand was circling rapidly. "I'm so ready. Touch me and you'll find out."

She was gorgeous and sensual and responsive…and right now, she was a distraction. Thalia was self-aware enough to know that if she obliged Dani, she would get caught up. Now, more than any other time in her life, she had to remain focused. The dream was in reach. Nothing else mattered.

"You're beautiful," she said as she hurriedly tugged on her pants. "And I feel like an ass for having to leave. I wouldn't go if I didn't have to."

"Your loss," Dani gasped.

It was incredibly awkward—and frustrating—to walk past her on the way out. As Thalia waited for the elevator, the thin cry of Dani's climax reached her, and her own body tightened in unfulfilled desire. She didn't believe in delaying gratification, and now her lack of practice was working against her. She might be her own worst enemy, but there was nothing she wanted more than Formula One.

Thalia wasn't going to let anything get in her way. Including herself.

CHAPTER TWO

Her Serene Highness Princess Pommelina Alix Louise Canella felt like a stranger in her own sitting room. She had always been the odd child, set apart from her siblings by a preference for books over ball gowns and studying over soirees. But exceptions to the rule had their place, and for the most part, she had been content to accept hers on the fringe of her family. Now, as she perched on the sofa beside her older sister and sipped at her espresso, she felt a jarring sense of dissociation.

Only yesterday, she had departed by horseback at sunrise from the tiny *manyata* in northeastern Uganda where she had spent the past three months doing fieldwork. February was planting season, and in between running her clinic, she had pitched in to help with the backbreaking work. How could she not? Farming was the work of women and children there, while the men drove their cattle far across the plateau in search of food and water. Claude and Eric, the two men in her security detail, had been strange to the villagers not for the color of their skin, but for their insistence on remaining in the community, at her side.

Balancing the bone china saucer on her knee, Alix rubbed a thumb across the calluses on her palm, ears ringing with the songs the women had sung in the fields. Even the frothy surface of her espresso reminded her of the colors of the savannah, its sere plains waiting anxiously for the spring rains. The dusty, arid breeze had chapped her lips and coated her lungs, lending her voice an unfamiliar, gritty quality. Now, the cool, moist air of Monaco soothed her parched throat, fooling her body back into complacence. Were she to go to the window and pull aside the heavy brocade curtains, the familiar, sparkling expanse of the Mediterranean would greet her, its surface reflecting the sky. All her life, she had taken it for granted. What was that verse from the Bible? *For now we see through a glass, darkly; but then face to face.*

She drained her demitasse and set it aside, where it was removed within moments by a swift, silent member of the palace staff. Across the low marble table, her father was parceling out royal duties for the coming months. Florestan, who for years had been more interested in enjoying his A-list status as much as possible, had recently become more interested in his role as hereditary prince. In his relief, their father had begun to increase his royal duties, and Florestan was already beginning to shoulder the burden of certain affairs of state. He had also recently begun dating Princess Monique of Luxembourg, and their mother made it no secret that she hoped this relationship resulted in marriage and several grandchildren. Alix thought of all the babies she had delivered over the past few months—children brought into a world that revolved around cattle, not casinos. Florestan's child, by a mere accident of birth, would never want for food or water or health care.

Guilt swept through her, leaving nausea in its wake. Her eyes were open now, yet here she sat in the lap of luxury, breakfast roiling in her stomach while women across the Karamoja labored under the pounding sun, bellies taut with hunger. Her presence among them had made a difference in small ways, but she wanted to do more. Last night, alone in her own space for the first time in months, floating on a mattress that felt like a cloud and cocooned in sheets scented with lavender, she had tossed and turned. Finally, she had gone to her desk and read article after article on humanitarian efforts in East Africa. Some of the organizations were familiar to her, but others she knew nothing about. The Princess of Wales was also apparently interested in the region, and Alix had been intrigued by reports of her efforts to stimulate economic development through micro-financing initiatives aimed at women.

Watching the slow progress of dawn across the surface of the sea, she had felt suddenly empowered by a fierce conviction that now was the time to *do* something. Thus far, she had devoted her adult life to studying medicine and the law, but now it was time to set the books aside and act. With three degrees to her name and the access and connections afforded by her royal pedigree, she could muster the necessary resources to create a foundation of her own. Not one to merely pay lip service to, as Florestan did in his patronage of marine conservation and Camille in her support of Monegasque cultural heritage.

"Are we almost finished, Father?" Camille's bored, soprano voice sliced through Alix's introspection. "I have an appointment."

Their father looked up from his leather bound notebook with a stern expression. "Since it isn't on our official calendar, it can surely wait a few minutes longer."

Camille sat back with a huff. As she almost certainly had an appointment at the spa or salon, Alix didn't feel an ounce of sympathy.

"However," he continued, "you will be relieved to hear that there is only one item left on our agenda: the British Princess Royal's... ceremony." His upper lip curled as he spoke the word.

Princess Sasha, second in line to the British throne, would marry her fiancée later this year—Alix wasn't sure when, exactly. Staunchly Roman Catholic, her father had been clear about his disapproval since Sasha had publicly come out as a lesbian. Even as same-sex marriage advanced across Western Europe, Monaco remained a bastion of social conservatism. Alix, for whom science was religion, thought the whole controversy rather silly.

Their mother, silent until now, shook her head in clear dismay. "That poor girl has been a lost soul since her mother's death. Why does her father allow her to flaunt herself in this way?"

"Sasha has never understood the value of discretion," Florestan said.

Florestan's hypocrisy was hard to swallow, but he had a point. Even Alix, who didn't care about celebrity gossip, had heard reports of Sasha's hedonist lifestyle. They hadn't crossed paths in years, since before Alix had gone to study in America. She couldn't recall the exact occasion, but it was impossible not to remember how Sasha had outshone every woman in the room—including Camille.

"She could have any man she likes," Camille chimed in, her tone caught between jealousy and admiration.

Alix was tempted to retort that logically, that was entirely beside the point for someone who preferred women. Fortunately, their father curtailed any further discussion by returning his attention to the calendar.

"The ceremony is in London in three weeks' time, and one of us must represent the family. Florestan will be at the Oceanographic Institute's conservation summit, and the twins, of course, must prepare for their exams."

"I need to be here to open the Garden Club's first flower show of the year," said Camille.

"Very well." Their father scribbled a note while Alix tried to get over her surprise. Camille was turning down an invitation to a party? "I will ask one of your cousins to—"

"I'll go."

Silence, as every head turned in her direction, each face registering surprise.

"You will?" said Florestan.

"Seriously?" said Camille.

"How wonderful!" Initially thrilled, their mother suddenly clasped her hands. "But you have nothing to wear! I'll call for one of the tailors immediately."

Their father was regarding her intently. "You're quite certain, Pomme? I know you prefer to avoid these kinds of large social gatherings."

The nickname she'd been saddled with since infancy grated on her ears, but Alix tried to mask her annoyance. "I won't embarrass you, Father," she said, working to make light of the situation. "And yes, I'm sure. I'll turn it into a business trip. The Princess of Wales has a charity that is very active in East Africa and I'd like to speak with her about—"

The wood-paneled door swung open with a loud creak. "Madam, you wish to see me?"

Felicite, the younger of the two royal tailors, stood framed in the gap. Dressed in a black and white checkered suit that had doubtless been created by a designer Alix had never heard of, she radiated a compassionately judgmental aura—as if her calling in life was to painstakingly educate the aristocracy on the changing landscape of the avant-garde in fashion.

"Yes, so good of you to come quickly." Alix watched her mother meet Felicite halfway across the room, gesture in her direction, and begin to confer in hushed tones.

And that was that—a description of her charity work eclipsed by the royal tailor. Alix couldn't say she was surprised. Fortunately, after so many years of disinterest from her family, the slight barely stung. Alix had faced the facts long ago: she was much more productive when she was neither seen nor heard.

❖

Petrol Macedonia's corporate park sprawled over five hundred thousand square meters on a plateau overlooking the Ribble estuary in western England. The office of Sir Alexander Rufford, seventh Earl of Rufford and company founder, looked out over the network of small streams branching out from the River Ribble like the tendrils of a jellyfish. Beyond them, the Irish Sea stretched to the horizon—now blue, now gray, as clouds streamed across the face of the sun. Thalia sat at the conference table, watching their shadows race along the distant marshland and trying not to fidget. A manila folder containing what she presumed to be her contract rested on the glossy surface only a few feet out of her reach, and in the far corner of the room, three bottles of champagne were chilling in a bucket stand. So long as she didn't make a mistake within the next few minutes, their popped corks would herald her long-awaited triumph.

To her left sat Peter Taggart, three-time Formula One champion and her new teammate. Peter's hair was tinged with silver at his temples, but otherwise he looked much as he had for all the years he had been her idol. His square-jawed, rugged good looks had not diminished with age, and he was just as fierce a competitor as he had been at the height of his career. From their first meeting at one of her father's dinner parties, Peter had always been kind to her. He had also been among the few to take her seriously as a driver early on, going so far as to keep tabs on her Karting career and offer her the occasional piece of advice. When Aiglon Motors had jettisoned him after one rocky season in favor of rising star Lucas Mountjoy, she had lost a large chunk of respect for them. Fortunately, Peter had landed on his feet at Petrol Macedonia, having exceeded all expectations by coming in third place last year— quite the feat for an organization brand new to F1. And now he was her teammate.

Teammate. The familiar thrill shot up her spine. She was about to be a Formula One driver. How long had she dreamed, how hard had she worked, how much had she hoped? And now it was a reality.

Surreptitiously, she took stock of the man to her right: Alistair Campbell, team manager and world champion driver in his own right. Alistair was a contemporary of her father's but nothing like him. Naturally reticent, he radiated a quiet intensity at all times but shunned the spotlight. Thalia wondered how much convincing he had needed to offer the second seat to her.

Behind the large, polished desk, Sir Alexander was expressing his displeasure with the person who had called in the middle of their conference. He scowled at the screen of his computer, the blinking blue light on his earpiece keeping time with the tic beneath his right eye. Like every other corporate executive she had ever met, he was always stressed and sought out high-adrenaline hobbies as therapy. His F1 team might not be one of the venerable dynasties of motorsport, but he was passionate about racing, smart enough to hire good people, and most importantly, wealthy.

"By end of day," he barked into the phone. "Otherwise, no deal." He hung up, and his expression cleared as he returned to the table. "Now, where were we?"

"You were just stroking Thalia's ego," Peter said with a grin. Unlike everyone else she had seen today, he treated Rufford more like an equal than like the man whose munificence made it possible for them to race. Last year's performance on top of his already stellar record may have earned him that right, but she was unproven and needed to mind her p's and q's. Especially until she signed the contract he was about to offer. Still, meek and mild was not in her nature.

"Jealous?" she fired back at him.

"Me? Jealous of you?" He flashed perfect white teeth in a mocking grin.

"I'm glad to see you two get along so well," Alistair said dryly. "Let's hope it extends to the track."

"Is there a particular strategy that you have in mind for this season?" Thalia asked, partially because she wanted to know his philosophy for the team, and partially to show him she could be serious.

"The only strategy I know is to win." He paused to look between them. "We're fairly confident in the performance of the cars. Theoretically, we have a fair shot at the Constructors' Championship."

The Constructors' Championship, awarded to the team to win the most points between their two drivers, was the prize sought after by a team manager. Often, the team that won the Constructors' Championship included the individual who won the World Championship, but not always. Alistair's taciturnity may or may not have been for the sake of diplomacy. Peter might be the team's first driver and she the second, but depending on skill and the vicissitudes of fate, she could outperform him once the season began. There had been years when both members of a team were competing for the World Championship title, and that often got ugly, with teammates forcing each other off the track, or capitalizing on each other's weaknesses rather than working together. In some cases, such high jinks had cost teams the Constructors' Cup. But even if they did both end up in title contention, Thalia would never throw Peter under the bus and was reasonably sure he wouldn't turn on her either.

"When Peter suggested you for our second seat, I initially had my doubts," Rufford said. "But then I watched a few of your races and asked Alistair to do the same. You're skilled, you're scrappy, and you're hungry for the podium. We're still the underdog, and we need those qualities in our drivers."

His candor roused her defensiveness, but she pushed it aside to focus on the positives. He was willing to give her a chance. Right now, that was all that mattered. "With all due respect, Lord Rufford, for years now, I've watched every male colleague who even approaches my winning record get promoted to Formula One. I have something better than a dick to swing around: I have a score to settle. I belong in F1 and will consider it an honor to hitch my rising star to yours." She held out one hand, praying it wouldn't tremble and betray her nerves. "Shall I sign to make it official?"

Silence. Drawing on all her experience keeping calm in the cockpit, she met his gaze without flinching. Finally, he smiled and pushed the manila folder to her side of the table. "My wife is going to like you."

Peter laughed. Alistair looked down at the tabletop. Thalia paused in the act of uncapping her fountain pen, alert to the presence of what could be a rhetorical trap. "I look forward to meeting Lady Rufford," she said carefully.

"Like you, she is formidable. And she is a great champion of women's and children's rights across the globe. She may well want you to serve as a spokesperson."

Thalia wondered whether they would be having this same

conversation if she were male. Well-intentioned misogyny was still misogyny. "I'd be happy to," she said, even as she hoped that Lady Rufford might find her an unpalatable spokeswoman and leave her to focus on driving.

"Go on and sign it, then," Rufford said, "so we can enjoy this very fine champagne."

Thalia's fingers closed around the barrel of her pen. It had been a gift from her mother and she had only used it once before—to sign the paperwork on the apartment she owned in London. Flipping through the contract, she initialed each page and then signed at the end. When it was done, she sat staring at her signature—the autograph of the seventh woman ever to claim the status of Formula One driver. None of her predecessors had ever won a race, or even come close to standing on a podium. Silently, she vowed to be the first to do both.

CHAPTER THREE

Thalia hated being driven by other people. Unable to relax into the leather embrace of the Rolls Royce, she tapped one foot against the immaculate mat, prompting a curious glance from her "plus one." Maeve Moynihan, Irish-born actress on a newly popular British sitcom, was about to make a splash, but if she felt anxious, she gave no sign.

"Nervous?" Maeve asked, resting one hand briefly atop Thalia's.

"Impatient," Thalia said. "I prefer to drive myself."

"Of course you do," Maeve said with a laugh. "But you couldn't make this car go any faster even if you were behind the wheel."

She had a point. The approach to Westminster Abbey was lined with people waving Union Jacks and rainbow flags. Police were stationed regularly along the route, directing traffic with crisp, efficient, utterly British movements. Thalia tried to push down her restlessness and enjoy the view. The first gay royal wedding ever in the history of the world, and she had been invited. She might not be the most modest person on earth, but that plain fact was humbling.

When the pale façade of the cathedral came into view, Maeve leaned across the seat to adjust Thalia's narrow tie. "Have I mentioned yet today how good you look?"

Thalia was certain that plenty of media outlets wouldn't see it that way, but she refused to be apologetic about her choice of formalwear. The world would be watching, and today, she wanted to remind them of her queerness.

"You're pretty spectacular yourself," Thalia said, not only because that was the expected response, but also because it was true. Maeve's dark blue dress clung to her slim figure, and its deep neckline allowed the string of sapphires around her neck to stand out against her pale, freckled skin.

As soon as she followed Thalia out of the car, the media would have a field day. Thalia's sexual orientation was ancient history, but Maeve would be the latest in a succession of women to use their dating relationship as a springboard for coming out. Thalia didn't mind; it only enhanced her reputation. And she was almost positive that she could trust Maeve not to fall in love with her, which made their dynamic so much more relaxed.

When the car began to decelerate, Thalia caught and held Maeve's gaze. "You sure?"

"Never more certain."

"Here goes." As soon as the car stopped, Thalia opened the door and stepped out. The snap, crackle, pop of a dozen flashbulbs punctuated the shouts, cheers, and boos from the crowd. Fleetingly, she wondered whether the latter were motivated by her sexual orientation or her affiliation with Petrol Macedonia, before she turned to assist Maeve from the vehicle. Silently, she counted down to the audience's inevitable gasp. They reacted right on cue, and for one precarious moment, she struggled to school her features.

"Is that Maeve Moynihan?"

"Maeve, are you a lesbian?"

"Are you two dating?"

"How long have you been together?"

"How did you meet?"

As the horde of journalists, bristling with microphones, surged forward, the police formed a loose circle around them. Thalia murmured her thanks as the escort cleared a path to the entrance. The tall wooden doors whooshed shut behind them like gigantic wings. Blinking hard to adjust her vision to the dim lighting, she squeezed Maeve's hand.

"All right?"

"I think so. Even knowing what to expect, it was rather overwhelming."

"You can never know what to expect." When Thalia realized that some bitterness had crept into her tone, she forced a quick smile. "Except for the talk show invitations. You'll have more of those in the next week than before a film premiere."

"I'm ready. I wouldn't have come with you today if I wasn't."

"Outing yourself at the first gay royal wedding. How apropos." Thalia turned to face the impassive Beefeaters guarding the entrance to the nave. "Good morning, gentlemen."

A short, stout man in royal livery stepped out of their shadow. "Good morning, ma'am. May I inspect your invitations?"

Thalia handed over the embossed note card, smothering a flash of resentment that she wasn't recognizable enough to dispense with the security precaution. Not yet. But she would be.

"Thank you. You may be seated in any row that is not marked as reserved. Should you like an escort to assist you—"

"We'll be fine, thanks."

"Very well." The man murmured into a wrist microphone, and a moment later, the double doors swung open.

Thalia had been inside Westminster Abbey before, of course— once as a reluctant child-tourist, and once as an even more reluctant adolescent on a school-sponsored trip. Despite her lack of enthusiasm on both occasions, she had marveled at the pale columns that jutted out of the earth like the skeletal remains of a massive creature. The Abbey lived in her memory as monochromatic, but today, it exploded with color. Rows of flowers lined the central and side aisles, dazzling the eye and scenting the air: red roses, orange lilies, yellow sunflowers, blue hydrangeas, and violets the shade of summer twilight. All the colors of the rainbow.

And then she laughed. The rainbow. Of course.

"What is it?"

"Just admiring Sasha's choice of floral arrangements."

"Oh! I see it. Clever." Maeve took her arm. "Where shall we sit?"

"Along the central aisle, if we can. That will make for the best people-watching."

They found a suitable place halfway to the sanctuary, but getting there proved to be rather an odyssey. Maeve paused to exchange greetings with two different actors, and then Thalia caught sight of her father. She had known he would be here, of course, but had hoped— perhaps unrealistically—to avoid him. He looked exceptionally British today in a charcoal morning coat and blue tie, his artificially dark hair neatly swept back from his forehead save for one errant strand. Beside him stood his wife, shimmering in a silver floor-length gown, her platinum-blond head crowned by a thoroughly ridiculous, vaguely aquatic-looking hat. The longer Thalia stared at it, the more it resembled a besequined octopus caught in the act of sucking out her brains. After acknowledging them with a slight nod, she looked away.

"That's your father, isn't it? And your stepmother? Shouldn't we say hello?"

Mildly annoyed by Maeve's use of "we," Thalia picked up her pace. "No."

"All right then," Maeve said peevishly under her breath, but Thalia pretended that she hadn't heard.

Once they took their seats, the conversation naturally turned toward the other guests. Thalia spotted several football stars and two other F1 drivers before her attention was arrested by a tall, red-haired man who strode smiling up the aisle, comically outpacing his escort. His dark suit was punctuated by the orange sash across his snowy white shirt.

"Is that the crown prince of the Netherlands?"

"Oh! Prince Ernst!" Maeve seemed seriously in danger of running out into the aisle after him.

Thalia shot her an amused glance. "Does someone have a crush?"

She colored. "I told you when we first met that I'm bi—"

"And did I bat an eyelash? No. Relax. I'm just teasing. Maybe you can get on his dance card later." Thalia turned to keep him in view, but rather than sitting in one of the roped off front rows, he carried on into the sanctuary beyond.

"Looks like the royal guests will be sitting in the choir," Maeve said.

"And probably some of the family members too, I'd guess." Thalia craned her neck in an effort to see all the way to the high altar where, presumably, the vows would take place. Only then did she notice the two large projection screens flanking the choir area. It seemed that Sasha and Kerry cared enough about the "plebs" at their wedding to want to make the particulars of the ceremony viewable to all. Not even her golden child older brother Arthur, dubbed "the world's favorite prince," had thought to make such a provision at his own ceremony two years prior. Thalia had watched that one from a hotel room in Belgium where she had been test-driving Ferrari's newest car on the Spa Francorchamps circuit.

Her introspection was interrupted by the arrival of another royal, whom neither she nor Maeve recognized. Fortunately, the Americans sitting behind them excitedly referred to her as Princess Monique of Luxembourg. She was followed a few minutes later by the Belgian Prince Sebastian, who was in turn succeeded by an Asian woman in a pearl-studded gown. Word spread through the crowd that she was the eldest daughter of the king of Japan, but no one knew her name.

The nave was nearly full, and the ceremony only ten minutes away, when Thalia noticed the woman in the green dress. She walked slowly, face upturned, staring avidly into the cathedral's arches. Wavy auburn hair fell to her collarbone, below which a string of emeralds adorned her tanned skin. So intense was her expression that Thalia looked up, but saw nothing remarkable. Was she simply admiring the architecture? And did she realize that she was about to cross the invisible line separating those of royal blood from the rest of the populace?

But instead of triggering a security response, the woman was allowed to pass unchallenged behind the lattice, gold-plated screen separating the nave from the choir area. When neither she nor Maeve could identify her, Thalia turned to consult the Americans. One of them, a tall man, flushed and fidgeting, set off her gaydar. The other, a Latina woman, seemed much calmer (and probably straight).

"Do you know who that was?" she asked them.

"One of the princesses of Monaco, I think," said the woman. "Do you remember her name, Harris?"

"Excuse me?" Harris, who had been rather blatantly ogling Manchester United's goalkeeper, refocused on his companion with evident effort. "I didn't catch what you said."

"The woman who just walked by—she's a Monegasque princess, right? Do you know which one?"

His broad brow furrowed in thought. "Not Camille—she's a platinum blonde and would've worn something much more revealing. And Soraphine, the female twin, has dark, curly hair. So that must've been the princess in the middle. Keeps a fairly low profile, and I'm embarrassed to admit that I can't remember her name. It begins with a P, I think."

"It must be Pommelina." Maeve was peering at her phone. "That's the only option."

He snapped his fingers. "Right! Pommelina. I'm surprised she's here. She doesn't get out much."

Thalia couldn't believe the amount of useless information he had in his head. "Are you an expert on the royals?"

"An expert? Oh no. I just enjoy following celebrit—" Suddenly, he grabbed the woman's shoulder as if she were the only thing keeping him upright. "Oh my God! You're Thalia d'Angelis!"

"Guilty as charged." Pleased he had recognized her, she stuck out one hand. "And you're Harris…?"

He pumped it enthusiastically. "Whistler. Harrison Whistler. Friend of the bride."

"Which one?" Thalia struggled to stifle her laughter at his earnestness.

"Kerry," his friend supplied with an affectionate eye roll. "And I'm Julia."

Thalia was about to ask them what Kerry was like, when Harris launched into a passionate monologue about how excited he was by her promotion and what a positive development it was toward true gender parity in sport, and how it would change the face of Formula One.

"How are you feeling about Spain next week? I've read that the changing wind directions at Catalunya can make for a crazy race."

Was he a walking trivia machine? "That's true. But I've done a lot of testing there, and I'm confident in my ability to—"

Trumpets pealed in a triumphant fanfare, setting the air afire with anticipation. As the last echoes rang through the cathedral, the organ hummed into life. Maeve gripped her arm in excitement as they both craned their heads for the best possible view. First to process down the aisle was the beaming Archbishop of Canterbury, his bald pate mostly concealed by his gold and white mitre. The Archbishop of Canterbury, officiating a gay wedding! Thalia wanted to cheer.

He was followed by three girls in white dresses who periodically pitched handfuls of white rose petals into the air. The youngest of them couldn't stop giggling.

"The King's nieces," Harris stage-whispered.

The King himself came next, escorting his youngest daughter Elizabeth, who wore a shimmering, sky blue gown. King Andrew, immaculate in some kind of military regalia Thalia couldn't place, looked grave—but then again, when didn't he? He was here, and that was what mattered. Thalia wondered, fleetingly, whether her own father would afford her the same courtesy if she ever chose to marry.

The King was succeeded by his heir, resplendent in a navy Royal Air Force uniform as he escorted his wife. Ashleigh, Princess of Wales, wore a form-fitting rose gown that flared at her ankles. Only last week, she had announced that she was pregnant, but she hadn't remotely begun to show. Her smile was genuine and her bearing relaxed. Clearly, she was enjoying herself.

Once Arthur and Ashleigh had passed into the sanctuary, the music changed key, shifting from a light and airy melody to a deeper and more viscerally powerful tune. Another fanfare rose in a descant over the triumphantly bellowing organ, and beneath it all, the scuff of two thousand feet against the floor as everyone rose to greet the brides.

They walked down the aisle together, hand in hand: Kerry in a silver tuxedo and matching boots, Sasha in a white silk dress with a short train. They took their time, savoring the moment. Kerry's smile was impossibly wide, but it was Sasha's expression that stood out the most to Thalia. They had attended the same secondary school and done their fair share of partying in the same crowd. At times Sasha had been almost desperate in her rebelliousness, as though she had something to prove. But now, that restlessness had disappeared, supplanted by an internal peace. She was radiant with it. Beyond happy. Joyous—that was the right word. And content.

In a way, it made Thalia sad. Not for Sasha, of course, but for herself. For a while, she had felt as though Sasha were a kindred spirit of sorts—always moving, always seeking, never complacent. Not that finding contentment equated to complacency, of course, and if there was ever anyone who could toe that line without going over, it was Sasha. But a silly, selfish part of Thalia couldn't help but feel…abandoned? No, that was too strong a term. She and Sasha were friendly, but not close.

Left out—maybe that was better. But "left out" implied that she wanted to be included in the "married" club, and she didn't want that at all. Serious relationships required work, and work required time— time she could be spending in the gym or in a simulator or test driving. Especially now that she had caught her big break, she had to be ruthless in eliminating anything that would detract from her focus. Catalunya was now less than one week away, and her performance there would set the tone for the entire season.

But as Sasha passed within an arm-length and shot her a brilliant, contagious smile, the promise and pressures of Spain temporarily faded in urgency. Yes, she had to prepare for the future, but she could also be wise enough to live in the moment. And in this particular moment, Thalia wasn't a racecar driver or an activist, but a queer woman fortunate enough to be witnessing part of her own history.

CHAPTER FOUR

Alix wished she had brought a book. Everyone originally seated at her table had gone off to enjoy the dancing in the Throne Room-turned-nightclub, and even she could only admire the intricacies of the wall paneling for so long. Pretending to inspect the oil painting hanging above her chair, she took stock of the room through her peripheral vision. A few small groups of people remained, chatting over their hors d'oeuvres and drinks. No one else was alone.

Beset by self-consciousness, she extracted her phone from her purse and checked her email. She had no unread messages, and her to-do list was up to date, but if she looked busy, at least she wouldn't seem pathetic. After aimlessly scrolling through her inbox, she switched over to her browser and pulled up a blog she had already reread several times, by a French colleague affiliated with Doctors Without Borders who was now working in the Karamoja region. Every ten days or so, he managed to travel into the town of Moroto, where there was just enough of an Internet connection to post an update on his work, along with a few photographs. They made her nostalgic—especially the picture of a lone black rhinoceros standing in a water hole, set in a naturally picturesque fashion against the volcanic mountain range in the background. She had grown up in beautiful places and among beautiful things, but there was something about the wild splendor of Karamoja that filled her with longing.

In the weeks between returning home from Africa and leaving for London, Alix had been furiously researching the legal intricacies of starting up her own not-for-profit organization, but before she began filing any of the paperwork, she wanted to hear Ashleigh's advice. Fortunately, booking a lunch meeting with the Princess of Wales had been a simple matter of asking her secretary to contact Buckingham Palace.

"Oh, how striking!" The sentiment came from just behind her, and Alix turned to see none other than Ashleigh herself, one hand resting on the back of her chair as she leaned in to gaze intently at the photograph. Up close, she somehow managed to be even lovelier than at a distance—softer somehow, in a way that made her feel more accessible, more human.

"Yes, it's one of my favorites," Alix said, surprised at Ashleigh's informality. They had met a few times, but never to do more than exchange small talk. Wanting to be certain not to offend, Alix rose and extended her hand as protocol demanded. "It's good to see you. Thank you for agreeing to meet with me tomorrow."

Ashleigh ignored her hand and instead stepped in to embrace her lightly, ending with a kiss to each cheek. "I'm so glad you reached out. We can save all talk of business until tomorrow, if you wish, but I wanted to touch base tonight to let you know that I'm looking forward."

"As am I," Alix said, even as she automatically catalogued the pallor beneath Ashleigh's subtle makeup. Fatigue, most likely. "Please, sit. I hope I don't appear antisocial, but I'm not much for dancing."

Ashleigh's laugh was just like the rest of her—refined yet genuine. "No need to explain. It's been a very good day, but a very long one." She settled herself in the chair. "You recently returned from Uganda, is that right?"

For the next half an hour, they traded stories about their time spent on the African continent. Most of Ashleigh's experience was in rural South Africa and Lesotho, and it was illustrative for Alix to hear about the circumstances of the people there. In Lesotho, almost one quarter of the population was HIV positive—a much higher number than in Uganda—and Ashleigh spoke eloquently about the foundation that Arthur had founded before they had met, which supported children orphaned by AIDS.

"And your foundation takes a business development perspective, is that right?" Alix asked.

"Yes, I'm hoping to—"

"Ash!" The soprano call came from across the room. "*There* you are! We've been scouring the world for you!"

Alix turned toward the noise to see Sasha approaching them, dragging her bride by the hand, a few other women following in their wake.

"The party's found us," Ashleigh murmured with a smile. "To be continued tomorrow?"

"Of course." Alix rose as they approached, but Sasha waved her back into her seat.

"Oh please. We're not standing on formality tonight, Pommelina." She collapsed into a chair and Kerry took the one beside her. "Are you enjoying yourself, I hope?"

"We've been chatting about Africa," Ashleigh said. She turned to Alix. "And you generally go by 'Alix' these days, correct?"

"Yes." Alix was grateful to Ashleigh for having brought it up. "I've never been very fond of my first name."

"Alix it is," Sasha declared. She gestured to the other women who had just joined them. "I'm sure you know Thalia, but have you met Maeve? She's a fantastic actress in one of the new BBC sitcoms."

Maeve, slender and pretty and all smiles, extended her hand. "It's a pleasure," Alix said. "But I'm not acquainted with Thalia either."

The woman in question was taller than her companion and wore a black tuxedo accented by a thin, silver tie. Dark, glossy hair brushed her broad shoulders, framing an oval face from which her eyes, bright blue and almond shaped, stared curiously into Alix's. To her embarrassment, she found she couldn't look away. Despite her unorthodox attire, Thalia was the most striking person Alix had ever seen. Her exotic beauty combined with an aura of easy self-confidence to lend her a palpable magnetism that Alix stubbornly wanted to resist.

In an effort to dispel the unwelcome feeling, she forced herself to notice details rather than the whole. Thalia had a small scar two inches below her left eye, and a golden lightning bolt stud in the helix of her left ear. The colorful hint of a tattoo peeked out from beneath her right cuff. When Alix caught herself making assumptions about Thalia's sexuality, she mentally scolded herself.

"Excuse me?" Sasha's tone betrayed her disbelief. "You two have never met? How is that possible?"

Her name did seem vaguely familiar, but Alix was certain they had never been in the same room together. Why was Sasha being so adamant?

"Thalia d'Angelis," Her accent was curious—mildly British, but not as clipped and with the hint of a drawl in some syllables. "Formula One driver. I met the rest of your family last year at the Grand Prix."

Realization dawned, and with it came relief. Alix had met plenty of F1 drivers over the years, and they were all the same: arrogant, thrill-seeking men obsessed with running in circles. Impossibly beautiful or not, Thalia was cut from the same mold.

"I see," Alix said, careful not to betray any of her dismissiveness. "I was out of town for last year's race."

"I think I heard you were studying in America?"

"Yes, for a master's in public health." Alix tried to remember what she had heard her family members saying about Thalia. Florestan's speculation that her recent promotion to F1 had been a publicity stunt certainly didn't bear repeating. But before she could find the right words to move their conversation forward, Kerry spoke up.

"How interesting. Did you have a particular focus?"

"Global health," Alix said. "My capstone project involved fieldwork in northeastern Uganda. I just returned a few weeks ago, and am interested in doing more to benefit the region—hence my interest in speaking with Ashleigh."

"I wish you all the best with that," Sasha said. "But forgive me if Uganda is not one of my favorite places in the world at present."

"The institutionalized homophobia there is certainly a problem," Alix said carefully, wondering if Sasha had any inkling that the Monegasque royal family was its own small bastion of social conservatism when it came to LGBT rights. "But I think it's a more significant issue in the urban centers than outside them. Where I was, in the rural northeast, the central government has very little sway. For the most part, the tribes make their own laws."

"But are the tribes any more accepting?"

"That's a good question," Alix conceded. "I honestly don't know."

A waiter stopped by to ask if they wanted anything from the bar, and in his wake, the conversation veered off toward lighter topics. As time passed, Alix realized that their group had unsurprisingly become the hub of the party. They were soon joined by Arthur, who brought with him two other princes—Ernst from the Netherlands, and Sebastian from Belgium. Maeve immediately monopolized the former, and Alix wondered how Thalia felt about that, since it appeared they had come together. But rather than seeming affronted, Thalia joined in to a conversation between Arthur and Kerry about football. Content to watch and listen from the periphery, Alix fell back on a mental trick she had learned as an adolescent for surviving high society parties—to play the anthropologist and study the social relations in the room.

As their group continued to expand, the first thing she noticed was the number of congratulations attended by caveats. Roughly three-quarters of those who stopped by to deliver their "best wishes" prefaced their remarks with some variant of "I never thought I'd see this day, but…" or "You've become downright respectable, Sasha," or "Kerry, you must be very special to have convinced Sasha to settle down." Each time someone delivered such a line, Alix wanted to wince. Why couldn't people simply express happiness for them, no matter what they might be thinking? She watched as Kerry, who had yet to let go of Sasha's hand, stroked her thumb lightly across Sasha's knuckles. They were both maintaining grace under pressure, but at what cost?

Alix had never had an interest in actively following the sordid affairs of her fellow royals or other celebrities, but news had reached her of Sasha's many peccadilloes throughout the years. The tabloids loved her, and she had seemed more than willing to feed their salacious appetite. But now here she was, cuddling close to her *wife*—the word felt strange in her mind, but it was undeniably the correct one now—not only happy, but also unafraid to champion social justice.

The sudden pang of loneliness was unexpected, but as her analytical mind took over, it made sense. Alix had yet to experience the kind of emotion that made a person want to share their life with someone else. She had never made relationships a priority, and as both the most introverted and plainest of her siblings, she had never been pursued by a man who was more interested in her personality than her royal titles. Those kinds of suitors were easy to spot and even easier to turn down. Once in a while, she thought she must be missing something important, but that feeling always passed. Relationships involved work, energy, and sacrifice—she knew that much from watching her parents.

But Alix was enjoying the work she had chosen, and she didn't want to have to negotiate with or worry about the opinions of someone else.

"Mind if I sit?"

Alix looked up to see Thalia patting the back of the chair next to hers. "Not at all," she said, anticipating that Thalia would return to her conversation with one of the others. Instead, she found herself once again the focus of those brilliant blue eyes.

"So, Alix—it is Alix, right?"

"Yes."

"Where in America were you studying? I was born and partially raised in Arizona."

"I was in Boston." Alix remained purposefully vague, not wanting to seem like a snob.

But Thalia grinned knowingly. "Let me guess—Harvard?"

"Yes." Alix felt silly at having been found out so easily, and she despised feeling silly. "And you?" she asked, hating the defensive impulse even as she succumbed to it.

"I never even tried to go to university. Secondary school was more than enough for me. All I ever wanted was to race professionally."

Alix had suspected as much, but Thalia didn't seem the least bit ashamed. "And now you have your wish. Congratulations." Alix hoped that would be the end of their conversation. She found Thalia's intensity rather disconcerting.

"Thanks." But instead of taking the hint, Thalia crossed her arms on the table and leaned in. "You're the first Monegasque royal I've ever met who has shown zero interest in Formula One."

Alix couldn't help but be impressed by her forthrightness. "Every family has a black sheep." When Thalia laughed at her rejoinder, Alix felt absurdly proud.

"Isn't that the truth. That's me as well."

"Oh?"

"I was a mistake," Thalia said with a self-deprecating grin. "Back in his glory days, my father won the American Grand Prix and then painted Phoenix red. That involved knocking up my mother, who was dancing at a club at the time."

Taken aback, Alix had no idea how to respond. Her panic must have been blatant, because Thalia leapt into the sudden silence. "Don't feel sorry for me. My father's guilt has always made him overly generous."

At last, Alix could empathize. "I've never lacked for anything, either. But sometimes that makes the longing even worse, doesn't it?"

Something subtle changed in Thalia's expression, like ice slowly breaking its bonds to become water. As her bravado fell away, she became even more beautiful. "Yes," she said softly, as if speaking to herself.

That single syllable was laden with a dozen emotions: pain, nostalgia, wistfulness, even a hint of anger. Instinctually wanting to comfort her, Alix reached out…only to pull back her hand as though she'd been burned when Sebastian, crown prince of Belgium, stepped into her field of vision. Feeling herself blush, she struggled to meet his eyes. She hadn't done anything wrong, so why did it feel like she had?

"Hello, Pommelina," he said in French. She didn't bother to correct his use of her first name and instead returned his salutation in kind. When he remained standing, she reluctantly rose to join him. Thalia stayed seated.

Sebastian, five years her senior, had once been a ranked professional golfer. Now that he had retired from the sport, genetics had caught up with him, lending his face and physique a puffy plumpness. Camille had dated him briefly before deciding that he wasn't nearly interesting or edgy enough for her.

After some small talk, he leaned in closer. "I need to step out to take a call, but when I return, would you like to dance?"

Dread filled Alix's chest like a balloon, but she tried to remain nonchalant. "Oh, I wouldn't make a very good partner. I haven't danced in years."

"That's fine. We'll take it slowly." He reached into his pocket and pulled out a buzzing phone. "There's my call. See you soon."

Alix watched him go, wondering whether she should confront him about his proprietary attitude or simply ignore it and give him what he had asked for.

"What was all that about?" asked Thalia, who clearly did not understand French.

"He asked me to dance, over my own protests," Alix said, trying to let go of her frustration. "I'm afraid he'll find me a poor partner; I was never very good to begin with, and I'm horribly out of practice."

In one graceful movement, Thalia stood and extended her hand. "Let's practice now."

Alix's first impulse was to look around the room for anyone who might be watching them, intentionally or accidentally. What would they think of this scene: Thalia, one arm outstretched, clearly propositioning her for something? Would they assume she was a lesbian by association?

And then she realized the homophobic turn her thoughts had taken and was ashamed. Talking to Thalia, taking her hand, and even sharing a dance did not make her a lesbian. And besides, no one was watching her. No one ever did—that was the upshot to keeping a low profile.

"Come on." Thalia was grinning again. "You don't want to trip over his feet, do you? And become a social media sensation tomorrow?"

"When you put it that way…" Alix let her palm slide against Thalia's.

"You have calluses." Thalia's tone betrayed her surprise. Had she taken Alix for some kind of fragile feminine flower who refused to threaten her manicure?

"So do you," she fired back.

"I race cars for a living."

"And I spent much of the past three months planting crops and digging wells."

Thalia had the wits to look somewhat chagrined. "Touché. I'm sorry for making ignorant assumptions."

"Apology accepted." Alix realized they were moving in the opposite direction of the Throne Room. "Where are you taking me?"

"There's a small antechamber between this room and the Grand Staircase or whatever they call it. Perfect for a dancing lesson."

Alix worried that someone from the palace's security detail would take exception to them leaving the drawing room, but nothing happened when Thalia opened the door and slipped through. They emerged into a rectangular, wood-paneled chamber, its walls lined with upholstered benches.

"Okay." Thalia stopped and turned, but retained Alix's hand. "The DJ's been playing a good variety, but I'm guessing Prince Sebastian will ask for something slow." She paused expectantly but rolled her eyes a moment later. "What, no swooning?"

"I've never swooned in my life," Alix said firmly, even as she felt another pang.

"That sounds like a challenge." Thalia winked as she pulled her closer.

Alix didn't resist the movement, but neither did she allow Thalia to completely eliminate the space between their bodies. Other women might find Thalia's playfulness endearing, but she found it rather manipulative. "Why are you flirting with me? Won't your date be upset?"

"Maeve is busy reaching for the next rung on the social ladder." Thalia placed one hand on Alix's shoulder. "Mirror me. There you go."

Surprised at her nonchalance, Alix let her fingertips rest lightly in the dip of Thalia's collarbone as she debated whether to continue the conversation. But why not? She would probably never see Thalia again after tonight. "That doesn't bother you?"

"We were never serious. Just having fun."

"I don't understand that." Alix hadn't meant to speak that thought, but Thalia didn't seem affronted or uncomfortable.

"That's because you are oh-so-serious." Thalia stepped closer, shifting her palm to the bare skin between Alix's shoulder blades. "Lighten up. This is a wedding, not a funeral. Dance like no one's watching. Maybe try having some fun with your Prince Sebastian tonight."

Before Alix could retort that he most certainly was not "her" Prince Sebastian, Thalia began to move—at first slowly, and then in a more intricate pattern across the floor. Alix tried to anticipate her movements and keep pace, but the harder she tried, the clumsier she became. And the clumsier she became, the more she wished she had never agreed to this. She had let herself give in to peer pressure. What did it matter if she didn't enjoy, nor was particularly good at, dancing? She was under no obligation to play the role of Cinderella.

"Whoa, whoa," Thalia said after the third time that Alix stepped on her toes. She halted unceremoniously. "You have *got* to stop trying to lead."

"Excuse me?" Alix could feel herself blushing, but she refused to be apologetic.

Thalia shot her a bemused look. "I get it. You're an empowered, twenty-first-century woman who actively resists stereotypes and has no patience for chauvinism. Fine. But someone has to lead in a dance, and Sebastian isn't going to follow." She pulled Alix closer, until the space between them had all but disappeared. "Relax. Being pliant on the dance floor doesn't mean you have to sacrifice your feminist ideals."

The absurdity of that statement made her have to laugh. "I certainly hope not." She took a long, deep breath. "I'll do my best to *temporarily* give up control."

A current of emotion, raw and powerful, rippled beneath the surface of Thalia's eyes. For a moment, Alix felt the brush of the sublime on her mind, an echo of the awe and longing she'd experienced only when alone in nature. But then Thalia blinked and grinned and said, "All right, here goes," and they were dancing again.

Alix fixed her gaze on the slim knot of Thalia's tie and breathed deeply, hoping to reach something like the meditative state she sometimes found while doing yoga. Incredibly, as Thalia guided her across the floor, she neither stumbled nor misstepped. It was strange to be dancing with another woman, but not unpleasant. The difference was subtle. Thalia was taller, but only by a few inches. She moved confidently, but her physical cues weren't heavy-handed. And there was a kind of softness about her—not that she ever would have verbalized it in those terms to Thalia—that helped Alix relax into their shared movements.

"There, that's it," Thalia murmured, warm breath washing over the sensitive shell of her ear, raising goose bumps on her arms. "Less thinking. More feeling. I know that's tricky for you brainy types."

Discomfort at her own visceral reaction gave way to vexation at being manipulated. "Less flirting. More practice."

Thalia laughed in evident surprise at being called out. "This is practice. Sebastian will definitely be flirting with you."

"I suppose you're right."

"You're really not interested in him?"

"No."

"Let's try a twirl." Gently but firmly, Thalia pushed her away, retaining the grasp on her hand as she initiated the spin. When they reconnected, Thalia continued her inquisition. "Why not? Is he not your type?"

"My priority right now is founding a not-for-profit, not finding romance."

"And you can't multitask?" Thalia twirled her again.

Once the world had stopped spinning, Alix decided to give her a taste of her own medicine. "Why the interrogation?"

Thalia cocked her head and took a long moment to reply. "You're not stereotypical, and that's interesting."

Alix was pleased by that assessment but didn't want her to know it. "I'll take that as a compliment."

"It was intended as such. Ready for a waltz?" Without waiting for her reply, Thalia led her in a sweeping series of turns along the periphery of the room. Their self-created breeze swept her hair back from her face, and a smile tugged at her lips before she could remember to suppress it.

"You have a beautiful smile," Thalia said.

Alix narrowed her eyes, more in a mockery of irritation than from true annoyance. "Is this another attempt to prepare me for Sebastian's advances?"

"No. This is me trying to beat him to the punch."

Alix couldn't tell whether she was joking, and the uncertainty sobered her. "I'm afraid you'll be disappointed," she said, trying to walk the line between gravity (in case Thalia was actually serious) and good humor (in case she wasn't).

"Possibly." Thalia slackened their pace, returning to the more conventional slow dance. "To make it up to me, why don't you explain how someone born and raised in Monaco, with motorsport in their blood, has such a distaste for Formula One."

"When did I ever use the word 'distaste'?"

"You didn't have to." Thalia grinned. "Don't worry. I'm not offended—just curious."

Alix didn't know how to respond. No one had ever questioned her lack of interest in racing or asked her to justify her opinion of the sport—either because they didn't care, or because *she* never had. Unlike Florestan, she had always been more interested in books than in cars, and unlike Camille, she preferred a quiet corner or solitary walk to the glamorous party scene that attended the circuit.

"It simply isn't how I want to spend my time. I don't understand its allure."

"Because?"

Out of patience with Thalia's needling, Alix abandoned politeness.

"Frankly, I don't see the point of driving grossly inefficient gas-guzzlers around in a circle, repeatedly, at suicidal speeds. It's wasteful and reckless. You don't even go anywhere!"

Thalia halted their swaying movements. "Jeez, tell me how you really feel. You do know that Formula One has all kinds of regulations to protect the drivers, right?"

But Alix refused to back down. "Are you trying to tell me it's safe?"

"Of course it isn't safe. What would be the point if it were?"

"That right there," Alix said, raising her hand from Thalia's shoulder to jab her finger emphatically, "is my problem. I am a medical doctor. How could I possibly enjoy a sport in which the practitioners voluntarily throw themselves in harm's way at the highest possible speeds?"

"Plenty of doctors are huge Formula One fans," Thalia said dryly. She captured Alix's hand and returned it to her shoulder. "Their enjoyment has nothing to do with the Hippocratic Oath and everything to do with being human."

The implied jab stung Alix more than she wanted to admit. It wasn't the first time she had been referred to as something less than human. "Robot" or "machine" were the usual epithets, delivered most frequently by people trying to commend her work ethic and accomplishments. But the implication always bothered her.

"Everyone craves an adrenaline rush from time to time," Thalia was continuing, heedless of Alix's discomfort. "You're the doctor—you know what it does to the brain better than I do. But instead of having everyone run out in search of thrills, isn't it better for most people to get the rush vicariously? All sporting events fill that need: the anticipation, the suspense, the triumph."

Alix had to admit to herself that she'd never thought of sports in quite that way, and that Thalia's logic did make a certain amount of sense. "I can see your point," she ventured, "but there are plenty of sports to choose from."

"None so viscerally satisfying as racing." Thalia cocked her head to meet Alix's gaze. "Come to Spain in two weeks for the first race of the season. Let me try to prove it to you. I'll even make it worth your while—you can sit in the Gambizi Tire box. Lord Rufford, the owner of my team, will be there with his wife, who does all kinds of charity work. If you spend some time schmoozing with her, maybe she'll be interested in helping your charity get started."

Still smarting emotionally, Alix had to remind herself that she was filtering this entire conversation through old baggage and that Thalia hadn't intended an insult. Even so, despite the olive branch, a part of her wanted to retort that she didn't need help. But that kind of attitude was ridiculous and would be counterproductive to her mission. If sitting through a silly race would benefit her nascent project, then that's what she would do.

"I appreciate that," she said. "And I accept." After releasing Thalia's hand, she took a long step backward. "I had better find Sebastian. Thank you for the refresher."

"Anytime."

"I hope you have an excellent season." Not waiting for a reply, Alix turned and walked briskly toward the drawing room. Despite the finality of her parting shot, she found herself wanting to look back and resisted. She wasn't a robot, but it would be better for them both if Thalia thought of her that way.

CHAPTER FIVE

Through the closed partition between the back and front seat of her car, Alix could hear her bodyguard talking excitedly to her driver about the Spanish Grand Prix. Normally taciturn, Claude spoke rapidly and his voice crackled with excitement, but she couldn't make out the words. For what seemed like the hundredth time, Alix examined the open portfolio on her lap containing the most recent draft of her business plan. But when her concentration began to waver, she closed it and set it aside. She didn't need to cram the latest details of the plan into her brain before encountering Lady Rufford socially. On the other hand, she could use a crash course in Formula One. As embarrassing as it was to admit her ignorance to her staff, she could potentially undermine her project by being woefully ignorant in public. Suddenly determined, she opened the screen and pressed the button to activate the intercom.

"Would one of you mind briefly explaining the current Formula One scene to me?"

They shared a glance before Gilles quickly returned his gaze to the road. She could only imagine what they were thinking—how was it possible for a princess of Monaco to have to ask that question?

"I know the basics," she clarified. "Twelve teams, two cars each, Grands Prix around the world. Ours—that is, Monaco's—is considered the crown jewel. Points are awarded for the top ten finishers of each race. The driver with the most points at the end of the season is the world champion."

"The last race counts for double points, ma'am," Gilles added. "And the team with the most combined points wins the Constructors' Cup."

"Thank you, Gilles. What is the current lay of the land? Is there a favored team this season?"

"Aiglon Motors won the Cup last year, and their first driver, Lucas Mountjoy, was the world champion," said Claude. "The formula hasn't changed all that significantly this year, and so they remain the favorites."

"The formula? What do you mean?"

"That's the set of rules that govern how the car is built, ma'am—the engine, the chassis, the electrical systems, and all other components."

"I see. Do you each have a favorite team?"

"I was raised a Ferrari supporter," Claude said.

"I used to favor Aiglon," said Gilles, "but I didn't appreciate how they treated Peter Taggart, so now I support Petrol Macedonia."

That was Thalia's team, Alix knew that much. And she had heard Peter Taggart's name before. But the rest of Gilles's logic was completely opaque. "Taggart was the world champion at some point, is that correct?"

"Three times," said Gilles. "But after one bad season, Aiglon sacked him along with their team manager, Alistair Campbell."

"Before last year, Petrol Macedonia didn't even exist," Claude added. "A British lord founded the team and snapped up Campbell to run it and Taggart as their star driver."

"The Earl of Rufford," Alix clarified, glad she could finally contribute to this conversation. Being so ignorant bothered her, though of course it had been her choice not to do enough research into the sport. "His wife is the one I'm here to meet. How did the team do last year?"

"Not bad. Taggart came in third." When Gilles had to stop at a security checkpoint to enter the VIP parking lot of the Circuit de Barcelona-Catalunya, Claude took over.

"Their other driver didn't perform well, so they jettisoned him and were poised to sign a Brazilian superstar when he suddenly decided to race in America instead."

Alix put two and two together. "Which is when they signed Thalia."

Claude turned with a quizzical expression. "Yes. Do you know her?"

Buckingham's security had been judged strong enough that she hadn't needed a guard inside, and the relief she now felt about that fact was tinged with an unfamiliar guilt. If Claude had seen them dancing together, what might he think? Despite having done nothing wrong, she felt oddly ashamed.

"We met in London two weeks ago. At the wedding."

He nodded and then turned his attention to the window. Alix did likewise, watching as the shapes of the track grew larger and more distinct: a rectangular, red-capped tower; the triangular white roof of a nearby building; the slate gray half-moon of the nearest grandstand. Soon, it dominated the skyline.

Alix preferred to conduct her own affairs whenever possible, and generally insisted that her security detail hover in the background. As she disembarked from the car before the main entrance, however, she was happy to let Claude take point. He was grave and expressionless now as he surveyed the hordes of fans trickling in through the gates. Perhaps, once they were safely ensconced in their box, she could convince him to relax and enjoy the race.

"Here you are, ma'am." Claude held out her badge and she slipped it over her head, then adjusted the collar of her shirt. Having resisted her mother's attempt to foist the royal tailor on her yet again, she had chosen a light khaki pantsuit for the occasion. She was here to do business.

Claude ushered her past three separate security checkpoints and into an elevator. Discreetly, she checked her reflection in its mirrored walls. Would she see Thalia before the race began, or was she deep in preparation? Not that it mattered, of course. She wasn't here to see Thalia, though it would be only polite to thank her for the connection she had made to Lady Rufford.

In the two weeks since the wedding, Alix had been working diligently on everything from acquiring not-for-profit tax status for her organization to beginning the delicate process of reaching out to the Ugandan government. Ashleigh had been able to offer a great deal of pragmatic advice—including the necessity to budget for "tips" to be distributed to government officials. A year ago, Alix would have balked at creating a line item for what essentially amounted to bribes, but having spent time with her boots on the ground, she now understood the necessity. Not to mention the value of perspective.

Now, with a mission statement and business plan in hand, she was ready to begin seeking out investors. Alix had read everything on the Internet about Lady Rufford, who had three grown sons and had apparently channeled her wish for a daughter into working to ameliorate the plight of female children in China and India. Alix could only hope to present a convincing case on behalf of women in East Africa. By turns optimistic and anxious, she had rehearsed her speech at least a dozen times.

The doors opened into a spacious room buzzing with conversation and a faint undercurrent of jazz music. Upon stepping over the threshold, Alix was struck by two features: the floor-to-ceiling windows on the far side, presumably overlooking the track; and the ridiculous number of televisions peppered across the room. They covered almost every available square inch of wall space and also hung above and beside the bar. No seat was positioned without direct line-of-sight to a screen.

"Your Serene Highness, welcome!"

The man bustling toward them parted crowds without having to ask. As she watched him approach, Alix was exceedingly conscious that she had yet to command anything close to that level of respect. Most of Western Europe had probably forgotten she existed. Under normal circumstances, that was exactly how she preferred it, but now that she had a company to think of, she would need to keep a more public profile. Perhaps showing up to this event would be useful in more ways than one.

"Stanley Rabeck, head of Gambizi Tires," Claude murmured discreetly. Gambizi was the official tire supplier of Formula One. This, she realized belatedly, was his box.

In the next moment, they were face-to-face. She offered her hand. "Mr. Rabeck, thank you for your hospitality."

"It is an honor to have you here," he said. "Would you care for some champagne?"

She rarely drank and was about to decline when she realized that might be perceived as a slight. "Please."

He snapped his fingers and a waiter in a white jacket materialized at his side. "Champagne," Rabeck said, and the young man was gone as quickly as he had arrived. "This is your first time at Catalunya?"

"Yes."

"Then you must have the tour." Smiling too brightly, he gestured to the clusters of couches in the foreground. "We have the most comfortable seating at the track, and our waitstaff will attend to your every need." He then pointed to the nearest television. "Our screens display the race in progress and real time updates on positional changes, so that you will never be in the dark about the standings."

The waiter returned with a tray of brimming flutes, and as Alix plucked one, she turned to Claude. "You too. I'm as safe as I've ever been."

After a moment's hesitation, he took a glass and Rabeck led them in a toast. "To Formula One."

He led them to the wall of windows, and Alix looked out over the dark pavement that, snakelike, folded in on itself before stretching into the distance. Unbidden, her imagination conjured the image of Thalia—except the only memory of Thalia that she had was from the wedding, and the Thalia who would ride out today in search of victory wouldn't be wearing a tux or a tie or an insouciant smile.

On the news early this morning, she had watched a piece about Thalia's ability to make history today. Apparently, she had qualified for this race in eighth place, and if she finished anywhere in the top ten, she would become the female F1 driver with the most points. If she finished above sixth place, she would become the top-finishing female F1 driver in history. Intrigued, Alix had turned to the Internet for more details, where she learned that to date, the top-finishing female driver had taken sixth place in this very race, the Spanish Grand Prix, in 1975. The race had been cut short due to a terrible accident in which several spectators were killed in a crash. At the moment of cancellation, Italian driver Lella Lombardi had been in sixth place, which at that time was worth a single point toward the Championship. Because of the accident, half points were awarded. Lombardi had not won points in any subsequent race, making one-half the benchmark for her female would-be successors to surpass. Nowadays, sixth place was worth much more—Alix couldn't recall how much—and so Thalia had the potential to break the points record as long as she finished tenth or above.

"Do you have a favorite team or driver, Your Highness?"

The question roused Alix from her introspection. "I'd like to see Thalia d'Angelis break the points record." The more she thought about it, the more Thalia's position in such a traditionally patriarchal sphere seemed like a golden opportunity from which to demonstrate gender equality.

"An intriguing driver, with a great deal of talent."

Alix resisted the impulse to frown at him. His words were perfect, but the tone was off. Was he one of the "good old boys" who believed that women had no place in Formula One? "And an inspiration to young women who aspire to male-dominated careers," she said, doing her best to keep an edge from her tone. "Don't you think?"

"Of course," he said smoothly. Too smoothly. She could recognize pandering when she heard it.

In the ensuing pause, she was startled to hear her own name being called from across the room. As her memory registered the voice, dread blossomed in her stomach. Sebastian. She should have known he would attend an event like this. Resignedly, she turned to face him. As at the royal wedding, he was wearing a suit, this one a navy pinstripe that accentuated his long legs and minimized the signs of his weight gain. Curly brown hair tumbled across his forehead, nearly falling into his equally brown eyes. He wasn't unattractive, but neither did he make her pulse jump.

"What an unexpected pleasure," he said in English, presumably for Rabeck's benefit. And then he leaned down to kiss her. She had expected the customary series of cheek kisses, but instead, Sebastian boldly kissed her on the mouth. His lips were moist and warm, and his breath smelled of mint and some kind of alcohol. Not entirely unpleasant, but certainly unwanted. She pulled away as quickly as she could without betraying her surprise and displeasure at his familiarity.

"Hello, Sebastian," she said, proud of the coolness in her voice.

"Your Highness," Rabeck said, inclining his head in Sebastian's direction. "Is everything to your liking? May I make any other arrangements for either of you?"

"I'm perfectly well, thank you," Alix said. When Sebastian echoed her sentiment, Rabeck took his leave, presumably to greet some other VIP.

"I had no idea you were interested in Formula One," Sebastian said, now in French, as he linked their arms together.

Discomfited by his closeness, she debated asking him to respect her personal space before deciding that would be uncharitable. "I'm not, especially. I'm here to meet with Lady Rufford about my charity."

Sebastian seemed mildly disappointed to hear that, for which she was glad. "Which team are you supporting?" she asked, in the interest of making conversation.

"I've been an Aiglon Motors fan since birth," he said. "Literally—my mother has photographs of me wearing a 'Red Eagle' bib."

Despite her interest in keeping him at arm's length, Alix found herself laughing. "That is true dedication."

"And you?" As they spoke, Sebastian steered her toward a nearby sofa.

"Oh, I don't particularly care. But I do hope Thalia does well, this being a potentially historic occasion." A sudden hubbub from the direction of the elevators made her pause in mid-stride, also forcing Sebastian to halt. "What's that, I wonder?"

Claude immediately stepped in front of her, poised for an altercation, but his shoulders dropped at the smattering of applause from those nearest the entrance.

"Speak of the devil and she shall appear," Sebastian murmured, craning his neck.

Since he had several inches on her, she had no reason to doubt his vantage point. A moment later, Thalia emerged into view. She wore a white jumpsuit trimmed in red and blue and covered with sponsor patches. The smile with which she favored her audience was nothing like the flirtatious grin she had flashed at the wedding. Everything about her, from the way she held herself to the way she moved across the room, telegraphed a coiled intensity waiting to be unleashed.

She seemed to be looking for someone, and Alix was just wondering whether that someone was her latest fling, when Thalia's gaze met hers and recognition flashed across her face. When she changed course, Alix realized the "someone" had been *her*. It was an unexpectedly heady feeling.

Thalia stopped a few feet away, her gaze sweeping over Alix's body and lingering on where her arm was linked with Sebastian's. Alix had to suppress a sudden urge to pull away from him.

"You made it," Thalia said quietly.

"Hello. And yes. Thank you for your help with the arrangements."

"No problem." She stuck out her hand to Sebastian. "We met in passing at the wedding, Your Highness. I'm Thalia."

"Yes, I recall," was all Sebastian said.

Alix saw a way to distance herself from him, and to prove to Thalia that she was less ignorant about Formula One than when last they had met. Not that that should matter, but somehow it did. "Don't mind him. He's been an Aiglon fan his whole life."

"I see." Thalia had picked up on her mood, and her blue eyes were glinting with humor. A secret understanding seemed to pass between them, though Alix might have imagined it. "That's very respectable and I certainly won't hold it against you." Thalia returned her focus to Alix. "I need to get back to the paddock soon. Have you met Florence yet?"

"I haven't."

"Then allow me to introduce you." She held out her hand, and Alix used the invitation as an excuse to slip her arm out from the crook of Sebastian's elbow.

"Enjoy the race," she told him as Thalia tugged her away.

"Someone has a crush?" she murmured as soon as they were out of earshot.

"I don't know. I hope not." Alix tried to remain matter-of-fact. She also tried not to worry about how any observers would perceive their clasped hands. "How are you feeling?"

"Fine." Thalia seemed distracted as she scanned the crowd, but Alix wondered whether that was simply a front to avoid having to talk about what she was on the verge of attempting. "Oh, there she is. Come on."

Thalia led her toward the bar, where a slender, middle-aged woman was holding court with two of her contemporaries. Pearl earrings adorned her ears and a matching pendant encircled her neck. As they drew closer, Thalia let go.

"Pardon me, Lady Rufford," she said deferentially, "but may I introduce you to Her Serene Highness Pommelina Alix Louise of Monaco? She is currently in the development stage of a not-for-profit to benefit women in eastern Africa. We met a few weeks ago and I suggested she speak with you based on your interest in philanthropy."

"It's a true pleasure, Your Highness," Lady Rufford said.

"Alix, please. And likewise. Perhaps we could arrange to talk at some later point?"

"Nonsense. You should join us."

"And I should leave you," Thalia chimed in. "My work here is done, anyway."

"On to your work out there." Lady Rufford gestured at the track.

Alix wanted to tell Thalia to be safe, but that was ridiculous. Jostling for position around a narrow track for two hours at speeds upward of three hundred kilometers per hour could never be safe. "You're insane" would be a more accurate, though not socially acceptable, sentiment.

"Good luck," she said instead, wondering if Thalia could tell she meant it more with respect to her safety than her position across the finish line.

As Thalia walked off, a few others in the room called out to her, but most simply watched. Some looked skeptical, and a few positively annoyed, but others were visibly excited to have her there. Thalia had a real opportunity to serve as a role model, not only to women who wanted to race cars (of which Alix hoped there were few) but also to any woman—any*one*, really—who found themselves in a minority position where people wanted them to fail. Thalia could still fall on her face, of course—the next few hours would be the test of that—but no matter what happened next, she had gotten this far.

Realizing she was staring, Alix turned back to Lady Rufford and her friends. "Please don't let me interrupt you," Alix said. "It was a pleasure to—"

"Do sit, Alix. And call me Florence." Lady Rufford gestured to a barstool to her left, and Alix perched on it with as much grace as she could manage. On high alert, she took only the tiniest sips of champagne as Florence introduced her to her two companions, Lady Bruxton and Lady Southey, both of whom were also the wives of British aristocracy and apparently *de facto* interested in charitable endeavors.

"What sort of NPO are you planning to found?" Florence asked.

Wanting to tread carefully, Alix opted for a conservative approach. "I'm very happy to provide all the details, but I don't want to interfere with your enjoyment of the race."

"The race?" Florence laughed. "Darling, aren't you from Monaco? Have you ever *been* to a Grand Prix? It won't begin for another hour at least."

"I attended several as a child. I always had my nose in a book."

"A budding intellectual, I take it?" Lady Bruxton said.

"Guilty, I'm afraid." At the risk of being perceived boastful, she decided to lay out her credentials. "I've recently completed a master's of public health from Harvard, and my culminating experience involved working with women and children in eastern Uganda. That experience has fueled my desire to start a foundation."

"Eastern Uganda," Lady Southey said. "Is that where the Maasai live?"

"The Maasai are primarily in Kenya," said Lady Rufford.

"I lived with the Karamojong," Alix said. "Their history is linked to the Maasai, but they are now a distinct group."

When Lady Rufford began to recount details from her own experiences in Africa, Alix was content to sit back and listen. She had anticipated this might happen. She might not have much of a chance to pitch her own ideas today, but by doing little more than listening attentively, she had a strong chance of making a good impression. Lady Rufford wasn't about to dispense her money or her support on a whim. If Alix could establish herself as serious and level-headed enough to be successful, yet engaging enough to attract attention to her cause, she might earn herself a second meeting where matters of real business would be on the table.

But at first, she found it difficult to concentrate. Around their small group, the room buzzed with anticipation. Like distant thunder, the muted growl of warming engines outside heralded the theatrical display to follow, and she found herself wondering about Thalia's pre-race mentality. Did she have a preparatory visualization routine? Did she listen to music? Or was she a ball of nerves until the race began?

Annoyed at her lapse in focus, Alix waved aside a waiter's attempt to refill her champagne flute. She was not here to watch the race, and she certainly didn't intend to overindulge. She had clear objectives to meet today, and allowing anything else to get in the way would be self-sabotage. As Lady Rufford regaled them with a humorous anecdote, Alix let her laughter pull her back into the sphere of conversation.

CHAPTER SIX

Thalia jerked the wheel first to the right and then to the left, forcing her car to weave across the track. She was nearing the end of the warm-up lap before her first Formula One start, and the butterflies in her gut were the size of dragons.

"All right, Thalia." The calm voice of her engineer, Carl, filtered through her headset. "One more burnout."

"Roger that." She pressed down hard on the throttle, glorying momentarily in its responsiveness as the car leapt forward before necessity demanded she hit the brakes or ram into the driver just ahead. Hysterical laughter threatened to bubble up in her throat at the thought. What a field day the media would have if she crashed before the Grand Prix even began.

The grid came into view, then: a narrow chessboard of white squares against the dark asphalt. She caught a glimpse of Peter's car slipping into the third-place spot before she had to concentrate on sliding carefully into eighth. Silently, she prayed that her tires and brakes were warm enough to handle a bid for stronger position at the first corner. Eighth position might be in the points, and not a bad place from which to begin her F1 career, but she wanted the podium, and that meant working her way up five places in the pack. Making a good start was one of the best ways to improve upon position.

Keeping her eyes on the row of five as-yet-unlit lights suspended above the track, she swallowed against a fresh surge of bile. She always vomited before a race and had emptied her stomach like clockwork into the rubbish bin in Petrol Macedonia's garage just before climbing into her car. Usually, she felt good as new afterward. Then again, *usually* she was not racing a Formula One vehicle in what amounted to an attempt to make history.

When the middle light turned red, the answering surge of adrenaline hit Thalia so hard her vision blurred. Fighting off the impulse to jump the start, she sucked in shallow breaths and released one of the clutch paddles on her steering wheel while pushing lightly on the throttle with her right foot. *Lightly* turned out to be heavily, as the engine soared past the ideal bite point for the clutch.

"Easy there, Thalia," Carl said into her ear as a second light turned red.

Easing up on the throttle, she decreased the car's RPMs to as close to the bite point as she could manage. The third light turned red.

When she realized that her hands were trembling on the wheel, she willed them to stop. All her life, she had been training for this moment. And in the moment, who cared about history? This was her dream come true, and she was going to make the most of every hundredth of a second.

The fourth and fifth lights were illuminated in quick succession, and Thalia automatically sucked in a deep breath, preparing herself for the heavy hand of gravity that would make breathing temporarily impossible. In the next instant, all five lights went out. Exultantly, she released her other clutch paddle and the car leapt forward like a living creature. The driver directly in front of her hadn't been so efficient, and she quickly jerked the wheel to the left in order to pass him.

"Great start," said Carl. "Keep it clean going into turn one."

She entered the turn abreast of two other cars and fought hard to surge ahead of them, but one of the Ferrari drivers blocked her attempt, forcing her back into the seventh-place position she had earned off the grid.

"That's fine. Take it easy and settle in now. Plenty of time to challenge."

Thalia knew that was true, but her failure to get ahead at such an opportune moment was still difficult to swallow. Forcing down her self-recrimination, she focused on driving cleanly even as she challenged the car in front of her at every good opportunity.

For the next twenty laps, Carl was mostly silent. Periodically, he delivered updates on Peter's position and on the cars directly ahead of and behind her. By the twenty-first lap, she agreed that she needed to come in—her rear tires were shot and the driver behind her was gradually gaining.

Pit stops always filled her with helplessness. All she could do, she did: gliding in as efficiently as possible and leaving the same way. But she hated giving up control of her car to other people—hated feeling the bump as the chassis was lifted into the air, rendered impotent however briefly. When she merged back into the race, she temporarily found herself in ninth, and fretted about her position until both cars in front of her pitted on the very next lap.

Back in seventh, with forty-four laps to go, she needed to strategize. Twice, she had come close to passing the sixth-place car, which Carl told her was currently eight-tenths of a second out of reach. She could make that up, as long as she drove efficiently.

But as lap stretched into lap, the goal seemed increasingly out of reach. Her opponent hovered between five- and eight-tenths ahead, and try as she might, Thalia couldn't make any consistent headway. In this situation, the only thing she knew how to do was to attempt to rattle him by making constant challenges at each of his positions on the track—even the relatively strong ones with little chance of passing.

Like a mosquito in search of that one uncovered patch of skin, she pursued him relentlessly, even as she continued to take stock of those behind her. The next car was just over two seconds back—not close enough to pose a constant threat, but close enough to capitalize on a mistake. As time passed, the temperature climbed in the cockpit. The sweat pouring from her forehead would have blinded her, had it not been for her balaclava.

By the fiftieth lap, her shoulders and neck were aching fiercely. Usually, she didn't feel this much pain during a race. She was too tense, and her muscles were fatiguing quickly. When she reached the next straight, Thalia pressed the "drink" button on her steering wheel only to find that after the initial surge of warm, sugary liquid, her fluids bag was depleted. Each turn became increasingly agonizing, as gravity conspired to make her head five times heavier than normal. And if she flinched even the slightest bit, she risked sending her car off the track.

By the time she had reached the sixtieth lap, the nerves in her arms and back were screaming for her to surrender. Every time she approached the pit lane, they urged her to capitulate. Pull in, slow down, give up. Let the critics have their day and find some other line of work.

And then, as she headed into the first corner for the sixty-first time, the car ahead of her swung too wide. With reflexes honed by instinct and training, she slammed down on the throttle and surged forward into the gap he had created on the inside, then braked hard to take the corner as tightly as possible. Pain shivered up her spine as she fought to keep the car steady despite the pounding g-forces. Her peripheral vision caught the metallic gleam of the car she had passed trying valiantly to keep abreast of her, and she accelerated hard out of the corner to complete the overtake. Exultation rose over her body's clamor, but there was no time to celebrate as seconds later, the tight chicane of turns two and three tested her stamina. More than ever, now, she had to keep her head.

Carl opened the mic channel and she could hear the cheers from their garage. "Nicely done, Thalia! Stay strong and protect your position."

Protect your position. She knew Carl was right, and that sixth place would be an excellent finish. But she wanted more. The podium might be out of reach, but fifth place certainly wasn't. Her tires were in decent shape—perhaps better than those on the car ahead. If she could make time on him during this next lap, another overtake might be a possibility.

That single lap stretched into an eternity, but by the time it was over, she had closed the gap enough to recognize the Ferrari logo on the car's wing. What a bonus—if she passed him, she would deal a blow to her father's team.

She opened her mic. "I'm going after the Ferrari driver. Is it Terrence or Hugh?"

"Terrence," Carl replied. Even in those two syllables, she could hear his uncertainty.

"I can do this. You know I can."

After a long moment of silence, the channel reopened. This time Alistair's voice greeted her. "His tires are shot from playing catch-up, and you're gaining on him. But don't be reckless. We need the points you already have."

"I hear you." Perhaps she should have phrased that more

respectfully, but she was the one piloting a vehicle with the power of six hundred horses in a cockpit that was by now well over one hundred degrees Fahrenheit. Surely her manners could be cut some slack.

Dimly, she realized that the physical preparation she had done for the GP2 season hadn't been enough to prepare her for the temperature and pressures of Formula One. By the time she had completed two more laps, the heat was starting to threaten her ability to remain conscious. A wave of dizziness nearly swamped her concentration on the final turn before crossing the line to begin her sixty-fifth lap. Tiny points of darkness shot through her vision as she struggled not to pass the car ahead, but simply to maintain a competitive line. But in spite of her relatively conservative driving, the gap continued to close. She could still capitalize on Terrence Delamar's mistake, if she could only keep her wits.

Her heart was pounding wildly, but she forced her breaths into a deep, rhythmic pattern, hoping to increase the blood flow to her brain. And then, halfway through the lap, she saw her chance—this time on the outside of a turn, as Terrence hugged the inner line. With her superior tires, she might be able to make a play around him.

Gritting her teeth, Thalia pressed on the throttle. As gravity tried to crush her skull, a moan slipped from her mouth, and tears rolled down her cheeks. A yellow haze tinged her peripheral vision, and she struggled to pull in deeper breaths. No. Not now. She could *not* faint now.

Terrence must have caught a glimpse of her approach, because at the apex of the curve, he began to swing wide in an attempt to force her to break. But Thalia slammed down the pedal, and her car leapt beyond the reach of his defensive maneuvering.

Fifth place. She was in fifth place. Her cheeks were tingling and her vision was shot with streaks of red, but she was in fifth place.

"Well fucking done!" Carl shouted into her ear.

She wanted to reply, but even the tiniest movement required a Herculean effort. She had to conserve every drop of energy for this final lap. There could be no mistakes, not even when the pain in her neck and shoulders sent bright arrows up into her brain to pierce her eyes; not even when her left calf muscle seized up in a cramp, making every touch to the brakes a hellish agony.

Twice, Terrence tried to slip past her, and both times she managed to fend him off. By the time she rounded the final bend, her slow, deep breaths had become gasps. Her parched throat burned with thirst, and her peripheral vision was gone. Slowly, the darkness closed in, until her entire vision telescoped down to two narrow cones of visibility. She couldn't see the checkered flag, but when she finally crossed the line, her ears were flooded with the sounds of celebration from the garage.

"Excellent race, Thalia," Alistair spoke calmly over the background exultation.

She wanted to thank him and ask after Peter but was using every ounce of her willpower to hold her head up as the car decelerated. Relief at not having blacked out momentarily eclipsed any sense of pride in her performance. It wasn't over yet—she still needed to guide the car around the circuit one last time to get back to the pit lane. And by the time she arrived, she had to pull herself together in order to function in the post-race media storm. Climbing out of the car only to collapse was not an option. She didn't want anyone to know how difficult that had been, or how close to the edge she had felt. Betraying any kind of weakness would play right into the hands of her enemies and detractors.

"Thalia?" Carl sounded concerned. "Are you okay?"

"Yes, of course," she forced out. "Thank you all. Brilliant job setting up the car. She performed beautifully."

"You made the magic happen out there. Come on in and let's have some champagne."

As she slowly piloted the car around the course for the final time, she tried to shove aside her physical discomfort and take a mental snapshot of this moment. In her first F1 race, she had improved her position from eighth to fifth—a personal victory, if not an actual one. She had won ten points for her team, and had stolen two from one of their main rivals. As her breathing finally began to slow and her heart rate came down to something closer to normal, she was able to smile.

"I did it," she whispered fiercely, rubbing her thumbs in a caress over the handles on the steering wheel. She found herself wondering whether Alix had watched any of the action, or whether she had been completely absorbed by her ulterior motive for attending the race. Might she possibly be impressed by Thalia's historical performance, or was history made by driving around in circles not impressive enough?

And then she laughed at herself, though it came out more like a croak. Why did she care what Alix thought? Plenty of people would recognize the magnitude of her accomplishment—not that she needed their praise, of course. What she needed was the first place trophy.

Thankfully, by the time the entrance to the pit lane appeared, she had regained her peripheral vision. Whether she could walk with the cramp in her calf was another question altogether. As she slid to a stop, her engineers crowded around boisterously, patting her on the helmet and offering their congratulations even as they went through their usual post-race systems check. This was it—the moment she had to stand on her own two feet.

In a motion she'd practiced a thousand times, Thalia pushed herself up and out of the car, putting as little weight as possible on her left leg as she landed on the garage floor. She disconnected her helmet from the head and neck support system and pushed it off, willing her arms not to visibly tremble. The afternoon air might have felt warm to everyone else, but to her it was deliciously cool. As she took a grateful breath, Carl stepped forward to give her a backslapping hug.

"How did Peter do?" she asked, catching sight of him sharing a moment with his wife across the room.

"Second place."

"And who won?"

"Lucas. Mason took third. Brilliant of you to steal two points from Ferrari at the end, there."

"I do have to say, it felt good." With twenty-five points going to the winner, Aiglon had earned thirty-three and was on top of the table. But with the twenty-eight points she and Peter had amassed, they weren't far behind. Trying to conceal her limp, she walked over to the nearest bank of monitors and peered at the leader board, but a sudden rush of dizziness forced her to clutch at the table edge. She needed the team doctor but didn't want to call attention to herself. Carefully, she moved toward the far corner of the garage, which was curtained off to serve as a small medical station. By the time she was close enough to quietly hail Dr. Stevens, her dizziness had returned and her ears were ringing. He took one look at her and ordered her to sit with her head between her legs.

"Privacy?" she managed to whisper, and only relaxed when he closed the curtains around them.

"I know you're dizzy. Headache too?"

"Yes."

"Heat exhaustion. Breathe slowly into this."

Thalia took the oxygen mask gratefully and held it over her face. Within a minute, the fog in her head had lifted and the pain was starting to diminish. She could hear her name being spoken in the garage beyond the curtain and didn't want to lose any more time. With one last grateful inhalation, she removed the mask and held it out to Stevens.

"Thanks. I'll be okay now."

"You should keep that on for at least another ten minutes."

"Can't." Carefully, she stood. "I will have more of that energy drink, if you've got it."

He reached into a nearby cooler. "I'll let you go back out there, but only if you promise to tell me if the dizziness returns."

"Promise." Now that she no longer felt as though she might keel over, Thalia was eager to be back in the crush of humanity. "Thanks, Doc."

When she pulled back the curtain, several team members nearby turned and frowned, Alistair among them. "Are you all right?" he asked.

She brandished her drink. "Never better. Just needed one of these. Is Peter already off to the podium?"

"Yes." He embraced her with his usual awkwardness, but his pleased expression was genuine. "Strong showing today. Let's go watch him get his hardware."

❖

From her position at the railing of the Gambizi Tires box, Alix had a perfect view of the podium. The awards ceremony was a remarkably efficient affair; after some opening words and brief interviews with each driver as well as the chief engineer of Aiglon, the trophies were distributed. The French national anthem was played for Lucas, and she overheard someone nearby explaining that had the constructor been of a different nationality, that anthem would have been played as well. The winners then popped their magnums of champagne, obligatorily spraying the scantily clad women, whom Alix had heard referred to as "grid girls," who shared their stage. They were dressed in identical outfits: low-cut red dresses stamped with the name of one of the circuit's sponsors. The hem barely reached mid-thigh. A few of them had circulated through their box midway through the race, and she had noticed Sebastian chatting with one for quite some time.

As the celebration continued, Alix tried to determine why the presence of those women bothered her so much. Revealing garb aside, they behaved discreetly. None of the "girls" who visited the box had touched a drop of alcohol despite several offers. Clearly, they had a rigorous code of conduct to uphold, no matter how the spectators might construe their presence. But if they were meant to be the circuit's ambassadors to the VIPs, then why were they exclusively female, clothed provocatively, and trained to exude sex appeal? Because most of the VIPs were male, of course. But was that an excuse to reinforce gender stereotypes (however misguided) and promote sexism?

Perhaps it came down to supply and demand. Men drove the cars, bet on the cars, and used the races as networking opportunities. Most men wanted women; therefore, women should be available as eye candy. But candy was something one consumed quickly. Ephemeral, it dissolved on the tongue within seconds to leave an aftertaste. The grid girls were objects to be consumed, not subjects to be conversed with. That was the problem, Alix realized—that the girls were *content* to be repeatedly objectified. It was their occupation, not an occupational hazard.

When the drivers went inside for a press conference, the box balcony began to empty. But Alix had caught sight of Thalia below, and remained outside to watch as the remaining members of the press corps surrounded her. She cut an impressive figure, her racing suit showing off her lean torso and sculpted legs. Dark hair swirled around her shoulders, and her cheeks were flushed. The reporters clustered around her like iron filings to a magnet. But where the grid girls existed to ornament the event, Thalia embodied its rush and thrill. The girls were meant to be seen and not heard, while Thalia's performance demanded she be taken seriously.

At that moment, she looked up to the balcony and found Alix. Raising one hand above her head, she pumped her fist. Alix, half pleased and half embarrassed, gave a brief wave.

"Thalia, your performance today was groundbreaking," someone from the BBC called out. "How do you feel about being the most successful female F1 driver ever?"

"It's an honor to have made history in this way." Thalia's voice rang out over the buzz of the crowd. "And I want to take this moment to salute all the women—drivers, engineers, and team managers—who have paved the way for me to be standing here. But I think they'd agree that making history isn't enough. Only winning is enough."

That was a near-perfect answer, and Alix felt absurdly proud of her for remembering to publicly acknowledge her predecessors. How strange, that she had met Thalia in her inaugural and groundbreaking season, just as she was launching her own women's rights initiative. The synchrony was eerie. Alix had stopped believing in God during her adolescence, and coincidence was nothing more than the human mind grasping at patterns within the chaotic framework of reality. But still—eerie.

"Do you see Aiglon as your main competition this season?" another reporter was asking.

Thalia brushed a strand of hair away from her mouth. "They're an impressive team, but in any given race, anything can happen. Everyone else on that grid is our main competition. Peter and I are going to work as hard as we can to both make it to that podium, every time."

Alix was quite frankly shocked by Thalia's restraint: rather than rising to the bait, she had emphasized teamwork and downplayed the tension between Taggart's former team and his current one.

"Last question, please," Thalia said. "I seriously need a shower."

That prompted a few chuckles. Alix had overheard part of a conversation about the extreme heat in a Formula One cockpit and could only imagine just how grueling it was to jockey for position at high speeds for over two hours while shedding every ounce of water weight. Not that she endorsed such behavior, but it *was* a feat of human stamina.

"You've already broken the record book, Thalia. What's your next goal for this season?"

When Thalia went very still, Alix knew the question had offended her. Apparently, some of the reporters felt the same energy, because the paddock grew noticeably quieter.

"I'm not in this sport to be the best female driver," she finally said. "I'm in it to be the best driver, period. See you in Italy, folks."

But instead of turning back into the garage, Thalia made her way to the barrier and spoke with one of the guards, then gestured to the balcony. Was she coming up? When they disappeared into the grandstand, Alix hurried back inside, discomfited by the elevation of her pulse. Of course Thalia would visit the Gambizi box to greet many of the most important race sponsors. She probably had all kinds of obligations built into her contract.

Wishing she could leave, but knowing she should stay, Alix decided to pay another visit to the bar. She hadn't touched a drop since that first glass of champagne. Now, she could use something to steady her nerves after such a protracted bout of extroversion.

"What may I get you, ma'am?" asked one of the many red-liveried bartenders.

"The punch," sounded a familiar voice behind her. "Two, please."

Shocked, Alix turned to find Thalia mere inches away. She smelled vaguely of heat and metal and motor oil, but somehow the combination wasn't unpleasant. For a moment, it was difficult for Alix to understand how the same person who had been hurtling around the track at over two hundred miles per hour mere minutes ago could now be standing there with a grin, placing a drink order.

In the wake of her surprise, Alix meant to say something suitably congratulatory. Instead, "You're here," was what slipped out.

Thalia's grin widened. "I sure am. Lived to race another day." She cocked her head. "So…what did you think? As mind-numbingly dull as you expected?"

"No, actually." As much as it might pain her to admit her error, Alix prided herself on honesty. "I still think you're a lunatic but was impressed despite myself." Their drinks arrived, and she held hers up between them. "Congratulations on breaking a record today."

"The first of many."

"How insufferably smug of you."

"Not smug. Just confident." Thalia clinked their glasses together. "Wait and see."

Alix drank and found the punch not overly sweet and pleasantly effervescent. "That's lovely, thank you." She sipped again in an effort to mask her own self-consciousness. She hadn't experienced this level of nerves around someone in quite some time. Why did Thalia bring out her insecurities?

"Was your day productive, I hope?"

"It was," Alix said, wondering how much of the question came from a genuine desire to know, and how much from a desire to reinforce her indebtedness. "Lady Rufford and I will be breakfasting tomorrow. Thank you."

Thalia waved her free hand in the air. "No thanks necessary." And then, as though she had read her mind: "I honestly just wanted to know."

At that moment, Rabeck approached with a group of young, well-dressed people in tow. "Thalia!" he called heartily. "Can we have you pose for some photos?"

"Of course." She drained her drink and deposited the glass on the bar. "You should come to Italy," she said under her breath, with a parting glance.

And then she was all practiced smiles as she laughed and posed with Rabeck's entourage, leaving Alix to wonder whether Thalia had been flirting with her and why the notion didn't bother her as much as perhaps it should have.

CHAPTER SEVEN

A lix knew something was wrong when her father joined her in the garden before the sun had fully risen above the horizon. She always breakfasted there when the weather was fine, preferring to savor her coffee. This morning was especially beautiful. Wispy clouds hovered at the horizon, a gauzy veil muting the vivid colors of the ascending star, spreading waves of pastel orange and purple and red and gold across the sky. Just like that, she had realized what her charity ought to be called: Rising Sun. A symbol of the hope and renewal she aspired to bring to the women of Uganda and, eventually, the rest of East Africa.

But then her father's tall form blotted out the light, filling her with a sense of foreboding.

Prince Raphael Pierre Louis Francois of the house of Canella didn't sleep very much. That was one attribute they had in common. But usually, he exercised at dawn and took his breakfast later, with her mother. As he took the seat across from her, she noticed that his eyes were bloodshot and the bags beneath them more prominent than usual. Something had happened.

"Pomme," he said, "I need to speak with you about Florestan."

"Is he all right?" she asked in some alarm. She had seen him earlier in the week, before he had left for a golfing trip to St. Andrews with his friends from university.

Her father's expression soured. "He is apparently in excellent health, seeing as he has gotten Monique pregnant."

"Another one?" Alix couldn't believe it. Florestan already had two illegitimate children with different women: one had been a flight attendant before her royal payoff, and the other had been an interpreter for the United Nations who was now a New York socialite. She had thought Florestan might be starting to settle down, but this latest incident made him seem as much a cad as ever. What on earth did he have against safe sex?

Her father winced. "Indeed. But this one, he will have to marry."

Alix stared at him in disbelief. The idea of Florestan married was about as easy to picture as a cat walking on its hind legs: theoretically, it might be possible, but it didn't seem likely. And then it clicked. This wasn't a matter of impregnating yet another commoner. He would have to marry Monique because she was a royal.

"How is Mother?" she asked, wondering whether she would be furious at the accident or blithely glad of the excuse to plan a wedding.

"She is already consumed with catering and color coordinating."

Alix shared a smile with him before deciding her humor was inappropriate and masking it with her cup. "How can I help?"

Her father steepled his fingers beneath his chin and regarded her thoughtfully. Alix met his gaze. They had always gotten along fairly well—unlike her mother, he had some appreciation for her intellectual ambition, while she seemed only to tolerate it.

"The wedding will be held in two months' time, before Monique's condition is obvious. Florestan will need to temporarily abdicate many of his responsibilities in order to make the preparations." He leaned toward her. "You did very well in London last month. I would like you to take over Florestan's position as our liaison to the Automobile Club de Monaco, if you are willing."

Alix flashed to the memory of Thalia after the Spanish Grand Prix, flushed and exultant, surrounded by fans and well-wishers. She thought of Lady Rufford and all of the other wealthy people in the room who gave to charity to assuage their guilt at their own good fortune. And she thought of the rising sun, that symbol of hope and perseverance.

"I am willing," she said, turning her face up to the light as she met her father's eyes.

❖

Thalia crossed her ankles and leaned back in her chair, enjoying a rare sunny day and an equally rare opportunity to relax. Peter had invited her to spend the day at his home in Tunbridge Wells outside of London. It was the calm before the storm: tomorrow, they would board a flight for Milan to begin preparations for the Italian Grand Prix.

He lounged beside her, holding hands with his wife, Courtney. On the patio, their three-year-old, Bryce, pedaled his tricycle in furious circles. The family dog, a mutt they had rescued long before Bryce came along, watched his progress avidly and heaved a jowl-flapping sigh.

Courtney laughed and reached down to give him a pat. "Rex and I are thinking the exact same thing at the moment."

Thalia could guess. "Bryce takes after Daddy in his need for speed?"

"And after Aunt Thalia," Peter protested.

"There's no pinning that"—she gestured at Bryce as he narrowly avoided clipping a planter containing a bonsai maple tree—"on me, my friend."

"I suppose not." He pushed himself up and gestured toward the outdoor bar, complete with a keg refrigerator. "Fancy another pint?"

"Is the sun hot?" She would need to stop drinking in the days leading up to the race, but for now, she was going to enjoy herself.

After refilling their glasses, Peter toasted their success in Monza. Thalia fervently echoed the sentiment and drank deeply. Fifth place had been fine for the first race of the season, but from here on out, she wanted to stand on the podium.

"So," Peter said into the conversational lull, "when are you going to settle down and invest in a country manor of your own?" He indicated his property with an expansive gesture.

Thalia, who had been about to take another sip, looked at him incredulously. "Settle down? I just got here!" Her life was crazier than it had ever been, and she couldn't imagine trying to cultivate a stable relationship on top of all the other demands on her time and energy. How Peter did it, she had no idea, though he had been racing much longer than she had. Perhaps the demands became more manageable with experience.

"Hon, really," Courtney chimed in. "Do you need to give Thalia the third degree this instant?"

"It's not unreasonable," Peter said. "We got married in my first year in F1."

So much for her theory. But when you purposefully dated people who wouldn't become attached, the likelihood of meeting someone interested in marriage was slim to none. She didn't want to tell him that the idea of settling down felt to her like *settling*, period. Instead, she fell back on humor.

"Well, find me a wife like Courtney and I'll consider it." She leaned forward to include her. "Do you have a sister?"

Courtney laughed. "Two strapping brothers, older, both with broods of their own. Sorry to disappoint."

Peter was like his dog with a bone. "You may be new to Formula One, but you've been racing for a while. Our life is crazy, but that's not a reason to give up on stability." He reached out for Courtney's hand. "Family grounds you. I love racing and I love winning. But having all this…it reminds me of the bigger picture."

The bigger picture. Thalia thought of Alix and her concern for the rural communities in East Africa. Where did that generosity of spirit come from? If she were being honest, she rarely thought of anyone except herself and her own goals. In GP2, she had participated in plenty of charity endeavors, but they were always a means to an end. Other people worried about the bigger picture. She worried about the racetrack. Was that a flaw? Was she missing something?

"You're happy," she said carefully, hoping she was choosing the right words.

"Damn right I am." He grinned. "Look, I promise I'll leave off lecturing you in a moment so we can get back to enjoying these pints. But you deserve happiness too."

"I am ha—"

He held up a hand for her to wait. "You're still near the beginning of your career. I'm getting closer to the end. Once, that would have terrified me. But because of my family, I'm not afraid of what happens when it's over. In some ways I'm even looking forward to it. That's all I wanted to say."

Thalia nodded slowly. She looked from Peter, to Courtney, to Bryce, and then beyond him, to the lush lawn of their spacious garden. It was beautiful. Comfortable. Orderly. But as much as she could appreciate its charms, she didn't want them for herself. The familiar restlessness, her constant companion, seethed beneath her skin, craving the rush of the track.

"I'm glad that's how you feel. You deserve all of this." She shifted her glass in her hand to let the amber liquid catch the sunlight. "But I don't ever want racing to be over."

CHAPTER EIGHT

As the bell tower at Monza struck the half hour, Thalia felt all of the trepidation and none of the anticipation she had experienced at Catalunya. In yesterday's third qualification session, her gearbox had failed during the *Variante Ascari* chicane, forcing her to pull into the pit. Her time had been strong enough to qualify for sixth place, but after the five-place grid penalty for having to replace the gearbox, she would begin the race today from eleventh position. As much as she had tried to put on a brave face for the media, she had to face reality: reaching the podium from eleventh position was nearly impossible.

"Stop psyching yourself out." Peter's hand on her shoulder was a merciful distraction.

"I'm good," she said, hoping she sounded confident.

"No, you're not. You're wallowing in a pity party. Knock it off." He leaned forward until their foreheads were pressed together, balaclava to balaclava. "Sure, you've had some shitty luck this weekend. But anything can happen out there. Claw your way back where you belong, okay?"

For one horrific, ludicrous moment, she thought she might cry. Ruthlessly quashing the impulse, she swallowed hard and pulled back enough to look him in the eyes. "I will."

He nodded sharply and was gone. As much as she was hoping for a chaotic race that would give her a stronger chance of making headway, Thalia wanted him to have a smooth ride. Peter had taken the pole position today, snatching it out of Lucas's grip by four hundredths of a second. Hopefully, he would never see anything but pure daylight for the next two hours. While Aiglon's second driver, Mason Chadworth, had taken P3, Thalia considered Ferrari to be the most dangerous threat in this particular race. Neither Terrence nor Hugo had qualified as well as they wished, but both would do everything in their power to claim a victory for the Tifosi on their home track.

"Time to saddle up, Thalia," Carl called.

As she slid into the car, the engineers swarmed around her like worker bees. She closed her eyes to escape their freneticism. The racetrack unfurled in her mind like a simulation and she saw herself in it—her car, shining silver and red and blue, slicing down the straights and effortlessly commanding the turns, overtaking rival after rival to join Peter at the apex of the pack. As she envisioned each subsequent meter of the track, she felt her pulse finally begin to steady.

"Fall asleep in there?" Carl asked with an affectionate thump on her helmet.

Suddenly invigorated, Thalia flashed him the finger. "Not likely!"

The next several minutes were a whirlwind of checking and double-checking before Carl finally started the engine. Her installation lap from the pit to the grid was thankfully uneventful, though she had to grind her teeth at watching Terrence pull into *her* sixth place spot. The team was protecting her from the media's intrusiveness, but Terrence had no compunctions about preening under the lights and before the cameras. Silently, she vowed to catch him.

With two minutes until the start, Alistair entered her field of view. "If you can get us at least one point, we'll call today a success."

Carl punctuated his words by starting up the engine again. Its roar thrummed through her body like the deep purr of a lion. She could feel it hovering—the elusive *zone* where her conscious mind was suspended in a state of hyperawareness even as her muscles reacted from memory. If she could only enter that headspace at the beginning of the race and remain there for its duration, she would be unstoppable.

The warm-up lap passed uneventfully, and by the time she had repositioned her car on the grid, anticipation had trumped her anxiety. She was an underdog. Everyone in front of her—and probably some of those behind—would underestimate her. Peter was right: she belonged on top of the grid, not at its midpoint. This was a golden opportunity to prove herself as the real deal and shut up everyone who was calling her a fluke, or a publicity stunt, or worse.

The world became five lights turning red. When they winked out, she was ready, surging forward to gain position on both cars in the row ahead. From eleventh to ninth in less than one second. Not bad. As the triumphant hollers from the garage echoed in her earpiece, Thalia remained aggressive, pushing hard in an attempt to overtake the eighth car on the first corner. Gravity knocked the breath from her lungs as she entered the chicane faster than she ever had, and she fought to keep the car on its line even as she hurtled past her opponent.

Eighth place. But by now, the field was beginning to spread out. Any other gains wouldn't come so easily.

Despite driving as efficiently as she ever had on this circuit, it took until the twenty-sixth lap for Thalia to make up another position. Once in seventh, she set her sights on Terrence. He was almost two seconds ahead, but she chipped and chipped away at the gap, gradually whittling it down. Unfortunately, by the time she was within striking distance, she had to pit.

"He'll have to come in soon," Carl said. "You'll have your shot."

He was right. A few minutes later, Terrence pulled into the pit lane, and several seconds after that, Carl jumped back onto the microphone. "Long pit for Terrence. Put him away!"

Jumping at the chance, Thalia took the final corner—the Curva Parobolica—as quickly as she possibly could. By the time she returned to the pit lane exit, they were on a collision course. Forcing her throttle to the floor, she blew past Terrence with what had to be scant hundredths of a second to spare.

He was going to fight her for the position, and so she focused on making her next circuit the most efficient yet. For the next few laps, he pushed hard, trying to force her into making a mistake. But that strategy went both ways, and if she kept her calm, perhaps he would eventually be the one to misjudge. She had to hold on. The cramp between her shoulder blades was nothing compared to the pain of the frustration she would feel if he managed to retake sixth place.

"Doing great, Thalia," Carl spoke into her ear. "Keep fending him off. He's burning more rubber than you."

That was true. Every time he swung wide or moved inside to challenge her, he was wearing down his tires more quickly than she was by maintaining the best possible line. She kept her car directly in the middle of the track on the penultimate straight and took a quick sip of her energy drink in preparation for the battle that was sure to come on the parabolic curve. Praying her new gearbox would continue to hold up, she downshifted and hit the brakes. Defending the corner was a matter of accelerating precisely at its apex in order to thwart his inevitable attempt to overtake. Even if she had wanted to breathe through it, the g-forces had temporarily paralyzed her lungs. Poised to open up the throttle and blast out of the turn, she waited for just the right moment—

The car shuddered and jerked toward the inside of the curve, its wheels scraping the turf. Thalia's teeth rattled in her head, and she accidentally bit her tongue as she desperately tried to wrest back some control. Reflexes honed by years of training were all that kept her from colliding with the barrier. She straightened out her course with mere inches to spare and let her car coast to a stop. Her ears were ringing and her mouth tasted like copper and she was dazedly captivated by the afternoon sunlight glinting off the spires of the main grandstand ahead.

"Thalia!" Alistair's voice sliced through her shock. "Are you all right?"

"I'm okay." She swallowed blood, gagged, and instinctively pushed the drink button. "What the bloody hell just happened?" she demanded, not even caring that her voice was trembling.

"Terrence clipped you. Wait for my word. Once the backfield clears, let's see if you can come in on your own."

"Are you fucking kidding me?" Thalia could feel the rage bubbling up inside her chest, threatening to drown her. With a supreme mental effort, she forced it back. For the moment, she was still in this race.

As precious seconds ticked by, fear warred with her anger. Here, on the inside of one of the fastest corners in the world, she was a sitting duck for anyone who happened to make a mistake or experienced a technical failure. When Alistair finally gave her the all clear, relief and nerves almost made her stall out.

The instant she pulled back onto the track, she could feel that something was wrong. The car was pulling hard to the right and responding sluggishly to the throttle. As she limped into the pit lane, hope drained away like sand from an hourglass. Even as she tried to convince herself that her damage was localized to a tire, every instinct screamed that it was much worse. This race was over for her—she would have bet on it.

Back in the pit, it took less than ten seconds for the engineers to corroborate her instincts. There was damage not only to the rear left tire, but also to the axle. In the blink of an eye, she had gone from sixth place to DNF—Did Not Finish.

After the crew guided her car back into the garage she waved off Carl's attempt to help her out, vaulted over the side, and barely resisted the urge to dash her helmet to the ground. "God damn it!"

Alistair was suddenly in front of her, gripping her shoulders. "You need to see the doctor."

"No, I'm not hurt. You're sure he clipped me?"

His mouth tightened. "Come and see."

At the nearest bank of computers, he called up her on-board camera. It showed two points of view, one behind and one ahead, and she gripped the table's edge as Alistair homed in on the rearview vantage point. As he replayed the footage from her last few minutes on the track, Thalia felt as though her brain had split in two: one half was critically analyzing her own driving, while the other focused on Terrence's maneuvers. At some points, she had done an admirable job of defending her position, while at others, she had created more space than she should have.

Thalia could see now that as she had gone into that final turn before the collision, she had left Terrence more of an opening than she had intended. But instead of taking the space he'd been given, he had pulled up close beside her in his overtaking attempt. Just as she'd been about to pull away—even now, she could *feel* that instant of anticipation before slamming home the accelerator—his front wing had nicked her rear left tire.

"What the fuck!" She brought her fist down on the tabletop, rattling the entire row of flat screens. "He could have gotten around me!"

"I agree." As always, Alistair was calm. Too calm. How could he be so even-keeled about something that had taken one of his drivers out of the race? Now, instead of the eight or even ten points they might have earned from her position, they had none. Peter would have to carry them both, and through no fault of her own.

Thalia wanted to scream. The rage bubbled up inside her, hot and fierce and animal, begging for an outlet. But she couldn't scream. She was supposed to be a professional. A true professional would be asking all the right questions right now, like whether they could file a formal complaint with the FIA and ask that they look into the collision. Thalia opened her mouth and the words just wouldn't come around the festering knot of emotion that clogged her throat.

At that moment, Alistair was called away to address a question about some of the telemetry data from Peter's car. Struggling to blink back tears at her own helplessness, Thalia forced herself to watch the end of the race. That's what Peter would have done, had their roles been reversed, and it was the least she could do now.

But as she watched Terrence lock in his sixth place finish while Lucas and Peter dueled for first, envy and bitterness rose up to choke her. Clutching the edges of her stool, she prayed for the race to be over quickly so she could begin drowning her sorrows with the very expensive spirits that would doubtless be provided at the after party.

❖

Alix's second Grand Prix had been nothing like her first. Last time, she had been a prized spectator, valued for the prestige her royalty automatically bestowed on those with whom she associated. Now, she still felt objectified, but at least she was a member of the club—albeit still on the fringes. As the official guest of Franz Mueller, the FIA president, she had spent the day in his box. Mindful of her own lack of fluency in F1 jargon compounded by her relative ignorance of the rules, she had spent most of her time hovering at the periphery of conversations and paying special attention to the behavior and responsibilities of those in charge of the event. In a few months, she would be in their shoes.

Since her arrival on Friday morning, Alix had been swept along with the other VIPs from event to event: the free practice and qualifying sessions at the track, a tasting at a nearby vineyard, a charity gala in Milan. The gala had inspired an epiphany; if she were to solidify the creation of Rising Sun before the Monaco Grand Prix, couldn't she hold a similar event? Energized by the revelation, she had stayed up late into the night struggling through what felt like endless paperwork.

She had needed more than her usual two cups of coffee to feel alert today, and the extended extroversion of the weekend was starting to take its toll. Fortunately, she wasn't a recognizable enough face that people constantly sought her out, and she had managed to retreat to a corner of the sofa in order to alternatively watch the race and the other spectators.

Like the Monegasque committee, the Italian organizing team appeared to be composed of both government officials and businessmen. Benito Brunardi, the Italian Prime Minister, was rather aloof and standoffish, but his wife did a fine job of playing the role of hostess. Their adolescent son was completely obsessed with Ferrari, and his enthusiasm was charming. Thalia's historic race in Spain had helped her understand how a racecar driver really could be a true hero, and Alix decided then and there to allocate some of the reserved Monaco GP tickets to children and their families who otherwise wouldn't be able to attend.

Thalia. The thought of her inspired a rush of sympathy. The crowd had erupted in confusion after her collision, and Alix could only imagine how discouraging it was for her to be unable to finish the race. Among those gathered in the box, debates had sprung up about whether the FIA should penalize Terrence Delamar and Ferrari. Despite the fact that the television announcers had been unanimous in their attribution of the fault to Terrence, Alix had overheard more than a few uncharitable comments about Thalia's racing ability. Each time, she had felt the urge to intervene and point out Thalia's detractors' obvious misogyny, and each time, she hadn't dared. Did that make her a coward?

Her self-recrimination was interrupted by Mueller's invitation to join him and the Brunardis on the track for the awards. When the elevator doors opened, a wall of sound assaulted her. Claude stepped out in front, fully on alert, but Brunardi's security detail had already taken care to create a clear passage. They were going behind the scenes to prepare for the award presentation, but Alix declined to join them. She wanted to try to touch base with Thalia, and Thalia was most definitely not getting an award.

Claude guided her to the VIP paddock, which commanded a perfect view of the stage. Thalia's teammate Peter had taken first place, but if Alix understood the rules correctly, Thalia's "DNF" meant that she had not been able to contribute even a single point, despite the strength of her position before the collision.

Alix forced herself to pay close attention to the intricacies of the podium ceremony. After brief interviews with all three drivers for the benefit of the grandstand and television viewers, each man raised his magnum of champagne. While everyone else in the paddock was pressing forward, she did her best to move out of the range of the bottles. Fortunately, her father would be presenting the trophies to the competitors in Monaco, so she wouldn't have to risk a close encounter.

The grid girls noticeably steeled themselves, freezing their smiles in place and narrowing their eyes. Alix couldn't blame them—being sprayed with champagne had to sting. At the last minute, all three drivers decided to coordinate, and their corks arced into the air in near synchronicity. As they drank and laughed and delivered a few more comments into the microphone, Alix looked again for Thalia, and this time she found her.

She stood on the track below the far end of the stage, surrounded by a clump of reporters. In the scintillating sunlight, her dark hair gleamed purplish-black like a raven's feathers. As she spoke, her hands sliced through the air, and while Alix couldn't hear her words, she could read the tension in her body language.

The stage emptied as the winning drivers headed for their press conference, and the VIP paddock began to clear out as well. But Alix remained, wanting to see if she could catch Thalia's attention. At the very least, she wanted to convey her sympathies.

And then Terrence Delamar emerged onto the track from below the stage, precipitating a chorus of quickly hushed exclamations. He headed in Thalia's direction, and someone must have warned her of his approach, because she spun to face him. Trailing reporters in her wake, she marched up to him, drew back her fist, and punched him in the face.

Terrence staggered away, clutching at his nose, blood leaking through his fingers. When he pulled his hand away and found his palm swathed in red ribbons, he shouted a string of obscenities in a mix of French and English. Thalia shouted back, gesturing sharply in the direction of the corner where they had collided.

"You pulled that shit on purpose! You had no move there, and you know it!"

Terrence spat blood onto the ground and rounded on her, clenching his own fists. "I was quicker coming into that corner!"

Alix watched in disbelief as the crews of both drivers converged on their positions to hold them both in place. One of Terrence's engineers was trying to staunch his nose with a towel, despite Terrence's attempts to get around him. Within moments, they were joined by a few security guards.

"Watch the video!" Thalia yelled. "You had nothing! You purposely sabotaged me!"

"You were too loose, you fucking cunt! You weren't on the line!"

Stunned by his language, Alix was even more shocked to see Thalia struggling furiously against the men who held her. Was she so far beyond reason that she wanted to attack him *again*? Her intensity must have caught the guards flat-footed as well, because she nearly broke free before one of them firmly grabbed her by the shoulders. She struggled with the officer, and in resisting, handed over the authority for him to be much more severe. Even as he pinned her hands behind her back, she continued to shout.

"Too loose? I was on the perfect line! Watch the goddamn replay, you misogynistic prick!"

More guards arrived, then, closing ranks around both Terrence and Thalia. Still battling her disbelief, Alix watched as the men escorted both drivers into racing headquarters. The crowd, which had gone silent, now began to murmur its disapproval. She had no doubt that the media had captured the entire altercation. This incident would not only taint the entire race weekend, but also the image of women in motorsport. Alix felt betrayed on behalf of her entire sex. She wanted Thalia to raise the bar of the sport, not sink to its lowest level of mudslinging.

Even if Thalia was correct about Terrence's motivation, the rules were clear. The FIA was the arbitrating force, not her fists. They could investigate if they felt something illegal had happened during the race. Her frustration and disappointment were understandable, especially given the strength of her position before the collision. But did that excuse the kind of violence and vitriol she had just witnessed? Of course not. Assaulting another driver was unsportsmanlike and indefensible. If Thalia was going to be competitive in Formula One, she had to first of all not sabotage herself.

Mueller's aide approached, hands clasped before him. "Your Serene Highness, I'm so sorry you had to witness that. Would you like me to escort you elsewhere?"

"I'll be returning to the box," she said, "but no need for you to be inconvenienced. Claude will see me there safely."

"Very well." The man quickly moved off.

"What are your plans for the remainder of the evening, ma'am?" Claude asked quietly as they returned to the elevators.

Alix could feel a headache threatening behind her eyes, and part of her longed to ask Claude to put the helicopter on standby so she could be in the air and headed for home within the hour. But if she left now, she wouldn't experience the full arc of a Formula One race weekend. For the next six weeks, the Grands Prix would be held in Oceania and Asia, and she had too much work of her own to consider accompanying the circuit south and east. She needed to see this circus through.

"I'd like to return to the hotel for a while," she said, "before putting in a brief appearance at the after party. Emphasis on *brief.*"

Once she had shown her face and witnessed the arrangements, she could retreat to her suite and spend what was left of the night in peace.

CHAPTER NINE

The official Formula One after party, known as the Onyx Salon, was held at an exclusive venue near each track. In Milan, this amounted to booking Giorgio Armani's nightclub. As soon as Alix was waved inside, claustrophobia rose up to choke her. Having already spent too many hours in the presence of too many people, she was more sensitive than usual to the constricting sensation that lodged in her throat. Two hours of much-needed solitude at the hotel hadn't been nearly enough to recharge her batteries.

She hadn't been able to stop herself from turning on the news to see what the pundits were saying about the race. They had vacillated between analyzing the collision and criticizing the altercation afterward. Alix had seen clips from an interview with Terrence—who was well on his way to having a black eye—in which he claimed to have been on his way to check on Thalia when she attacked him "out of the blue." When the interviewer pushed him on the obscene and degrading language he had used in response, Terrence said he had been shocked and upset and couldn't remember what he had said in the heat of the moment.

Alix, who thought that the "heat of the moment" tended to be when a person's true character was revealed, didn't believe his convenient story about shock-inspired amnesia. Terrence was probably the "misogynistic prick" Thalia had accused him of being, but he was doing a good job of portraying himself as a victim in this case.

The television program had then turned to clips from a press conference with Thalia and Alistair Campbell, in which Thalia expressed remorse for giving in to her anger and frustration. She informed the media that she had already apologized to Terrence, and that she wanted her fans to understand that her behavior had been reprehensible. But as Alix watched her say all the right things, she wondered whether Thalia meant any of them. Campbell said very little except that they would be subsidizing Thalia's participation in an anger-management workshop and had asked the FIA to look into Terrence's overtaking move. The remainder of Campbell's response was interrupted by breaking news that the FIA would not, in fact, be launching a formal investigation, calling the collision a "racing incident" that did not require an official inquiry, and that they had sanctioned Thalia with a "heavy fine" for her unsportsmanlike behavior.

Alix wondered what Thalia thought of their decision. She didn't quite know what to think of it herself, though the fine did seem appropriate. But was it equally appropriate for the FIA not to investigate what had happened during the race, or was their hands-off response more evidence of misogyny?

Mercifully, the club's VIP host arrived, interrupting her pointless introspection. After expressing his delight at her presence and his willingness to provide any amenity she wished, he led her upstairs to the VIP area. The semicircular bar was surfaced with burnished copper that reflected the spinning lights above the nearby dance floor. Most people were either dancing or seated in small groups in the lounge, but Alix opted for a small table tucked into the back corner of the room.

She had already consumed more alcoholic drinks today than she usually did in a week, but as soon as she caught sight of Thalia, she wanted another. Dressed in a pair of threadbare jeans and a white collared shirt, she blatantly flouted the club's dress code. She was leaning against the bar, and snugged between her legs was one of the platinum blond grid girls. As Alix watched, Thalia cupped the woman's waist, then skimmed her palms up until her thumbs could reach the undersides of her breasts.

Blindsided by a wave of fury, Alix had to turn away. Despite all the controversy earlier in the day, Thalia was now choosing to make even more of a spectacle of herself? Alix felt as though she were observing the behavior of a completely alien species. How was this Thalia even the same person as the one who had given her dancing lessons only a few weeks ago? At the wedding, Thalia had been playful and flirtatious, but also insightful and kind and sympathetic. Now, she was playing into every single chauvinist stereotype about racecar drivers without even being male. The disconnect was so severe that Alix found herself wondering whether Thalia might actually have multiple personality disorder.

The host, who had stepped away discreetly as she settled in, now returned to take her drink order.

"A sidecar, please," Alix replied, because that was exactly how she felt at the moment—a sidecar to the real action and politics of racing. She had chosen to become a part of this world for selfish reasons, true, but also because Thalia's presence in it had led her to believe that Formula One was on the verge of becoming more inclusive. Thalia had the opportunity to advocate for that inclusivity, and to model what true equality looked like. But judging from what Alix had seen today, Thalia wasn't interested in using her position for anything except her own self-interest. She couldn't even put aside her own hot-headedness for the sake of her team's status and reputation. She wanted to be a member of the good old boys' club, not work to transform it from the inside out.

In an effort to slow her hyperactive brain, Alix looked deliberately around the room, everywhere except near Thalia. Liquor and laughter dominated the scene. The music, loud and unfamiliar, was trying to burrow itself into her head. Her birthright entitled her to enter any conversation in the room, and she *should* be out there, beating the metaphorical bushes to drum up support for her charity. But even the prospect of turning herself back "on" socially was utterly exhausting.

It was suddenly all too obvious that she didn't belong here. And if she didn't belong here—if she couldn't muster the will and energy to advocate for her own project—what did that say about her likelihood of success? Maybe she wasn't cut out for this kind of philanthropy. Perhaps it would be better to give her time and money and expertise to other organizations, rather than found her own. Maybe this entire project was a fool's errand, and she the fool.

"Why so serious?" At the sound of Thalia's slurred voice, Alix's chest tightened. She forced herself to look up slowly. Thalia was alone. Even flushed and glassy-eyed, she was stunningly beautiful. Uncomfortable with the thought, Alix reminded herself that Thalia's beauty was only skin-deep.

"And why are you sitting by yourself?" Thalia pressed, sliding into the chair across from hers. "Don't you know it's a party?"

"You certainly look like you're having fun." Alix wanted to take the words back as soon as she spoke them, but now that they were out, she couldn't help adding, "Where is your friend?"

Either Thalia hadn't picked up on her sarcasm, or she didn't care. "Victoria? She stepped out for a cigarette."

"Lovely." Alix had no desire to hide her disdain. And all health-related feelings about smoking aside, how could it be enjoyable to kiss a smoker? Not that she wanted to think about Thalia kissing anyone.

Thalia frowned and, leaning forward, she squinted dramatically in the way intoxicated people do when they are trying to focus. "I know smoking's pretty bad. But c'mon. Don't you have some vices? At least one?"

"I have flaws," Alix said, thinking of her impatience and of her pride. "I don't have vices."

"What's the difference?"

"Flaws are embedded in a person's character, like..." Struggling for a comparison, she fixed on a loose thread in the collar of Thalia's shirt. "Like an imperfection in a fabric. And repairing them is the struggle of a lifetime. But a vice is a choice—something you choose to do, despite knowing it's bad for you."

Thalia cocked her head, visibly thinking over the distinction. "If that's true, then flaws can lead to vices."

"Yes," Alix admitted, wondering how on earth they had managed to get into a philosophical discussion in a nightclub. "But someone who is actively working to mend their flaws will have an easier time resisting vice."

The bridge of Thalia's nose wrinkled. Alix would have called the expression "cute" if she hadn't been so frustrated. It was taking all her self-restraint not to refer specifically to Thalia's shortcomings during this conversation. She would have made quite the case study.

"What are your flaws, then?" Thalia asked.

Alix appreciated candor in herself and others, but every instinct screamed at her not to reveal any vulnerabilities to Thalia. She sipped from her drink in order to buy enough time to consider how to answer. "I'm not in the mood to discuss them," she said finally.

"C'mon." Thalia apparently had enough control remaining over her fine motor skills to waggle her eyebrows. "I'll show you mine if you show me yours."

The mental image of Thalia unbuttoning her shirt, revealing inch after inch of pale, golden skin, took Alix's mind by storm. She barely held back a gasp at the intensity of her physical response. And then the image was gone, leaving her hollow. Fear rushed in to fill the empty space, with anger close behind. Why was she letting Thalia affect her this way?

"Yours are already on display for the world to see," she snapped.

Thalia drew back, her gaze sharpening. "I get it. You're pissed off that I hit Terrence."

The rules of politeness dictated that Alix should keep her mouth shut, or tell Thalia that she didn't want to discuss this either. But the pressure of her anger and frustration—both at Thalia and herself—had reached a boiling point.

"Why? Just…why? Why would you ever do something like that? Why would anyone?"

Thalia crossed her arms over her chest. "He deliberately took me out of the race. They're hazing me because they don't think I belong!" When she realized the volume of her voice was starting to elevate, she hunched forward. "And they're getting away with it."

"'They' who?"

"The other drivers."

"How do you know?"

"I just know! They don't want me here."

Feeling a headache coming on, Alix rubbed at her temples. She didn't know enough to be able to judge whether there might actually be some sort of fraternal conspiracy against Thalia, but without any evidence, her accusations seemed baseless.

"What?" Thalia asked belligerently. "You don't believe me?"

"To be honest, you sound quite paranoid right now." When she opened her mouth to retort, Alix forestalled her. "I'm not saying the other drivers aren't going to test your limits. That makes a certain kind of sense. And I'm not saying that Terrence didn't do something wrong, because it sounds like he did. But when you react the way that *you* did, you sink to their level. Below it, even, because at least Terrence hit you in a race while he was trying to pass you."

"You're taking his side." Thalia's jaw was tightly clenched in obvious anger, but she at least had the presence of mind to keep her voice down. "I can't fucking believe this."

"Taking his side?" Alix bristled. "I was there today. I heard what he called you, and I am absolutely not taking his side. I'm taking yours, though you don't seem to have the ability to see it. All you're interested in doing is self-destructing."

The flush spread down Thalia's neck, mottling her flawless skin. "How am I being *self*-destructive when fucking Terrence fucking *hit* me?"

"Have you ever considered that if you had gone straight to the FIA and presented your case, instead of throwing a fit and punching another driver, they might actually be opening a formal investigation right now? You made it easy for them not to take you seriously. Not to respect you. And not only them—everyone. Reporters. Fans. Little girls everywhere who like to go fast on their scooters and bicycles.

"Imagine the father who loves Formula One and wants to share it with his daughter, especially now that there's a female driver who seems so promising. They sit down together to watch the race. When the female driver gets hit by someone who clearly wasn't following the overtaking rules, they both shout at the screen, and once the girl has calmed down, her father has a talk with her about sportsmanlike behavior. And then, in the post-race coverage, the girl's hero *punches* the driver who caused the collision." Caught up in the story she had spun, Alix jabbed the table with her forefinger. "Now you've lost her admiration and her father's respect."

Thalia tugged at her collar as though it were suddenly too tight. "For God's sake, I never asked to be anyone's role model."

"But you are. Don't you see? You have a gift, and you've worked so hard, and you're squandering it. You could be the change you want to see in this world, instead of perpetuating what's worst about it."

Alix sat back in her chair and realized she had just delivered an unintended lecture. Her heart was pounding and her breaths were coming quickly, and as she squared off silently with Thalia across the table, she wondered whether anything she'd said had hit its mark. The small muscles around Thalia's jaw continued to clench and unclench as she stared at her, but Alix couldn't read the expression in her eyes. Did Thalia hate her now? The thought was unsettling, though she wanted not to care.

"I'm not the person you want me to be." When Thalia finally spoke, her voice was surprisingly devoid of inflection. "I like to drive fast cars and fuck fast women and drink too much and watch the sun rise before I sleep. That's who I am. I'm here to win, not to be a hero or make a point."

Fury broke over Alix like a firecracker, flaring briefly before winking out into darkness. In its wake, exhaustion came crashing down. She was beyond finished with this conversation. She raised her glass in mockery of a toast, then downed its contents and pushed back her chair.

"Best of luck with that."

She left the club without a backward glance, regretting her decision to ever become involved in Formula One in the first place. At least it would be well over a month before she would have to see Thalia again. Hopefully, after a long separation, the intensity of her visceral reactions would subside.

CHAPTER TEN

Every second of the Malaysian Grand Prix was torture. It was always the hottest race of the season, and even the most experienced drivers had been known to grow dizzy or confused with dehydration and heat exhaustion by the last several laps. A few had even fainted and crashed. During the nearly three weeks they had to prepare, Thalia increased her cardio regimen, even going so far as to crank up the heat in her gym in order to simulate the racing temperature. She hydrated religiously, sucking down liters of the electrolyte-heavy drink as she practiced repeatedly in the simulator.

But that was during the day. Work hard, play hard—and at night, she did. Her fame was now sufficient to catapult her into an entirely new class of celebrity, with all the rights belonging thereto. She went out to the hottest clubs and promptly undid all her hydration. She attended exclusive private parties and brought a new date to each. As her fame increased, so did the invitations…along with the attention she was receiving from the public. Photos of her began to appear regularly in the tabloids and on entertainment news shows. Suggestive nicknames were invented for her. Internet articles speculated on her allure. One of her dates ended up on a sleazy morning talk show.

Her critics were eager to point out her active social life as evidence of a lack of focus. They were desperate to get hold of every glossy image taken by the paparazzi—and every grainy video captured by the amateurs—that revealed her hedonism. They debated her on sports television and radio, on blogs, on social media.

When she managed a seventh place in Malaysia, she thought she might have silenced them. But after video emerged of her feeling up a grid girl at the Onyx Salon that same evening, the murmurs once again became shouts.

Shortly after the F1 coterie arrived in Melbourne for the Australian Grand Prix, her father summoned her to his hotel room. They rarely spoke at all, but had become virtually noncommunicative since the beginning of the season. What would have been the point? He was focused on managing his Ferrari drivers, and she was focused on trying to beat them. But when he opened the door for her, she expected some gesture of recognition that their relationship wasn't purely professional—a paternal arm squeeze, or a grudging word of praise. She got neither. Without a word, he led her into the seating area of his suite.

"Your behavior has been untoward," he said once they were seated on opposing couches.

"Has it really?" she asked sarcastically. "According to whom?"

"According to any decent person."

"Not you, then. So you're worried about what everyone else thinks of me. How sweet."

His eyes narrowed. "Stop trying to be smart, because you're not."

Thalia winced inside and hoped she had not done so visibly. She was swimming in shark waters. There could be no sign of wound or weakness.

"I didn't call you here for my own sake," he continued in that crisp, infernally proper British accent that suggested he was civilized and she barbaric. "But for yours. Your actions have become increasingly self-destructive."

"You'll have to be more specific." Thalia decided to willfully misinterpret his concern. "Am I too loose on the corners? Not quite catching the proper bite point? What exactly is not to your liking?"

"Stop being deliberately obtuse." In a rare show of emotion, he ran one hand through his steel-gray hair. "This has nothing to do with your racing and everything to do with what happens off the track. The booze, the women—"

"At least I can't get any of them pregnant."

He flushed a dark scarlet and went perfectly still. "As usual, you are twisting everything I say."

"And as usual, you are being a condescending bastard. Where you get the nerve to lecture me about my life choices, I'll never understand." Thalia stood. "If you approach me again, I'll report it to the FIA as a case of tampering with another team's driver."

When she turned to leave, he called after her. "I'm not finished with you yet!"

"See if I care." Thalia opened the door and didn't look back.

❖

In China, she qualified in fifth place but dropped down to eighth by the end of the race, while Peter took second. It was the car, she claimed, and switched over to the team's spare. But two weeks later in Australia, she managed only ninth while Peter claimed another victory.

It wasn't the car.

After falling three places in Shanghai, video of her doing a keg stand at a private after party had found its way online. When she barely squeaked into ninth place two weeks later, photographs emerged of her getting a lap dance at an exclusive club in Melbourne. Because Peter had won decisively, no one was in a forgiving frame of mind.

On the day after the race, Thalia was sleeping off her hangover when she was awakened by a phone call: Lord Rufford's assistant, summoning her to brunch with his wife. Thalia lurched out of bed and into the bathroom to lean against the shower wall under a stream of nearly-scalding water. She made herself as presentable as she could as quickly as she was able, all the while battling the premonition that she was about to get a dressing-down. An hour later, she stood outside the door to their presidential suite, feeling rather like a wayward child who had been summoned to the principal's office.

But she hadn't done anything wrong. She had to remember that. No, she hadn't raced as well as she had hoped, but she had still finished in the points. And what she did on her own time, when she wasn't training or in the car, was her business. If the press chose to make it theirs and then pillory her for it, that was their problem. This entire so-called "scandal" was completely a product of the pervasive double standard that denied women the same social freedoms as men.

When she was ushered inside, Lady Rufford was already sitting at the table, sipping from a delicate china teacup. She looked Thalia up and down, and her mouth compressed.

"You look like something the cat dragged in." She gestured to the food. "Sit. Eat." She snapped her fingers at the hovering waiter. "You there. Pour Ms. d'Angelis some much-needed coffee."

"Thank you," Thalia murmured, resentment simmering beneath her meek comportment.

The waiter removed the lids from several dishes: scrambled eggs, French toast, sautéed mushrooms, roasted potatoes. Thalia's stomach turned, but she forced herself to take a little of everything except for the toast.

Lady Rufford made no move to pick up her fork, which suited Thalia just fine. The silence stretched between them.

"My husband took a risk on you," Lady Rufford finally said.

Her accusatory tone got under Thalia's skin, fraying the shreds of patience she had tried to pull around her like a tattered jacket. "Your husband hired me as a publicity stunt."

"Does that matter? If you do well, everyone wins. You're here, in Formula One, where you have wanted to be all your life." She leaned closer. "There are drivers who would give their firstborn child for the chance you've been given."

"For the chance I've *earned*."

"If you've earned this position, then why are you acting like a publicity stunt?"

Thalia felt as though she were taking a tight corner—unable to breathe, unable to blink, unable to do anything more than endure the terrible pressure. "Excuse me?" she finally choked out.

"Whenever I see you, you're either whining petulantly about something out of your control, making some kind of ridiculous demand like a prima donna, or hanging all over a grid girl. You need to change your attitude, your behavior, and the company you keep. Then, perhaps people will believe you've earned your way onto this stage."

Resentment churned sluggishly in her chest, stirring up the long-buried sediment of guilt. Obstinately, she resisted the emotion. "All of the most successful male drivers—except for Peter—are exactly what you just described. Why should I need to behave differently from them? If you claim to be a feminist, then why are you reinforcing the double standard?"

"Because you *are* different. And you should be. Men and women should always be equal, but never the same. The double standard may be ridiculous, but why would you want to play into that kind of male chauvinism in the first place?" Lady Rufford pointed an elegant finger at her chest. "Do you really want to objectify a woman, clumsily seduce her, bed her, and then forget her name the next morning? Or do you want to be different?"

Thalia stood up and pushed back her chair. "I want to be myself," she spat.

"I'm relieved to hear that." Lady Rufford looked up at her, unfazed. "Because it seems to me as though you've been trying awfully hard to be exactly like those men you mentioned."

❖

Thalia leaned against the balcony and looked down at the ocean foaming against the coral reef that stretched invisibly below the surface. She wished she could sprout a pair of gills and lose herself in it—become something not human for a few hours and escape into the simplicity of an animal brain.

Did animals feel shame? Dogs, perhaps, though that might also be anthropomorphization. Nothing that swam through that coral reef felt shame, she was sure.

You need to change your attitude, your behavior, and the company you keep.

Every word was a bitter pill to swallow, but she would have to internalize them if she wanted to succeed. How could she not have seen what Lady Rufford had perceived so easily: that in her quest to legitimize herself as a Formula One driver, she hadn't been original or authentic in the slightest. All she had done was parrot how the men around her acted.

She thought of Alix and how passionately she had tried to make that very point at the Onyx Salon after the Italian Grand Prix. Thalia hadn't been willing to listen then, but she was now. Had Alix been watching these past few races as Thalia continued to fall apart? Had she felt vindicated? She didn't strike Thalia as the kind of person to buy tabloids, but when the papers were staring you in the face at every supermarket, how could you avoid them?

Then again, Alix was a princess. She didn't need to go to the supermarket.

Alix deserved an apology. Perhaps that could be her first step on the road to following Lady Rufford's command. She would mend her—relationship? friendship? acquaintance?—with Alix and try to remain in her orbit for the time being. In so doing, she would also remove herself from the temptations of her usual social scene. It was as good a plan as any—assuming, of course, she could convince Alix to go along with it.

"Hey." Peter had found her.

"Hey." She glanced at him quickly, then away. "Where are Courtney and Bryce?"

He pointed behind them, toward the pool. "Happily splashing away."

She watched as Bryce, his arms enveloped by a pair of Batman floaties, doggie-paddled enthusiastically toward his mother. For one ridiculous instant, she wanted to trade places with him. And then the feeling passed.

"So…what's going on with you?" Peter asked.

"What do you mean?"

"I mean that I feel sometimes like I barely know you anymore." His stare bored into hers. "The Thalia I know is a fighter. She would never be content with these kinds of results. She'd find a way to pull herself back up to the top, instead of letting herself sink to the bottom."

"Yeah, well, maybe you don't know me." Chest aching with a fresh surge of shame, she returned her gaze to the ocean.

"Bullshit." Peter spoke the word in an oddly conversational tone. "I've watched you race with a giant chip on your shoulder since you were a teenager. You raced to get your father to act like he loves you, and when that didn't work, you raced so he would respect you. But underneath all of that bullshit, it was always clear that you were racing because it was your vocation." He shrugged. "That's what you've lost."

Frowning, she turned back to him. "But it *is* my vocation. It's the only thing I'm good at."

"Now you just sound desperate. Desperation breeds fear, and fear breeds failure. Don't you think Terrence is patting himself on the back right now for getting into your head with that dick move of his at Monza? You haven't been the same since, because you've been afraid."

"I'm not afraid," she shot back. "I've always known the risks."

"Not afraid of dying. Afraid of losing." His gaze held hers. "You and I both know you can't win if you're afraid of losing."

Thalia felt close to tears for the second time that day. "Fuck." She clutched at the railing.

"You have the talent. No one worth their salt who has seen you race doubts that. But right now, you're wasting it." He squeezed her upper arm. "Stop wasting it. Find your way back to who you really are."

"Who I really am." Thalia could hear the hollowness in her own voice. "What if I don't know who that is?"

Peter stood with her for a long, drawn-out moment in silent sympathy. Or perhaps it was empathy, Thalia thought. Had he ever been in a similar position? Lost in the maze of his own making?

"Talented. Intense. Focused. Driven. Humorous. Generous. Playful." He squeezed her arm again, punctuating the list of attributes. "I know who you really are," he said quietly. "I bet there are plenty of other people out there who do too. If you've forgotten, stick with us. We'll remind you."

CHAPTER ELEVEN

Alix was in the process of composing the invitation to the Monaco Grand Prix's Onyx Salon charity fashion show—all proceeds from which would benefit Rising Sun—when her phone rang. Caller ID revealed the number of her secretary, but past nine o'clock was rather late for him to be contacting her.

"Yes, Alain?"

"Your Serene Highness, I apologize for the hour. But Ms. Thalia d'Angelis is on the line for you. Would you like to speak with her, or shall I take a message?"

Confusion filtered through her anticipation. She and Thalia hadn't parted well in Italy, and Alix had heard nothing from her for nearly two months—though she had certainly seen plenty of images suggestive of just how thoroughly Thalia had been "enjoying" herself. The media fallout had been unkind, but she didn't know much more than that. Reading about Thalia's misadventures "Down Under" hadn't rated on her to-do list. If she were being honest with herself, she hadn't wanted to know the gory details.

"Ma'am?"

"I'll speak with her," Alix said quickly.

"Very well."

"Hello," she said coolly into the receiver, wondering why she felt nervous. Thalia was the one who should have a case of nerves, given how their last conversation had concluded.

"Alix. Hi. Thanks for taking my call, especially since we didn't exactly leave things well last month."

Alix didn't know what to say. For the first few weeks after their last encounter, she had alternated between waiting for word from Thalia, and hoping they never had another conversation. After the Australian Grand Prix, when photographs had surfaced of Thalia getting that ridiculous lap dance, Alix had vowed never to take her call, even if she did reach out. And now she was breaking her promise to herself.

"Are you there?"

"I'm here."

"Okay." Thalia sounded uncharacteristically meek. Had she finally found some measure of shame and humility, or was it all, as Alix feared, an act? "Can we talk?"

"We're talking."

"I mean in person. That's how I want to apologize to you."

Alix was surprised and pleased, and hated herself for being the latter. "Maybe. Where and when would you like to meet?"

"Well…I'm actually at the Meridien right now. So anytime you'd like."

Alix felt her pulse shoot through the roof and took a deep breath in an attempt to curb it. Thalia was here, in her city. Just a few blocks away.

"Sure of yourself, were you?"

"No. Just hopeful."

It wasn't possible to feign the slight quaver in her voice, was it? Alix hoped not. As far as she could tell, Thalia wasn't good at pretending. Perhaps that was a kind of salvation.

"I'll come to you," she said after a long moment of consideration. While she would rather meet Thalia on her own turf, she didn't feel comfortable inviting her to the palace. Thalia's paparazzi tail would likely catch wind of her visit, and then her own family would be in the news again—this time linked to Formula One's wayward daughter. For her parents' sake, she wanted to avoid that.

Before she left her apartment, Alix changed her clothes. She had been lounging in yoga pants and a tank top, but abandoned them for jeans and a loose linen shirt. She looked nothing like a stereotypical princess, which suited both her and her needs just fine. David, her security detail for the evening, was surprised to see her at the door.

"I need to go to the Meridien to discuss business with Thalia d'Angelis. She's a Formula One driver," Alix added, perhaps unnecessarily.

"Yes, ma'am," was all David said before trailing her out of the palace.

The breeze off the Mediterranean cooled her face as they walked, for which Alix was grateful. She tried to imagine the conversation she was about to have with Thalia. If she could predict it, she could solve it—like a mathematics equation. Alix knew she should be the one to speak first in order to keep the power firmly in her court, but she had no idea what to say. And after the impromptu lecture she'd delivered in Monza, might it not possibly be more daunting for Thalia if she presented a silent and impassive front?

That was when Alix realized she wanted Thalia off-kilter. She couldn't talk to the version of Thalia who was always "on"—always plugged in, always fully charged. Despite her better judgment, Alix wanted to see below the layers of studied extroversion, beneath the devil-may-care aura she projected to the rest of the world.

As she walked into the opulent lobby, Alix considered presenting herself to the front desk with an alias. The past few weeks had revealed the extent to which Thalia's private affairs were under scrutiny by the media, and the last thing Alix wanted was to become grist for the rumor mill. But then she realized that the name by which Thalia knew her was probably enough of an alias, even here in the heart of Monaco. And sure enough, the clerk didn't so much as blink when she gave her name. Being the forgettable princess certainly had its perks.

By the time Alix stood before the door of Thalia's suite, she was no closer to knowing what she should say. Perhaps this had been a mistake, and she should just turn around, leave the hotel, and feed Thalia some story about a sudden crisis—

The door opened. Thalia stood in the frame, barefoot and dressed in a tight black Petrol Macedonia shirt and matching sweatpants. The shirt clung to her sculpted arms and pulled across her breasts. Her dark hair curled around her shoulders, still visibly damp from what must have been a recent shower. As always, the magnitude of her physical beauty caught Alix off guard. But unlike the last time they had been in the same room, this time Thalia's body language was uncertain and her expression uncharacteristically vulnerable.

"Hi."

"Hello," Alix said evenly, empowered by Thalia's evident discomfort.

"Thanks for being here on such short notice. Come on in."

The act of moving past her in the narrow space felt oddly intimate. She smelled of soap and a hint of jasmine, and the combination was pleasant. Needing some distance, Alix walked quickly through the small entryway and into the suite's sitting room, where Thalia gestured to the wet bar. "Can I get you a drink?"

"Just some water, please," she said, watching to see whether Thalia would follow suit or choose the liquor she enjoyed so much. But instead of going behind the bar, she reached into the refrigerator and brought out three water bottles, one of which she handed to David.

"I'll need to do a quick sweep of your rooms, Ms. d'Angelis," he said.

"Of course." Thalia looked to Alix and gestured to a pair of sofas arranged before a coffee table. "Shall we sit?"

When she did, Thalia chose the other couch. She appeared to have abandoned the aggressive flirtatiousness of their last meeting, which was a relief. Why, then, did Alix also feel a twinge of disappointment? So much for being a robot. Computers couldn't hold a "1" and "0" in the same memory space, but apparently, humans managed quite well with self-contradiction.

"So," Thalia said into the silence. "How have you been?"

Flustered, Alix fell back on habit. "Fine. Busy. You?"

Thalia's grin was more tired than wry. "Not so red hot."

Alix felt like she had to apologize for being so callous. "I'm sorry. That was an instinctual response, not a real question. I know the last few races have been difficult."

"And here I was hoping you hadn't been watching." Thalia rolled her as-yet-unopened water bottle between her palms.

Alix didn't know what to say. Thalia had claimed that she wanted to apologize, but now it seemed she was more interested in girl talk. She might be sober and contrite at this particular moment, but all Alix had to do was think back to the scandalous photographs and videos that had set fire to the Internet, and her teeth were back on edge. Refusing to make this easy for her, Alix said nothing.

"Okay." Thalia put the bottle down and leaned forward. "I invited you here to apologize for my behavior back in Italy. You were right about…well, about all of it. My conduct after the race was unsportsmanlike and unconscionable."

Alix could tell she had rehearsed that little speech. "What's changed?"

This time, Thalia didn't have a ready answer. Her left leg jittered as she stared at the table, and when the awkward silence became prolonged, Alix started to wonder whether she had any answer at all.

"I'm not doing as well as I should be. A few people in my life have recently helped me understand that I've been making excuses instead of confronting my challenges. That despite the ups and downs of Formula One, I'm in charge of whether people take me seriously or not." She finally looked up to meet Alix's gaze. "But they're not the first person to deliver that message. You were, and I refused to hear it."

Alix held Thalia's eyes. Her words sounded good. But was there any substance behind them? Then again, what did Thalia have to gain by dissembling? Alix wasn't one of the people she needed to impress in order to return to the good graces of the FIA or the public.

"I accept your apology," she said.

"Thank you." Thalia nodded and finally looked away, out toward the Mediterranean.

Alix followed her line of sight, but instead of focusing on the dark expanse dotted with lights, she was caught by the elegant lines of Thalia's profile. Regardless of how she felt about Thalia's choices, she could never help being struck by her beauty. Even after weeks of separation—weeks in which Thalia had, by her own admission, behaved badly—her magnetism had not diminished. It was confusing and irritating and suffocating, and Alix wanted to leave. Immediately.

But just as she was about to rise and make her excuses, logic intervened. Why was she letting Thalia's attractiveness get under her skin? Thalia had control over what she said and did, but not over her physical features. To resent her for being beautiful was beyond ridiculous. So what was the source of her resentment? Did it stem from feelings of jealousy?

No, that didn't make any sense. Camille was beautiful too, and Alix wasn't jealous of her anymore. She had accepted long ago that she was the relatively ugly duckling in her family. Searching for answers, she scanned the bland prints on the off-white walls without really seeing them. What was it, then? Did Thalia's sexuality make her uncomfortable? When the question jangled brightly in her mind, she knew she couldn't dismiss it. She had thought herself different from the rest of her family—more liberal and open-minded because of her intensive scientific and sociological training. The notion that she might still be bigoted, deep down, was disturbing. Could it be true?

Suddenly self-conscious, she leapt to fill the silence, lest Thalia perceive her internal struggle. What had they been discussing? Oh, yes—her apology. "What do you intend to do now?"

Thalia roused herself with a swift shake of her head. "Figure out how not to be volatile and self-destructive, I guess. Stop associating with the wrong people and going to the wrong parties…" She laughed, but without humor. "Change my entire lifestyle. Shouldn't be too hard, right?"

Frantically, Alix grasped to approximate the tone she had used before realizing she was thrown off by Thalia's sexuality. She had never given Thalia an inch, and if she began now, Thalia would know something was amiss.

"Now you're treating me like a therapist," was what she settled on. Good enough.

"You can bill me." Thalia smiled wanly. "As long as you help me find a new scene."

"A new scene?" As their banter picked up speed, Alix began to relax. "I don't have any kind of scene at all."

"What if that's exactly what I need?" At first, Alix thought Thalia was teasing her, but on second glance, she seemed entirely serious.

"Look," Thalia continued, "maybe this will sound crazy, but I'm starting to think we can help each other." Something in Alix's expression must have betrayed her doubts, because Thalia cracked a self-deprecating smile. "I can tell what you're thinking. You want to know what I can possibly offer you."

"The question had crossed my mind." There was no use in denying it.

"I can help with your charity. Help raise its profile."

Alix was more intrigued than offended, but she wanted to make Thalia sweat a bit. "Excuse me?"

"I didn't mean you're not already high-profile," Thalia said quickly, raising both hands in the air. "But I can reach a significant audience too—"

"When you're not alienating them," Alix said pointedly.

"Right, which is part of why we're having this conversation." Thalia leaned forward. "Really, though, think about it. We'd make a good team. We each have a unique kind of star power. And with the Ruffords backing your project, we'll also have capital."

Alix's heart was slamming against her rib cage at the thought of having to spend more time with Thalia, but perhaps that was exactly what she needed in order to get over her discomfort.

"What exactly are you proposing?"

"I can publicly endorse your charity and help out with some fundraising opportunities."

The mental image of Thalia doing a charity keg stand made Alix wince. She needed to be sure they were on the same page. "Help out in what way?"

"You know—autographs and signed paraphernalia, driving a high roller around in an old safety car—things like that."

Alix exhaled in relief. "On one condition."

"Name it."

"You don't publicly endorse Rising Sun until you've proven yourself. Right now, I can't trust you not to be volatile."

"Vola—" Thalia bit back her protest, and took a sip of water. Perhaps she really was capable of change. "Prove myself? How would that work?"

"I've arranged to visit a children's hospital in Graz prior to the Austrian Grand Prix." Alix watched Thalia's face closely for any sign of distaste at the idea. "Come with me. If you can manage to behave yourself, then we have a deal."

Thalia didn't hesitate. Leaning over the coffee table, she extended her hand. "You're on."

CHAPTER TWELVE

Thalia squared her shoulders and gave herself a silent lecture as she followed Alix into the Children's University Hospital in Graz, Austria. She hated hospitals, but Alix had made these arrangements with her in mind, and so she was going to make the most of the day. Dr. Konig, one of the lead researchers, was there to greet them just inside the lobby. Thalia used almost every German word she knew in the course of saying, "Hello and thank you for having us," while Alix launched into a conversation with him as though she had been born to it. English, French, and now German—that made three languages in which she was fluent. At least.

They walked through a series of corridors that had been brightly painted, presumably for the children. But there was no disguising the harsh, antiseptic scent that clung to the walls, and no hiding the faint beeping of heart monitors from behind closed doors. The children behind them had come here in hopes of some kind of salvation. As she obliquely caught sight of her reflection in a window, Thalia realized she had done the same.

Looking past herself, she focused on the distant, snow-capped peaks of the Alps. The closest major city to the Austrian Grand Prix, Graz was nestled in the shadow of the mountains but boasted a much milder climate. Thalia had been here twice before, but only to enjoy the nightlife after a long day of testing. By day, Graz boasted that appealing blend of Old World charm and twenty-first-century savvy typical of most major European cities.

The sound of Alix's amusement drew her attention. She was

laughing in response to something the doctor had said, and her fingertips briefly rested on his forearm. Thalia was abruptly overcome by a wave of jealousy and anger strong enough to make her flash back to Monza. She clenched her left hand, forcing her nails to bite into the meat of her palm.

No. She was not going to lose control—not here, not now. Her jealousy was unfounded. She and Alix were…what were they, exactly? Friends? They had clashed too much for that term to seem right, but they had shared too much to be acquaintances. Business partners? Not really—not yet. There was something happening between them, but it appeared to defy any term Thalia could think of. But did Alix feel the same way? Did she sense the subtle shifts in energy, like eddying magnetic currents, when they were in the same room?

Maybe she didn't. Maybe she was completely straight and flirting with Dr. Konig. He was decent looking, she supposed—not that Alix would pay any attention to purely physical attributes. She cared about what was going on in someone's head, not whether they had a pretty face. So much more the pity for the girl with the pretty face, Thalia thought wryly.

"I'm sorry," Alix said as they paused before a bank of elevators. "Here we've been chattering away in German. Dr. Konig has been telling me about the hospital's newest advancements in the treatment of juvenile diabetes."

Thalia wanted to ask what was so humorous about that topic but managed to restrain herself. "That sounds very interesting," she said instead. "Will we be seeing some of those patients today?"

"No, today we'll be in the pediatric oncology ward." He favored her with a quick smile. "We have several Formula One fans in that group who are eager to meet you."

Thalia's steps faltered. Ever since Alix's lecture about being a role model, she had avoided interacting with children. The last thing she wanted was to be a disappointment to someone battling cancer. And then she caught herself. Was she seriously having qualms about bringing a small ray of joy to a sick child? How selfish was that?

Suddenly filled with self-disgust, Thalia lectured herself silently all the way to the ward entrance, where a nurse greeted them and asked whether they were ill or had been in proximity to anyone with flu-like symptoms over the past forty-eight hours. Alix had already asked her the same question, so that was easy enough to answer. The nurse then explained how the visit would work—there were twenty-four beds in this particular ward and they would stop briefly at each.

"Doing okay?" Alix murmured as the doors swung open.

"Absolutely," Thalia said with more confidence than she felt.

The first child they visited looked so small and fragile in the hospital bed, ringed as it was by all kinds of monitors and devices. But when they entered, he sat up eagerly, introduced himself as Franz, told them he had just turned ten, and proceeded to talk their ears off—in English—for the next five minutes. Franz liked football better than motorsport but had an older brother who raced dirt bikes. He was confused by Alix's lack of a crown, but seemed to accept her explanation, delivered with a perfectly straight face, that it was too heavy to wear for long periods of time. Thalia tried not to laugh as he continued talking a mile a minute, until the nurse gently interrupted him with the news that his guests had to move along.

As they progressed through the ward, Thalia watched Alix interact with the patients. She seemed to feel none of Thalia's unease, and Thalia wondered whether that had to do with her personality, her medical training, or her experience as an older sibling. Regardless, the self-consciousness Thalia had sensed from Alix on so many occasions was completely absent here. Each time she pulled up one of the uncomfortable chairs to a new child's bedside, she made him or her feel like the only person in the room. When they spoke little or no English, she served as a translator. She made every single one of them laugh— even the little boy who had been in tears when they entered.

By the time their visit was winding down, Thalia had learned from Alix how to look past the illness to see the child beneath. They were people, not patients. It would be a great injustice to define them by their symptoms. So when they entered the last room to find a teenage girl who was practicing walking on a prosthetic leg, Thalia thought of the times she had been temporarily sidelined from driving by an injury—how she had hated seeing pitying looks and hearing sympathetic platitudes. The girl, who had turned at their entry, was now making slow progress toward them. When Alix started to move forward to save her the trouble of crossing the room, Thalia reached out and grasped her wrist to hold her back.

"Trust me," she said softly before releasing her.

Alix greeted the girl in German, and she replied in a deferential tone, introducing herself as Lena. That much, Thalia could understand. But when Alix introduced *her*, Lena's eyes went wide and her color rose.

"You are my favorite athlete!" she blurted out in charmingly accented English that Thalia was certain sounded better than anything she might say in any other language.

And then the meaning of the words hit her. She was Lena's favorite athlete. Lena probably watched Grands Prix from this hospital bed and cheered her on every time. Lena probably looked out the window toward the mountains and wished she could be in motion under her own power, instead of confined to her bed as her body coped with the loss of a limb. Would she have access to a running "blade," as Thalia had seen other amputees use? Was that kind of thing even covered by health insurance?

Lena halted in front of them, bowed formally to Alix, and then held out her hand to Thalia. Thalia stepped forward and embraced her instead. She was so petite, so thin, but not fragile. Strong. She clung to Thalia's shoulders for one brief, vulnerable moment before pulling away.

"It's an honor to meet you," she said.

"The honor's all mine." Thalia decided to take a gamble. "Mind if we sit?" If they took a seat, Lena might feel more comfortable about resting in their presence.

"Please." With all the maturity of a high society hostess, she gestured toward the plastic chairs.

Thalia could feel Alix's gaze on her as they settled themselves, and she knew it was up to her to guide the course of their visit. As she had seen Alix do, Thalia tried to steer the conversation away from why the girl was in a hospital bed instead of running around with her friends outside.

"So tell me, Lena, how did you become interested in Formula One?"

Lena smiled. She would mature into a beautiful woman, Thalia thought, if she had the chance. "My father..." She searched for the right words. "He is Tifosi."

"A Ferrari fan? I guess I can forgive him for that." She smiled to make sure Lena got the joke.

"I like Ferrari, but it makes me so happy when you joined Petrol Macedonia."

"Me too," Thalia said, and they both laughed.

"How did you start racing?"

"I've always loved to go fast," Thalia said, careful to speak slowly so she could follow. "First on my tricycle, and then on my scooter, and then on my bicycle. But I didn't start Karting until I moved to England when I was fourteen."

Thalia's trip down memory lane inspired an eager smile on Lena's face. "Really? I am twelve now." The smile abruptly disappeared, and she looked down at her left leg. "But I have to be…how do you say it? Real? About what I can do."

"Realistic?" Thalia felt a surge of anger at whoever had encouraged her to be realistic instead of aspirational. "Well, don't forget that most people drive with only one leg. Right foot for the brake and the gas."

Thalia wasn't about to tell her that while most *people* used only one foot for both, most F1 drivers used their left foot to brake. Lying by omission might still be lying, but sometimes it was necessary to keep hope alive. And there were plenty of successful drivers in the past who had both braked and accelerated with one foot. Just because left-foot braking was the general rule at the moment didn't mean it had to be that way forever.

They chatted for a few more minutes before the nurse popped her head in to announce that visiting hours were drawing to a close. Before they left, Thalia wrote down the contact information of her agent. "Call or send him an email, okay? I want to stay in touch to see how you're doing."

Lena clutched the slip of paper and nodded, eyes bright, blinking furiously to keep her tears in check. "I will. Thank you. Thank you."

As the nurse escorted them back through the ward, she and Alix struck up a conversation in German. Thalia was glad not to have to pay attention or contribute. Meeting Lena had rattled her. Thalia couldn't shake the memory of how crestfallen she had seemed when she remembered her limitations. The prosthetic blades for runners made it possible for them to run at fairly competitive levels, but there hadn't yet been a world champion or Olympic medalist with a prosthesis. Thalia wondered whether the same disparity applied to Formula One. The question of braking aside, one of the most important safety requirements—stringently tested at various points throughout the season—was that a driver had to be able to get out of the cockpit within five seconds of the car coming to a halt. The maneuver required a great deal of dexterity.

The nurse said her good-byes at the elevators and thanked them for making time for the children. Thalia snapped out of her introspection to chime in with Alix, insisting that the visit had been their pleasure. As the doors slid shut behind them, Thalia realized she owed Alix a separate debt of gratitude.

"Thank you for suggesting I come with you today. That was really hard, but also really good."

Alix regarded her silently for a long moment. "You seemed deep in thought just now. What were you thinking?"

They stepped out of the elevator and began to cross the lobby. "That we get to walk out of here," Thalia said, gesturing to the gleaming glass doors looking out onto a sunny afternoon. "And Lena doesn't."

"But she will," Alix said firmly. "She'll walk out on her own two legs." She met Thalia's eyes briefly. "You were a natural with her."

"And you were a natural with everyone else."

Alix smiled, but sadly. "As difficult as it is to work with children who are so ill, I enjoy it because of how hopeful they are. Nothing is impossible to them. Most of us lose that optimism by the time we're adults."

They stepped out into the fresh air and Thalia turned her face toward the sun, relishing the warmth and the breeze and the absence of antiseptic. They had some free time now, before a dinner with members of the hospital's Board of Trustees. She was tired, but it was a fatigue born in her head and heart, not her body. A workout would do a world of good in restoring her equilibrium.

As the car swept them back to the hotel, Alix turned to her again. "Could Lena really race in Formula One with a prosthetic leg?"

"I don't know," Thalia admitted. "But it might be possible. I really do want to stay in touch with her. Is she in good enough shape to come to the Grand Prix this weekend, do you think?"

"If she's still in the ward, it probably means they're worried about her immune system," Alix said. "So my guess is that this weekend would be too soon. But we can always check."

We. Thalia was glad Alix was thinking of them as a team. That was a good sign. "I'd like to do that. And if not this Grand Prix, then another."

"That's generous of you."

"You sound surprised."

"Maybe I am."

Irritated, Thalia met Alix's appraising gaze without blinking. "I know I have a deserved reputation, but not for being a miser."

Alix leaned forward. "I'm not talking about money. I mean in your heart." A faint blush colored her cheeks. "Not that emotions come from your heart. It's just a saying."

"Your Serene Highness," Thalia teased her, her irritation forgotten. "Are you getting sentimental?"

"Don't push your luck," Alix said, but she was smiling. "Especially since I've decided that you adequately proved yourself today."

Her approval meant more than Thalia cared to admit. "Oh I did, did I? So we have a deal?"

"You help me with my charity, and I help you stay out of trouble." Alix extended her hand. "Deal."

Her fingers were softer than the last time they'd touched. For the rest of the car ride, Thalia tried not to think of how they would feel on her face, stroking her cheeks as they kissed.

❖

The evening meal was a formal affair at the fanciest restaurant in Graz. Like all formal dinners Thalia had ever attended, the caliber of the wine couldn't make up for the stiltedness of the atmosphere. Alix did her best early on to play the role of the gracious and charming princess philanthropist, but by the third course, Thalia could tell she was running out of steam.

"Will I be seeing any of you this weekend at the racetrack?" she asked during a lull.

The ploy worked like a charm, immediately sparking debates about everything from the layout and condition of the A-1 track, to the science behind the structure of the HANS unit. When the waiter momentarily interrupted the conversation, Thalia leaned into Alix's space.

"Told you doctors love Formula One," she whispered.

"No need to be smug about it," Alix muttered back. But her lips twitched.

Once the last sip of the last cappuccino had been consumed, Dr. Konig asked them if they were interested in enjoying Graz's nightlife. Thalia had a split second in which to decide upon her best course of action, and she took a risk that also tested her willpower. Citing her need to rest and hydrate, she declined. While she hoped Alix would return to the hotel with her, she had given her a golden opportunity: if Alix felt anything for the doctor, she could turn the rest of the evening into a date. Like taking a hard corner, she held her breath through the tension.

"Regretfully, I'm rather tired," Alix said. "But thank you for the offer."

Thalia indulged in a mental fist pump. As they stepped out into the balmy evening, Claude in tow, she took another risk. "What would you think of holding off on calling the car, and walking for a while instead?"

Alix's face illuminated in that rare expression of pure, unmediated happiness. "That sounds perfect. Did you have anything in mind?"

"Let's meander through the Old Town for a while and see what happens." She nudged Alix's shoulder. "Or do you need a more concrete plan than that?"

"Not at the moment. I'm happy to be aimless."

They wandered along the narrow, sinuous streets, silent at first until Thalia, reflecting on how effortlessly Alix had interacted with the other physicians, decided to ask about her experience in the field. Most physicians had quite enough of school by the time they graduated, but Alix had felt as though something were missing. That feeling had motivated her pursuit of the master's in public health degree, and she had chosen Harvard specifically for its emphasis on fieldwork. As she spoke about her interest in East Africa, Thalia wondered what it must feel like to care so deeply for people you had never met.

Whether instinctually or by pure coincidence, they had worked their way into the town center where the Schlossberg rose like a hulking beast, blotting out most of the sky. Thalia looked from the lamp-lit zigzag walkway snaking back and forth along the ramparts, to the blue-lit glass elevator outside of which a bustling crowd was gathered despite the lateness of the hour.

"Let's take the elevator up and the path back down?" she suggested.

"Fine with me, lazybones."

"Lazybones?" Enjoying their banter, Thalia pretended offense. "Would you like to come to the gym with me tomorrow?"

Alix considered the request seriously. "All right, I will. If only to ensure you're not lying about the amount of weight you can neck-press."

The idea of Alix watching her lift sent a jolt through Thalia that she didn't want to feel. For days now, she had been avoiding acknowledgment of her growing attraction. Alix was brilliant and straight and conservative, not to mention *royalty*. After a rough start to their friendship, Thalia had finally managed to gain her trust. And now she had to go and develop a crush?

Why did she always have to push the boundaries, she reflected as the line to the ticket window moved forward. There were plenty of available women in the world, even discounting grid girls and starfuckers. Why did she have to be interested in someone who couldn't possibly return her attraction?

Distracted by her thoughts, she didn't realize that Claude had stepped forward and was about to pay for their trip to the top of the clock tower. "Let me," she said quickly, reaching for her wallet. But Alix stopped her with a hand on her arm.

"He's insisting that we go up just the three of us," she murmured. "Which costs extra."

Just the three of them. Thalia knew Claude would try to make himself as invisible as possible, but there wasn't much to work with in a glass elevator. After a brief negotiation, they were shepherded through by a security guard who blocked the passage of those behind.

"I always feel badly about causing a delay," Alix said, leaning close to her so Claude wouldn't overhear.

Thalia tried not to focus on the sensation of Alix's body pressed against hers, but without success. The urge to wrap one arm around Alix's waist and pull her even closer was nearly overwhelming. Fortunately, Alix moved away to follow Claude down the corridor.

The elevator operator was on the phone when they arrived but hastily hung up. "Good evening, Your Highness," he said, having clearly gotten the message.

They stepped inside, and Claude took up a position in the far left corner. Alix moved to the opposite side, leaning forward to admire the blue-veined stone walls.

"Look," she said, beckoning Thalia forward. "We're in the heart of the mountain. What an interesting design choice."

Thalia was careful to keep several inches of space between their bodies this time. As the elevator began to move, she looked up and caught her breath. The shaft was open to the night sky, and the moon hung above them like a suspended jewel. Her resolution forgotten, she reached out to touch Alix's arm.

"Look up."

"Oh!" Her cry of surprise was disconcertingly sensual, and as she angled her head to gain the best vantage point, Thalia felt Alix's warm breaths puff against her neck. Desire arrowed through her, swift and sharp, and she closed her eyes against it.

"What's the matter?" Alix asked. "Are you in pain?"

Thalia opened her eyes to find Alix's face upturned and very close. Concern had caused tiny wrinkles to form on the bridge between her eyes, and Thalia wanted so badly to smooth them away. She reached out for the railing to stop herself.

"No," she said hoarsely, knowing she should say something more to explain away her behavior, but unable to think of an excuse.

Today, Alix's eyes were more gold than green or brown—tawny, like a lion's mane. She didn't look away, her pupils expanding into dark pools in which the blue illumination of the elevator flickered like fairy lights. When her tongue darted out to moisten her lips, Thalia knew she wasn't imagining the connection that had just passed between them. Attraction. Alix felt it too. What did *that* mean?

The elevator jolted as it slid to a halt, breaking the spell. Confused and aching, Thalia gestured for Claude to precede her. They emerged into the courtyard of the Schlossberg, and Thalia welcomed the cool breeze against her heated cheeks. She spun in a slow circle to take it all in—the illuminated clock tower behind them, and ahead, a parapet overlooking the Old Town.

"How stunning," Alix said, gazing up at the tower. "I've read that it's from the thirteenth century and was very nearly razed by Napoleon."

"How did it escape?" Thalia asked, half relieved and half disappointed that they had moved beyond their charged moment.

She pointed to a nearby placard. "Maybe that will tell us."

The tower, called the Uhrturm, had only survived because the town burghers had been willing to ransom it with a large sum of money. Thalia quickly lost interest in the rest of what was written, and while Alix remained absorbed, she snapped a few photos. She wanted to suggest they take one together but didn't dare.

Feeling restless, Thalia went to the parapet and rested her forearms on it. It faced south, toward the racetrack. The Austrian Grand Prix awaited, and with it, the chance to redeem herself. She had to stay focused. Maybe she had misread that moment in the elevator. And even if Alix was queer and only just starting to realize it, now was not the time to bring someone out of the closet. That was almost always a messy and protracted process, and it would be a hundred times worse for someone of her stature. The media had gone berserk over Princess Sasha, and even though Alix wasn't as public a figure, the reaction would still be intense.

"Ready to walk down?" Alix called from behind her.

Thalia pulled the crisp alpine air into her lungs and steeled her resolve. Back down to earth, to reality, to the race.

"I'm ready."

CHAPTER THIRTEEN

"Well now, Your Serene Highness," Lord Rufford said congenially as they waited for the first of their VIP guests to arrive, "all that worry about the weather appears to have been for naught."

Alix glanced heavenward to where the flat disc of the sun was struggling to pierce gauzy gray clouds. It looked like a coin hanging suspended in midair, and for a moment she expected to see the familiar profile of her father's face etched on its surface and surrounded by the twelve stars of the European Union. But then the cloud thinned and the coin became the star, bathing them in brightness for the first time all morning. Quickly averting her eyes, she turned back to him.

"I'm so pleased that it will be a beautiful day."

"Good thing we decided on Brands Hatch. The storm system is passing north of London."

His use of "we" was generous. Lord and Lady Rufford had been instrumental in brokering the deal that had allowed Rising Sun to hold its inaugural fundraiser at one of England's most historic tracks. For many years, Brands Hatch had hosted the British Grand Prix. The more intimate setting—if one could use such a term for any sweeping stretch of asphalt designed for motorsport—suited her purposes. In a matter of minutes, VIPs would begin to gather for a day of exhibitions and performances that would conclude with a formal dinner and raffle. Admission was five thousand euro a head, and almost every seat had been claimed.

As matters currently stood, Rising Sun would be able to collect most of that money. Lady Rufford had persuaded the Brands Hatch management to charge only a nominal fee in exchange for a tax write-off and a promise of future patronage. Thalia was volunteering her time and had convinced Peter Taggart and Petrol Macedonia's two test drivers to do the same. She had even managed to persuade Gene Michaels, the world champion of Motocross, to dramatically reduce the appearance fee his agent had initially quoted.

Thalia. Since Graz, they had been in touch on a daily basis, working together to plan this event. Alix had initially been skeptical of Thalia's sincerity in wanting to help, but her enthusiasm in securing Petrol Macedonia's support soon proved that skepticism unwarranted. Such was the level of her commitment that Alix had begun to worry that Thalia might be neglecting her training and preparation. But Thalia's performance on the track was better than ever: she had placed fourth in both the Austrian and German Grands Prix, which had gone a long way toward silencing her critics and rehabilitating her place in the standings. With Peter having placed first in Austria and second in Germany, Petrol Macedonia was firmly in position as a top contender for the Constructors' Cup.

The growl of a revving engine intruded on her introspection, heralding the arrival of the first guests. Part of the VIP experience included being shuttled from the helipad to the racetrack by a chauffeur with a Superlicense. Lord Rufford had secured two Brabus Mercedes four-seat cabriolets for the experience—one red, one blue—and as they watched the latter accelerate onto the track, a scream of delight filled the air. The driver guided the car into the pit lane, taking the curve just fast enough to inspire another shriek, before coming to a stop precisely in front of the entrance to the tent. As Peter vaulted out of the seat and opened the rear door with a flourish, Alix summoned every shred of social grace she should have been born with.

"Your Serene Highness, my Lord Rufford," Peter greeted them as he extended a hand to the elder of the two beautiful women in the back seat, "allow me to present Mr. Clive Bassler, his wife Ariana, and their daughter Isabel."

Alix was woefully out of touch when it came to pop culture—a fact that had been driven home when she had examined the finalized guest list last night, only to find she didn't recognize half the names on it. In a panic, she had called Thalia, who patiently explained the celebrity status of the various models, actors, and reality television stars whom Alix had never heard of. The Bassler family were Hollywood royalty. Clive was an American actor who had met Ariana on the set of some action film that had long since been forgotten, and they had gone on to have a fairytale Hollywood romance. Twenty years later, Isabel was coming into her own as an up-and-coming model for a fashion house. Alix couldn't remember which, but doubtless it was one of the most distinguished. She was ethereally beautiful, with flawless pale skin and long, golden hair falling past her shoulders.

"Welcome," Alix said. "I'm glad you could join us and grateful for your support."

"We wouldn't have missed it, Your Highness," Ariana said as they clasped hands.

"Please, let's dispense with the formalities. Feel free to call me Alix."

Lord Rufford moved to her side and greeted Bassler like an old friend. Content to let him shepherd them into the tent, she remained outside to await the next guests.

"Thank you for your help, Peter," she called as he climbed back into the car.

"Anything for such a good cause," he said with a smile. "I just got word that my family is at the landing pad. I'm off to fetch them." And with a rev of the engine, he was gone.

As the minutes stretched into hours, Alix's feet began to ache in the new pair of heels her mother had insisted on purchasing for the occasion. Neither of her parents had been free to attend this event, but both had been generous in their donations for the raffle. Florestan and his bride were happily married and off enjoying their honeymoon. These shoes might be physically uncomfortable, but the ridiculous magenta taffeta gowns Monique had chosen for her bridesmaids had caused Alix psychological trauma. At the wedding, Camille and Soraphine, who had been blessed by genetic lottery with classically beautiful features and hourglass figures, had looked like fairy-tale princesses. Alix, on the other hand, had spent the day feeling like one of Cinderella's evil stepsisters.

Thankfully, Thalia's red car appeared on the track at that moment. While Peter had ceded his place to one of the Petrol Macedonia test drivers after the arrival of his wife and son, Thalia cheerfully carried on. On this particular trip, she had toned down her showboating antics, making Alix wonder who was in the car. No sooner had it come to a halt when Thalia leapt out, sporting an infectious grin.

"Guess who I've found?"

Kerry, who now shared the title of Duchess of Kent with her wife, emerged from the backseat and waved to Alix with one hand while extending the other to Sasha. On the other side of the car, Arthur was attending to Ashleigh.

Alix's fatigue receded at the sight of them, and her doubts about the success of the gala promptly disappeared. There was something special about this up-and-coming generation of the House of Carlisle—a subtle energy about both couples that transformed the space around them for the better.

"The party can start now," Thalia quipped, as though she had read her mind.

"Alix!" Sasha called as she hurried over to exchange the obligatory cheek-kisses. "Kerry and I *must* take a drive around the track with Thalia. She's promised to do one of those"—she circled one finger in the air, pantomiming a donut—"while we're in the car! Where do we sign up?"

Her childlike eagerness was charming. "On the right, just past the champagne," Alix said, pointing inside the tent. When she turned around, she found herself face-to-face with Kerry, who seemed bemused by her wife's enthusiasm. Dressed smartly in a dark green blazer and gray slacks, she looked both fashionable and comfortable. Alix couldn't help but envy her.

"Congratulations on your launch of Rising Sun," Kerry said politely.

"Thank you. I'm glad all of you could be here today."

Kerry's smile shifted into a more serious expression that spoke business. "I know today will be frenetic, but perhaps we can find a time to chat? I have a friend from the Rhodes who's now teaching at the London School of Economics, and he expressed interest in teaming up with you to create internships for his students."

"That's an exciting prospect," Alix said, her mind already racing ahead to canvas the possibilities. She had been so focused on raising the necessary capital to launch Rising Sun that she hadn't yet considered the possibility of forming relationships with academic institutions. "I'd certainly like to discuss it in more detail."

"I'll find you later," Kerry said. "For now, I'd better figure out what exactly Sasha has signed us up for."

"The ride of your lives!" Thalia called after her.

Kerry stopped and looked over her shoulder. Her cordial professionalism had abruptly given way to a cocky half-grin. "I'm not going to say what I'm thinking," she replied, "but I bet you can guess."

Thalia hooted in delight. "Ah, newlyweds."

Before Alix could connect the dots in an effort to follow their subtext, Ashleigh stepped forward, shaking her head. "Ignore those cretins." She embraced Alix warmly. "We've been looking forward to this since receiving your invitation."

"Though we'll be keeping our feet on solid ground," Arthur chimed in, accompanying his words with a gentle caress of Ashleigh's slightly protruding stomach.

"Perfectly understandable. And we have sparkling cider in addition to the champagne."

"That's very considerate." Ashleigh took her prince's arm. "We'll catch up with you later."

Once they were all inside the tent, Alix turned back to Thalia. "You've been driving back and forth all morning. Why don't you let one of the test drivers spell you and take a break before your exhibition?"

"Very well, Your Serene Highness." Thalia doffed an imaginary cap.

She rolled her eyes at the posturing. "Oh, stop." The role of humble chauffeur fit her about as well as the painfully fashionable shoes that chafed Alix's toes.

Thalia drew level with her and pressed the car keys into her palm. "For my replacement."

When their fingers brushed, a shiver ran through Alix before she could suppress it. Thalia's head jerked up and she took a step backward, reminding Alix of a startled horse. Had she felt it too—the tiny charge of energy that had passed between them when their skin touched?

With an awkward wave, Thalia turned and strode into the tent. Alix watched as she approached the knot of people that had formed around the British royals. She had just the right vantage point from which to observe Sasha's welcoming smile, and the elegant arm she threw around Thalia's waist to pull her into their midst. The prick of jealousy was like a bee sting, sharp and unexpected.

Sasha and Thalia had been schoolmates, but had there ever been more to their relationship? Alix had clear memories of the teenage Sasha, who had learned early on to wield her beauty as a weapon in the service of her own rebellion. And she could imagine a younger version of Thalia—skinnier and less jaded, but just as much a daredevil. They were a likely pair for finding trouble, but what about adolescent romance?

When she tried to picture it, her mind balked—but was that because Sasha and Thalia didn't have that kind of chemistry, or because *she* didn't have enough imagination? Or worse: was her inability the result of lingering prejudice?

The crowd shifted to reveal Sasha standing close to Kerry. As Alix looked on, Sasha reached for Kerry's free hand, and they shared a quick, private smile. Alix plumbed her own mind for any evidence of homophobia, but the sight of them together, so clearly in love, was simply beautiful. What, then, was the cause of her discomfort?

The only remaining option was the jealousy she didn't want to acknowledge. But Alix had never been in the habit of sticking her head in the sand. She had long ago accepted her position on the margins of her own family—partly a function of her personality, but also as a result of her own choices. Now, she needed to confront the fact that her jealousy was far more complicated than that of an unattached woman who sees a successful relationship and wishes for her own love story. Her feelings were much more focused.

On Thalia.

She watched as Thalia laughed at something Arthur had said. The quick flash of her smile, the dark glint of her hair in the lamplight, the lithe strength of her arms as she gestured while she spoke. She was beautiful. But it was not the kind of beauty Alix wished she possessed, like Camille's or Soraphine's. It was a beauty she appreciated in a way that ran deeper than pure aesthetics. It was a beauty she wanted to *know*. The warmth of Thalia's embrace, the texture of Thalia's skin, how Thalia's lips would feel as they moved against hers...

The intimacy of her desire was frightening in its unfamiliarity. Her own skin suddenly felt too tight, and panic rose when she couldn't manage a deep breath. *Adrenaline*, whispered the corner of her mind still capable of rational diagnosis. She had experienced attraction before, but always at a distance. Never like this—never accompanied by a visceral craving for touch. Her own private joke with herself was that Florestan had inherited her share of libido in addition to his own.

Apparently not. That part of her had only been asleep. Now it had woken and was inconveniently focused on Thalia d'Angelis— who, aside from being a woman, was about as incompatible with her temperament and priorities as another person could be. Yes, Thalia had been on her best behavior for the past few weeks, but Alix didn't for one moment believe that her urges had disappeared. She was either repressing them or sublimating them into her work on the racetrack. Regardless, they were still there, churning below the surface. What had Thalia said in Italy? *I like to drive fast cars and fuck fast women and drink too much and watch the sun rise before I sleep. That's who I am.* Could those traits possibly be part of what Alix desired? Was she a misguided moth, wanting to approach the flame of Thalia's intensity?

A low drumroll had begun in the back of her head, and she wanted nothing more than to escape into some quiet place to confront the magnitude of this epiphany. But on today of all days, that was simply not an option. She would have to muscle through the turmoil—to shove aside these nascent feelings and the anxiety they inspired. To remain calm, collected, and professional even as her own mind erupted, bubbling and roiling, contours shifting to become an unfamiliar landscape.

Isabel joined the group that had gathered around Sasha, and Alix watched as she was introduced to Thalia. Her eyes narrowed as she tried to catch any evidence of flirtation. Would Isabel entice Thalia to relax the iron grip on her self-control? This was the first week of a month-long break in the Formula One schedule, before it resumed with the Monaco Grand Prix. Would Thalia decide she had enough breathing room to let down her guard?

As the seconds ticked into minutes, Isabel deftly maneuvered herself to stand next to Thalia. She spoke; Thalia smiled and gave an answer. As their conversation continued, Isabel rested one hand on her shoulder. Jealousy returned, hotter and sharper, piercing Alix's chest. By acknowledging its root, she had given it power.

Her breaths hitched, making her dizzy. But with the weakness came a surge of anger. She *would* stop this. Logic *would* prevail over fear. And when this day was over, she would spend some much needed time alone where she could critically examine these new emotions and learn how to manage them without feeling as though they were tearing her apart.

❖

Thalia sat at the far corner of the bar at the Brands Hatch clubhouse, forcing herself to nurse two fingers of very fine scotch. This spot was partially obscured by a pole, which was why she had chosen it. If she was tired of interacting with people, she could only imagine how exhausted Alix must be.

The post-dinner party was finally winding down. Minus a few hiccups involving the vegetarian menu and an intoxicated DJ, the day had been a smash success. At her closing remarks, Alix had announced that Rising Sun had raised almost three million euro. For all her introversion, she was a polished public speaker and a consummate hostess.

Thalia craned her head, checking that Alix was still where she had been a few moments ago: deep in conversation with Arthur's uncle Edward, the Duke of York. That boded well, as Edward was a financier who ran his own hedge fund. Confident in her ability to remain unobserved, Thalia watched the many tells of Alix's body language. Fatigue was evident in the way she shifted her weight back and forth, but her shoulders were unbowed, and her hands moved crisply through the air in clear excitement.

Her hands. They had been the source of their first clash: when, at Sasha's wedding, she had taken Alix's hand and remarked on her calluses. She tried to recall her mindset in that moment. Had that first connection sparked the interest that had long since become attraction? Alix had challenged her from the very beginning, forcing her to reject any preconceived notions of what it was to be a philanthropic princess. *I spent much of the past three months planting crops and digging wells*. She had spoken in defense of her own choices and in defiance of Thalia's stereotyping, not to boast.

Alix's useful and competent hands, trained to plant and dig and heal. How would they move in a moment of passion? Would she be eager to explore, or shy of contact? A few days ago, in a moment of weakness brought on by insomnia, Thalia had consulted the Internet for evidence of Alix's past romantic liaisons. She had uncovered several rumors, of course—no contemporary princess, no matter how she might try to fly beneath the radar, was beyond the reach of human curiosity—but nothing that could be confirmed. Most of the relevant articles were in one particular French gossip magazine, and Thalia had been thankful for the translator built into her Web browser.

But the pieces were fluff, all mights and maybes and perhaps without a shred of real evidence. Having been the subject of more than a few such rumormongering articles, she could recognize the lurid glow from a mile off. The fact of the matter was that she had no reliable information about Alix's past love life.

Of course, she could always ask. Thalia took another sip of scotch to prevent herself from laughing. Her decade of practice spent flirting with other women notwithstanding, she could think of no possible way to bring up the subject of romance to Alix. For the past month, most of their conversations had revolved around the planning of this event. Occasionally, Alix would ask about her training, and of course they spoke of each Grand Prix as it happened. Thalia made an effort to periodically check in about Florestan's shotgun wedding, and in rare moments of candor, Alix would drop hints about the strained relationships she had with her siblings. Thalia had to confront the facts: she and Alix had a comfortable friendship, but not a particularly close one.

Thalia had expected that without fuel, her interest in Alix would die off. Instead, the opposite was happening. The more time she spent with Alix, the more intrigued she became. Alix might prefer to operate behind the scenes, far from the spotlight, but that only made her more fascinating. Unlike her siblings and peers—unlike Thalia herself—she wasn't in search of glory. Sometimes it almost felt as though Alix was doing the opposite: hoping to atone in some way for the accident of her privileged birth.

Deep waters, there. Deep waters that Thalia wanted to plumb.

Movement from across the room jarred her out of her thoughts. Alix and the duke were shaking hands, their conversation clearly at an end. Thalia slipped out of her chair and rested one hand on the pole as she entered Alix's unimpeded line of sight. When Alix shifted her stance, angling herself toward Thalia, she knew she had been noticed. A warmth distinct from the heat of the scotch settled in her stomach. That was worrisome—or at least, it should have been. Somehow, she couldn't muster enough concern about these feelings to take the steps necessary to quash them.

As Alix approached, Thalia pulled out the chair next to hers. "Your feet must be tired," she said.

Alix glanced down at her shoes. "These things are torture devices masquerading as footwear." A sudden thought wiped the hint of a smile from her face. "Has my control slipped? Am I wincing?"

"Your control is perfect," Thalia said, even as the devil on her shoulder prodded her to imagine how Alix might look in a state of sensual abandon. "It was a lucky guess. You've been standing all day."

Alix ordered a coffee from the bartender, shot Thalia a sidelong glance, and surreptitiously eased her feet free of the vise-like straps that held them. "Just for a little while."

"I'll never tell." Thalia clamped her lips together before she forgot herself and offered a foot rub.

"There's a part of me that can't believe this is over," Alix said into the lull. "The details have consumed my every waking moment, and I've forgotten how to live without this hanging over my head."

Thalia raised her eyebrows. "I hate to break it to you, but last-minute preparations for the Monaco Grand Prix will rush in to fill the void. It's a madhouse." And then she caught herself. "What am I saying—you know this. You've lived with it all your life."

"But until now, I never paid attention. I never cared."

"And now you do?"

Alix shot her a look that screamed "*Obviously*," but that didn't stop the warm feeling from intensifying in Thalia's chest. No. She couldn't fool herself. Alix cared about this year's Monaco Grand Prix because she was helping to organize it, not because she was coming to care for *her* in some way. Getting caught up by this crush would be a mistake. At this point in the season—in her career, in her life—Thalia couldn't afford sentimentality.

"There you are!"

Thalia looked up at the interjection to the sight of Isabel Bassler approaching, expertly threading her way around the tables on four-inch stilettos. Inwardly, Thalia groaned. Isabel's interest had been plain from the instant of their introduction, and Thalia hadn't been able to shake her all day. This, she was learning, was one of the many problems with having a reputation for being easy; people didn't pick up on your *I'm not interested* signals. Hours ago, she had cornered her friend Gene, who just so happened to be both the defending Motocross champion and an unrepentant bachelor, with one simple request: flirt adeptly enough with Isabel Bassler to redirect her attention. Apparently, he had failed.

"I've been searching for you since—" Isabel halted when Alix turned around, and her wine-flushed cheeks grew even darker. "My apologies, Your Serene Highness. I didn't recognize you."

"No apologies required, I assure you. And it's Alix, remember?"

The words were the right ones, but something in Alix's tone made the hairs on Thalia's arms stand up in warning. Alix was not pleased, but she was also trying not to show it. Why? And would Isabel pick up on the undercurrent of tension?

"Alix," Isabel said, and flashed her supermodel smile. "This has been a lovely day. Congratulations on your success."

"Thank you for helping to make it possible." Still the epitome of politeness, but the words were stilted.

"I wouldn't have missed it." She glanced between them. "A few of us have planned to carry on the party at *boujis*," she continued, naming one of London's most exclusive nightclubs. "Would you like to join?"

Thalia caught the intent look Isabel flashed her, and the subtle emphasis she placed on *you*. When Alix immediately replied in the negative, citing fatigue, Thalia would have laid down money that Alix was deliberately paving the way for everything Isabel's unspoken communication was hinting at. She should have been grateful. Would have been, half a year ago.

"And I'm in training for the Monaco Grand Prix," Thalia said. "As much as I enjoy *boujis*, it's not part of my regimen."

Isabel's alluring mouth turned down in a pout. "Oh, but that's weeks away, isn't it?" She leaned in closer to reveal even more of the milky curves of her cleavage. "Surely you can allow yourself a night of fun."

For a heartbeat, Thalia was tempted. The past few months had been ascetic by her standards, and her body was craving the physical release she continued to deny it. And why? Her will was strong enough to ensure that a single night of pleasure didn't become a downward spiral of debauchery. Or was she susceptible to the slippery slope? She didn't want to believe that about herself, but now—mid-season, when she was finally racing consistently well—was hardly the time to experiment with her own limits.

You need to change your attitude, your behavior, and the company you keep. Lady Rufford's admonition still echoed in her ears. The mantra had been working so far, and Thalia was superstitious enough to believe in the possibility of jinxing herself. Besides, she wanted to prove to Alix that her word meant something—that she was above succumbing to a beautiful and famous face simply for the sake of an evening's transitory pleasure.

"Every second counts," she said. "But thank you for the invitation."

Isabel closed in on herself and took a step backward. "Good night, then," she said frostily before turning on one heel and sashaying off. Thalia redirected her gaze to her scotch, not wanting to betray her appreciation of the seductive sway of Isabel's hips.

"Did you want to go?" Alix asked quietly, once Isabel was out of earshot.

"Yes." Thalia saw no point in denying the truth.

"Then why didn't you accept her invitation?"

Thalia raised her head but could find no trace of censure in Alix's expression. She looked a little sad, of all things, but perhaps that was a manifestation of her fatigue.

"After my poor showing in Melbourne, I promised myself that I wouldn't do anything to jeopardize my success," she said. "And I'm sticking to that."

Alix nodded but didn't reply. When her phone buzzed, she glanced down at the screen, allowing Thalia the opportunity to observe her at close quarters. She had accentuated the natural waviness of her hair for the occasion, and it curled around her shoulders, partially obscuring her profile. Thalia wanted to reach out and pull the curtain back to reveal the tan column of her neck. She wanted to lean in and kiss the corner of Alix's mouth.

This, too, was lust—but it was also more. Isabel had offered everything Thalia was accustomed to wanting: a conflagration that would consume itself, leaving nothing but a hazy and pleasant memory in its wake. But now she found herself wanting something different. The desire she felt for Alix was laced with an unfamiliar tenderness that frightened her enough to consider going after Isabel after all.

But then Alix looked up from her phone with an apology and reached out to touch the back of Thalia's hand. She froze. It was the second time today that their fingers had brushed. How could these tiny little touches feel so much more significant than the intimacies she had shared with dozens of lovers?

"Thank you again for your generosity today. And for your help with the planning." Alix moved her hand away, and Thalia clutched at the bar to stop herself from taking it back and lacing their fingers together. "Without you, this wouldn't have been a success."

Thalia shook her head, buying time to swallow past the tightness in her throat. "You're wrong about that. But I was happy to help." Alix seemed ready to leave, and Thalia lighted on a way they could spend a little more time together tonight. "Let me know when you're ready to go, and I'll drive you back to your hotel."

A frown line creased Alix's forehead. "Oh, that's not necessary. I can take the helicopter. Besides…" She eyed Thalia's empty glass.

Thalia started to bristle at the implication before logic interceded. She had never gotten behind the wheel of a car while drunk, but Alix couldn't know that. Her reputation's coattails were unfortunately long. "I've just had the one. And I promise you I wouldn't make the offer if I were intoxicated."

A light blush rose to Alix's cheeks. "I'm sorry. That was callous of me. I trust you."

"No, you don't." Thalia spoke without rancor, hoping her honesty would get through to Alix. "But I hope I can prove that you should. Someday."

Clearly flustered, Alix didn't have a ready response. "Let me drive you," Thalia repeated, keeping her voice soft in an effort not to seem pushy. "I'm heading back to London anyway. It's no hassle."

Finally, Alix nodded. "All right. Thank you. I just need to let my security detail know, and to say good-bye to a few more people."

"Take your time." Thalia hoped her voice wasn't betraying the triumph she felt. She signaled the bartender. "I'll be here. Drinking coffee."

She didn't turn around to watch Alix walk away. But she wanted to.

CHAPTER FOURTEEN

A lix sat in the boardroom, pretending to pay attention when in fact she had lost the thread of the conversation long ago. The Grand Prix was one week away, and last-minute planning was at a fever pitch. Hotel kitchen fires, double-booked mooring pins at the marina, and a water main break downtown were only a few of the inevitable, eleventh hour crises that had begun popping up. Fortunately, every event pertaining to the royal family and the palace was well in order, so Alix didn't need to scramble.

Surreptitiously checking her phone—though why she still felt the need to be sly when everyone else had them in their hands or out on the table, she didn't know—Alix reread the last text from Thalia. She was at a café across the street, waiting. As soon as this was over, they would spend the remainder of the daylight hours walking the Grand Prix course. It was a fairly popular activity for tourists, but once the barriers and grandstands began to go up, they were barred from certain sections. She and Thalia wouldn't have that issue.

She was looking forward to learning Thalia's perspective on her city. The better Alix knew her, the more she wanted to understand the intricacies of Formula One. After their walk-through, she would be able to picture the circuit through Thalia's eyes on race day.

When the chairman finally adjourned them, she quickly gathered her belongings and gestured to Claude that she wanted to leave quickly. When the president of the Casino de Monte Carlo tried to stop her, ostensibly to chat about some minor aspect of the Grand Prix weekend, she politely but firmly told him she had a prior appointment.

She found Thalia sitting at an outdoor table. Her lustrous dark hair was pulled back into a ponytail, and she wore a red and white Arizona Cardinals cap. That was apparently an American football team, and both the cap and hairstyle worked well as a disguise. Formula One fans were looking for the version of Thalia they saw before or after a race, or in a grainy illicit photo. This version of her was not that, and Alix much preferred her incognito.

Thalia was looking at something on her phone, and Alix was glad of the opportunity to observe her unawares. Instead of resisting the excited flutter in her chest, she relaxed into her anticipation. As the race drew closer, it would become increasingly difficult to find time to spend together. This afternoon felt like an oasis amid the stormy insanity of the world's most highly anticipated Grand Prix.

As she drew closer, she noticed that Thalia was drinking only water. The amount of self-restraint that demonstrated was a sign of just how badly she wanted to continue her upward trajectory in Monaco. If Alix were being honest with herself, Thalia's focus coming into this race rivaled her own as a student. When, weeks ago now, Thalia had apologized to her in the nearby Meridien, Alix had been skeptical of Thalia's pledge to change her ways. But she had delivered on that promise, demonstrating the kind of altruism, fortitude, and perseverance that Alix couldn't help but admire.

Thalia was absently tracing patterns in the condensation on the outside of her glass, and Alix found herself momentarily entranced by the gentle movement of her fingertips. Desire flared, and she shivered despite the warmth of the day. These sudden, visceral reactions were becoming less easy to manage. Until now, sexuality had never been an important part of her identity. She had never felt a strong biological imperative, and she had never dated anyone with whom she felt comfortable being so vulnerable. Since coming to realize the nature of her feelings for Thalia, Alix had been looking back on her life since adolescence with a critical eye. Had she been sublimating her sexual drive all along? Had she been attracted to women previously, without recognizing it?

Thalia looked up at precisely that moment, as though drawn by her busy thoughts. She smiled—not the practiced smile always ready for the media, but an eager, genuine smile that Alix had only seen directed at her. "Hi," she called.

"Hello." Alix took the seat across from her. "I'm sorry to keep you waiting."

"It's been a real hardship to have to sit outside in this," Thalia said dryly, indicating the perfection of the day with a wave of her hand.

"But I know you don't like to sit still. Shall we walk?"

Thalia stood, then reached for the small backpack beside her chair. It was the kind that had a pouch filled with liquid and a plastic tube for drinking. "I'd offer to share," she said as she put it on, "but trust me when I say you don't want to drink this stuff."

"Is it the same drink that you use in your car?"

"The very same. Chock full of vitamins and minerals. If you're really curious..." She held out the mouthpiece of the tube.

Alix was poised to make her excuses when she remembered that one of the reasons for their excursion was to help her understand how it felt to race in a Grand Prix. Her ability to empathize would only be improved by sampling the drink Thalia would be guzzling.

"I'll try it." In moving close enough to take a sip, their bodies were separated by mere inches. "You don't have any infectious diseases, do you?" Alix said, mostly to distract herself from Thalia's warm, vaguely herbal scent.

"You might catch the gay." Her face remained deadpan, but her eyes were sparkling.

A dozen replies leapt to Alix's lips: *So what if I do?* and *I think I already have*, and *Is that what you want?* She closed her mouth around the tube as much to keep herself from speaking as to take a sip. As soon as she got a taste, she stepped away.

"It reminds me of weak, too-sweet tea."

"I can see that." Thalia took a sip herself. "Unpleasant, but necessary. Now that we're fortified, shall we?"

"Lead the way."

"So, this is the start and finish line of the race." Thalia turned toward the train station. "The start is always insane, as you've seen, but it's especially important in this race because overtaking is almost impossible. I've been practicing mine intensely over the past week."

Claude fell in behind them as they began to walk. Alix was glad he hadn't insisted on more of a security presence, but she also resented that he had to be there at all. She couldn't tell where his loyalties lay. He was already privy to how much time they were spending together, and if she and Thalia were ever to share any kind of intimate moment, she wouldn't be able to keep it from him. Would he feel compelled to tell her father? Had he perhaps already done so? She thought back on her recent interactions with her parents, but nothing about them seemed suspicious. Her father was pleased that she was taking more of an interest in royal duties. Her mother continued to suggest beautification "remedies" and eligible bachelors, but that was nothing new.

"This is the first turn." Thalia's voice pulled her out of the whirlpool of her thoughts. "Named St. Devote for the church there. It's crazy on the first lap because of all the jockeying for position, but otherwise pretty standard."

"What's your plan for the race?" Alix asked as they continued on along Avenue d'Ostend. "Don't worry. You can trust me not to run to the nearest reporter."

"It wouldn't matter if you did. Most everyone has the same strategy here. Because overtaking is so difficult, qualifying becomes especially important. I just want to qualify as well as possible and then run a clean race."

Thalia led them past the marina, and they traded yachting stories. Alix tried not to be jealous when Thalia mentioned an ex-girlfriend. Not for the first time, she wondered whether the interest she could sense from Thalia was simply the result of her wanting another notch—a *royal* notch—on her bedpost. Their interactions didn't feel that way, but she couldn't help considering the possibility.

Trying to put aside her fears, she focused on enjoying the beautiful day, spent in the company of someone she liked. As they walked past Casino Square, home of the Monte Carlo Casino, Alix admitted that she had never gambled even once. Thalia was so incredulous that she could barely string together a coherent sentence. But when she tried to convince Alix to go inside and remedy that deficiency, Alix staunchly refused.

"It has no appeal to me. Absolutely none. And besides, as a citizen of Monaco, I'm not allowed to gamble there."

"Excuse me? Not *allowed*?"

"Mm." Alix couldn't help but enjoy her incredulity. "I'm not even allowed inside. It's an old law, from over a hundred years ago—ostensibly made to protect the locals from being exploited by their own government."

"You're honestly telling me that if we walked up to the front door, they would turn you away."

"They would. Very politely, but they would."

"Unreal." Thalia shook her head. They continued on in silence for a few minutes, before she said, "And in all your traveling, you've never gambled elsewhere?"

"I almost did, once, at a casino in Nice. Florestan was playing the slots." She laughed at the memory. "I asked how he chose when to pull the lever, and when he told me there was no strategy involved whatsoever, I was entirely turned off."

"Let me get this straight," Thalia said slowly. "You thought there was a way to influence a slot machine?"

"Why shouldn't there be?" Alix still felt a tiny bit indignant, even after all this time. "Why can't you try to anticipate the motion of the machine and pull the lever accordingly?"

"Because then it would be a game of skill, not luck," Thalia said. "And the house hates games of skill."

"Well, I hate games of luck," Alix fired back. "Risk is unacceptable unless I know I have the power to influence the outcome."

"You like to be in control," Thalia murmured.

The question was surprisingly sensual, and Alix felt herself blush. Unbidden, her mind called up a scene: a room overlooking the harbor; its windows open to admit a fresh, salt-scented breeze; she pinning Thalia's arms to her sides as they kissed slowly, deeply, sensually…

"I do when I'm taking a chance on something," she managed to have the presence of mind to retort.

Thalia looked like she wanted to reply right away, but apparently thought the better of it. "The Monegasque royal who has never placed a bet," she finally said, smiling. "I admire you, Princess Alix. You're the most independent person I've ever met."

Alix was more pleased by that assessment than she wanted to let on. "It has its drawbacks," she said instead.

"Oh?"

"Sometimes I find it difficult to connect with other people, because we don't have similar goals or values. And sometimes I can't tell whether I'm doing something—or not doing something—because it's really what I want, or whether I'm just being contrary. That's what my mother used to call me when I was younger. 'Princess Contrary.'"

Thalia looked thoughtful. "She thought you would oppose her wishes out of…what, exactly? Spite? Stubbornness?"

"The latter. But everything we've ever argued about has been silly."

"Such as?"

"As a young girl, I used to put up such a fight about having to wear a dress to every function or outing. And then, when I was older, she wanted me to care more deeply about superficial things—makeup, hair, clothing, boys." When they paused at an intersection, she glanced at Thalia to gauge her reaction. Attentive and sympathetic, she reached out as if to touch Alix's hand but then apparently thought better of it.

Alix wanted that touch, and she wanted to tell her so. But her throat closed against the words, and logic interceded to tell her that even though they had yet to be stopped by a tourist or fan, they were both recognizable. It wasn't safe to indulge in any kind of emotional or physical display, unless they were both prepared to face the consequences. And there could be no discussing consequences without first having talked about what was happening between them. Dating and relationships were complicated enough, she imagined, without also having to negotiate the minefield of celebrity.

"Listen to me, complaining," she said self-consciously. "I've grown up in a life filled with extraordinary privilege."

"Yes," Thalia said, "but that doesn't mean it's been perfect. You may have a lot of privilege, but with that comes expectations and responsibilities, some of which you may want nothing to do with."

"Well said," Alix murmured.

As if sensing she would prefer to drop this conversation, Thalia pointed to the road. They were coming up on the luxurious Fairmont Hotel, and the hairpin curve it overlooked. "The Fairmont hairpin," she said. "You have to take it very slowly, and the g-forces of decelerating into it and then accelerating out are just insane."

"A pain in the neck?"

Thalia rolled her eyes. "You're almost as sharp as that corner."

They walked on, skirting the ocean as they rounded the curve known as Mirabeau, which had an escape road where a driver could pull off in an emergency, and headed toward the double right-handed turn known as Le Portier. The barriers here were nearly flush with the ocean, which splashed against their feet as they made their way toward the tunnel. As Thalia explained the aerodynamics behind what made the tunnel so difficult—not to mention how quickly her eyes had to adjust if it were sunny outside—Alix felt a new appreciation for just how much mental calculation went into a Formula One race on the part of the drivers.

The walkway ascended out of the tunnel, past the theater with its tall, arching windows and distinctive rounded cornices. Thalia had decided to regale her with stories of the most outrageous racing incidents in the history of the Monaco Grand Prix, and Alix relaxed in the spell of her storytelling. It was nice simply to listen, and not to have to think too hard about what to say next. The longer they walked side by side, the stronger grew the urge to lace their fingers together in that simplest gesture of intimacy.

If she gave in to the urge, Thalia would be surprised. She would probably want to talk about it, and while Alix knew she should want to have that conversation, a part of her wished it could be skipped— that she could join their hands together and not have to explain her motives to anyone, least of all herself. That was cowardice, and she was ashamed of it. But shame didn't stop the wanting.

Even if Thalia asked no questions, they couldn't risk detection. The crowded streets were potentially filled with prying eyes, and the last thing she wanted was for an incriminating photograph to surface. The irony would be extreme—she would be branded a lesbian before she had the chance to determine whether that was, in fact, the case.

Even thinking the label made her wince. Sexuality had never been an important part of her identity, mostly because she hadn't ever felt a strong pull toward either gender. *Any* gender, she mentally corrected herself. Her medical studies may have taught her to think outside the binary, but she had never managed to internalize that skill. But if she were queer—and if she were being honest, signs pointed to precisely that—she needed to do better at acknowledging the continuum on which both gender and sexuality operated. Which only contributed to the irony, since her fear was of the media pigeonholing her.

The media cared, of course, because she was a princess. But she was a *princess*. Why was she thinking like someone without any resources? She couldn't find anonymity on the street, but she could certainly find privacy elsewhere. Thalia was in the middle of a lengthy discussion of tires and their impact on a Formula One race, but Alix decided to interrupt her.

"I'm sorry. I just had an idea."

"You were drifting off, weren't you?" Thalia said, seeming amused rather than upset.

"Maybe a little. I'm sorry. But my thought was that once we've finished our walk, we should take some refreshment on board my family's yacht. It's moored just down there." She pointed to the bay.

"Sounds perfect," Thalia said.

"Let me make a quick call to alert the staff." Alix felt at once competent and illicit. An odd combination, but one that made her feel very much alive. "And then you can keep telling me about tires."

❖

It had been so easy. "I'm entertaining a Formula One guest," she had told her secretary. "We'd like to spend part of the evening on the *Priceless Pearl*, including dinner."

"Very well, ma'am," Alain had replied. "I'll alert the staff. Do you have any dining preferences?"

After a brief consultation with Thalia, Alix had requested seafood. They had shared their meal on the highest deck at a table facing the city as the blue sky slowly gathered hints of gold. By some tacit agreement, the conversation had remained light. Thalia had regaled her with stories from her boarding school and Karting days in England, and Alix had reciprocated as best she could. She hadn't gotten herself into nearly as many humorous scrapes, but she did have a few funny anecdotes to share from Oxford, particularly in regard to her one, ill-advised attempt to partake in organized athletics. She had attempted to play field hockey, only to be summoned by the coach to a private meeting in which he very apologetically explained that despite her royal pedigree, she would be unable to earn a starting position on the squad.

"I'm much better at individual sports," she said. "Hiking and skiing, for example."

"Then you have the perfect temperament for a racecar driver," Thalia said with a grin.

Alix had very nearly blurted out something about her lack of a death wish, but caught herself at the last second. That would have been insensitive, bordering on cruel. Instead, she had deflected the conversation back to Thalia's trajectory as a driver and learned in the process just how difficult it had been for her to break into Formula One, despite equal or better racing records. Somehow, she had failed to realize just how deep the misogyny ran, and she was impressed by Thalia's perseverance despite having been passed over for years.

By the time they had finished their meal, Alix had a much stronger understanding of whence the chip on Thalia's shoulder derived. While throwing a punch would never be the answer to anything, she might at least be able to sympathize with the extreme frustration Thalia must have felt when confronting Terrence's actions. He easily stood in as a representative of the patriarchal history and structure of Formula One—especially since he seemed to actively embrace the role.

Once their plates had been cleared, conversation lapsed into silence. Alix, who had taken the seat facing west, couldn't help but admire Thalia's profile against the backdrop of what was turning into a stunning sunset. The intervening hours, supplemented by a glass of champagne, had done nothing to diminish her feelings of attraction, which were somehow enhanced by the magnificence of the horizon. Aching physically and emotionally, Alix felt paralyzed. All she could manage, through a throat tight with trepidation and desire, was, "Look behind you."

Thalia turned and exclaimed wordlessly. When she got up and went to the railing, Alix followed her. They stood alone at the stern of the boat. The setting sun was turning the water to fire, and she felt as though it was doing the same to her blood. She dared a quick glance at Thalia beside her, bracing her arms on the railing and staring pensively into the distance.

Alix was tired of fighting the impulse to touch her. Like Eve in Eden, she needed more than to admire from afar. She needed to *know*. That single imperative eclipsed the alarm bells in her brain. Heart hammering against her ribs, she raised one hand from the rail and gently rested her palm on Thalia's back, between her shoulder blades. The light shirt did little to mask the heat pouring off her skin—heat to echo the conflagration all around them. Thalia shivered, but otherwise remained perfectly still.

"What are you doing?" she asked in a low, gravelly voice.

"Touching you."

Thalia exhaled sharply and bowed her head. "You shouldn't."

"Why not?" Intoxicated by the power she appeared to have in this moment, Alix ran her fingertips down Thalia's spine, eliciting another shiver. She might not have any basis for comparison, but that didn't matter. Thalia's responsiveness made her even more alluring.

"Alix." It was one of the few times Thalia had ever said her name, and the way she half spoke, half groaned it now made Alix feel the kind of sensual urgency she had only ever experienced by proxy in a film or book. She had thought they—the authors, the directors, the actors—had been making it up. And now here she stood, living proof that they had been right all along. It would have been an eerie feeling, had she any brainpower to spare.

"You're beautiful." Unlocked by Thalia's reaction to her simple touch, the words came easily. She had always thought so, and the shame in confessing it had finally been eclipsed by desire.

"Why are you doing this?" The words were tortured in their uncertainty.

Alix moved her hand up, first to caress the nape of Thalia's neck, and then to massage the tense muscles along her collarbone. "Because I want to. I have for some time now."

"For some ti—" Thalia cut herself off and finally raised her head. Her eyes were darker than Alix had ever seen them. The pulse in her neck fluttered wildly like a moth against a lampshade. "Are you serious?"

"Yes." She had intended the syllable to sound firm and confident, but it emerged as a whisper.

Thalia straightened to her full height and turned so her back was against the railing. She slid one finger through the belt loop of Alix's slacks and tugged. "Then come here."

And finally, Alix knew how it felt to be fully pressed against Thalia's lean frame. Her arms encircled Thalia's neck as though they belonged there, and when Thalia tentatively cupped her waist, Alix finally understood why the romantic books she had read as a teen described this kind of moment in terms like "melting" and "dissolving."

"You feel amazing," Thalia murmured. "I've wanted this too."

"Really?" The word came out before she could bite it back.

Thalia frowned. "Do you not believe me?"

"I believe you."

But she must have said it too quickly, because Thalia's grip tightened, her thumbs sweeping in rhythmic arcs across Alix's hipbones. "You don't. Tell me why."

Alix cursed the inexperience that had left her unprepared to manage this kind of moment. Trying to collect herself, she looked down at their feet—her chestnut loafers alternating with Thalia's state-of-the-art trainers—and tried to think of a way through this conversation that didn't involve her confessing her insecurities.

But Thalia leaned forward to press her mouth against the shell of Alix's ear. "Tell me."

Now it was her turn to shiver. "Unfair," she said breathlessly, even as Thalia withdrew. Expecting to find her smirking, Alix was surprised to be met instead by the expression she associated with Thalia as a racecar driver—intense, focused, determined.

"You may as well walk away right now if you're not willing to tell me."

Alix couldn't have been more shocked. Thalia was notorious for being an unrepentant player who had never once claimed a steady girlfriend. She had witnessed it herself at Sasha and Kerry's wedding—though on that day, she recalled, Maeve had been the one looking to move on. But since then, Thalia's bad reputation had only become more firmly entrenched. She didn't seem to care about the emotional state of her conquests...although now that Alix thought about it, she had to admit that there was no way she could actually know that. In fact, the more she tried to analyze this situation, the less certain she became of anything except for the fact that Thalia was still holding her, and it still felt amazing.

She wasn't going to walk away. Not now. Not yet. And really, Thalia was right. No matter what else happened, she and Thalia had been friends first, and Alix did owe her honesty.

"I'm well aware that I'm not as attractive as the women you usually...associate with." There. Done. Her face was warm with shame, but the truth was out there.

Thalia's mouth twisted and her expression softened. "Hey." She raised one hand to brush Alix's cheek. "Please don't insult yourself. You are beautiful. Do you doubt me?"

"No, of course not," Alix said quickly.

"Liar," Thalia murmured, and kissed her.

She had been kissed before—awkward, too-eager kisses from men who wanted nothing more than to stake their claim on a princess. This was nothing like that. Thalia's lips were warm, and soft beyond anything she could have imagined, yet also firm enough to guide her in the subtle exchange. The kiss ebbed and flowed, and the longer it went on, the more Alix lost herself in it.

When Thalia's tongue pushed gently inside her mouth, a low moan caught her unawares. Immediately self-conscious, she tried to pull away. But Thalia's arms tightened and she deepened the kiss, proving to Alix through the gentle movements of her mouth just how avidly she wanted to be right here and now.

As her restraint disintegrated, Alix pressed closer, hips circling in an instinctual desire for relief. Some distant part of her mind knew she was being far too forward, but she simply didn't care. Her desire, so long in hibernation, had finally woken hungry and impatient. But instead of taking the blatant invitation, Thalia began to gentle their kisses, bringing Alix reluctantly back down to earth. Shifting away from her mouth, Thalia pressed her lips along Alix's jawline, then down to skate across her neck.

"Oh, yes," Alix murmured as her skin prickled delightfully in response.

It seemed, then, that Thalia spent years on her neck—first kissing, then gently suckling, then nibbling with a flash of teeth that would immediately be soothed by the soft heat of her mouth. Her attentions were utterly distracting, and Alix soon felt herself even more molten than she had been previously.

In a meager attempt at retaliation, she let her fingers play in the short hairs on the nape of Thalia's neck. Her first reaction was to pull Alix tightly against her thigh, and a jolt of need shot through Alix's body in response to the possessive action. Thalia's head jerked up, her expression panicked, and she tried to take a step backward. But there was nowhere to go.

"What's wrong?" Alix asked, not halting her gentle stroking.

"You need to stop doing that," she said through gritted teeth. "Please."

Alix stilled her hand. "This?"

Thalia exhaled slowly, as if in relief. "Yes. I'm sorry."

"Can you tell me why?" It wasn't because Thalia hadn't been enjoying herself—Alix was certain of that much. Rather, she seemed to be having some kind of internal battle.

"The way you were touching me..." She swallowed hard. "My body was interpreting that as a signal to do things you're not ready for. Please don't take this the wrong way, but I haven't taken this kind of thing slowly in a very long time."

Although Thalia's presumption of her naïveté was correct, Alix felt affronted. "How do you know what I'm ready for?"

"Okay, you're right," she said. "I don't. But I also don't ever want to assume, or presume, or do anything you'd find upsetting."

"I appreciate that," Alix said. "But not assuming goes both ways."

It took a moment for her words to register, but when they did, Thalia pulled her closer. Alix wondered whether the movement had been premeditated or involuntary. Presumably, the latter. "For my own peace of mind," Thalia said, despite their lips being mere inches apart, "I need you to answer some questions. Honestly. Will you?"

"Yes." Alix wouldn't have hesitated even had she wanted to. This was her chance to shatter Thalia's assumptions—or, of course, to fulfill them. She didn't want to do the latter by playing the role of the naïvely questioning woman, but what if that was the only role that fit?

"Have you ever felt this way about a woman before?"

"No." Suddenly, the way forward was clear. Her position was about parity, not exclusion. "But I've never felt this way about a man before, either."

Clearly nonplussed, Thalia blinked at her. "I'm sorry?"

Alix took a deep breath. If she confessed her inexperience, would Thalia read it as inadequacy? "I've never felt this way. Period."

"Describe to me how you feel."

"Exhilarated. Frightened." She swallowed hard. The truth was the truth, and sugarcoating it would only make everything worse. "Wanting."

Thalia's jaw clenched. "Have you ever made love? Had sex?"

Alix didn't want to admit the truth, and that made her angry at herself. There was nothing *wrong* with her. She had never wanted to explore that level of intimacy with anyone. It wasn't a flaw—just a fact. "No."

"And do you want to right now? Do you want your first time to be with me?"

Forcing herself not to look away despite the blush she could feel rising to her cheeks, Alix tried to process her reaction to the question. Desire, yes, but also trepidation. "I don't know," she finally said. It was the most honest answer she could offer.

Thalia's expression softened. "I'm relieved to hear you say that."

"Relieved?" Of all Thalia's possible responses, she hadn't expected relief. "Why is that?"

Her confusion only increased when Thalia also blushed. "Because if you had said yes, I would've known you just wanted to use me for experience."

"I was under the impression that you like casual, no-strings sex," Alix said, determined to call a spade a spade.

"Usually, yes," Thalia said, seeming increasingly uncomfortable. "When I'm sure of what the other person wants and expects."

"And you think I would want or expect more than that?" Alix's frustration was mounting again. Just because she'd never had sex before, she wasn't allowed to want it for its own sake? Did Thalia expect her to be pining away? Suddenly wanting space between them, Alix took a step backward. Thalia raised her hands in a pleading gesture.

"Hang on a second, okay? You're misinterpreting what I'm saying. I didn't just meet you at a club or at the track. We know each other. We work together. Anything that happens between us is going to be more than casual."

More than casual. The words pleased her more than she wanted to admit. Allowing herself to be pulled back into Thalia's orbit, Alix decided that she rather liked it when Thalia was a little off-kilter. "Is that a roundabout way of saying that you care about me?"

When panic was the first emotion to flash across Thalia's face, Alix felt the keen slice of disappointment. But then Thalia cupped her cheek, and her thumb ghosted across Alix's lips, and Alix couldn't help but lean into the gentle touch.

"I do care about you. But I'm not at a point in my life where I want to make promises."

"I'm not asking you to."

"What are you asking for?"

As Alix thought through how to word her answer, Thalia's hands skimmed over her rib cage—up and down, up and down. "That's distracting," she said.

"Is it?" Thalia asked disingenuously.

Teasing. Thalia was teasing her. And she liked it. Narrowing her eyes, Alix silently vowed not to turn into a puddle every time Thalia touched her. She had more backbone than that.

"It would appear that we're attracted to each other," she began.

"You think?"

Alix touched two fingertips to Thalia's mouth, and her eyes went dark again. "Don't interrupt me. I'd like to explore…this"—she gestured to the space between them—"slowly and without any strings attached. How does that sound to you?"

Thalia's smile seemed genuine. "Good. Really good." And tugging Alix closer, she bent to claim another kiss.

Alix gave herself up to it, fully relaxing against Thalia's body for the first time. Heat upon softness, the kiss went on and on, as the warm breeze sighed around them and the yacht rocked gently beneath their feet.

CHAPTER FIFTEEN

A s Thalia crossed the line just before the third qualifying session expired, she knew her time had been good. She also knew she could do even better. The more fuel she burned off, the lighter and faster her car became. This last lap would be her best one yet.

"Excellent work, Thalia," Carl's voice sounded in her ear. "You're P5 at the moment."

She spared a nanosecond for celebration—if she could hold on to it, fifth place would tie her highest qualifying result this season—before focusing on taking the St. Devote turn as efficiently as possible in order to carry every ounce of possible speed up the hill to the casino. As she accelerated along Beau Rivage, her peripheral vision registered the flicker of sunlight on the ocean to her right. In the next instant, her lips were burning—not parched with thirst, but aching in memory of the kisses she and Alix had shared on the yacht.

No. She bit down hard on her lower lip, willing the pain to restore her concentration. She could not lose focus—not here, not now. Not when she had the opportunity to reach even higher than P5.

As she accelerated through Casino Square's wide corner, Thalia steeled herself for the one-two punch that was Mirabeau and Le Portier. Gravity would paralyze her lungs for several seconds, and she took a long, deep breath in anticipation of touching the brake.

Suddenly, her earpiece crackled back into life at the same instant that the LED on top of her steering wheel glowed yellow. "Yellow flag, Thalia. Yellow flag."

"No! Goddamn it!" A yellow flag meant there was some sort of incident up ahead. Qualifying was over. Her flying lap would remain unfinished, and she would have to be content with P5.

Braking heavily, she coasted into Mirabeau, alert for debris or people. With a flick of her thumb, she turned on her mic. "What happened?"

And then she saw it: one of the Ferrari cars on the escape road, slowly backing toward the track. Rage hijacked her vision, tingeing the world red. She would have bet every penny to her name that that car belonged to Terrence, and that he had staged the emergency to put a stop to her lap.

"Terrence went off the course," Carl said. "Locked up, we think."

As she headed into the tunnel, Thalia double-checked that her mic was off and then shouted every vulgarity she could think of. None of the breathing rhythms or mental exercises she had learned in that ridiculous anger management workshop held any appeal. All she could think about was how much she wanted to hit him again. Seething, she took a long pull of her energy drink, wishing it were a whiskey.

Emerging from the tunnel was always tricky, and because of her low speed, she had been inside it longer than normal. Blinking fiercely, she negotiated the chicane mostly from memory. But in forcing her to concentrate, the shift from shadow to sunlight had the unexpected consequence of temporarily dulling her anger enough to allow reason a voice.

Terrence might have had a legitimate emergency. As much as she didn't think that was true, discounting the possibility would be a mistake. And even if he had been malicious, this time she had to be the "bigger" person. She certainly couldn't hit him again, or call him names, or curse at him. Somehow, she had to rein in her emotions enough to encounter him without incident, and to answer the media's inevitable questions without going off the deep end.

As she rounded the sharp Tabac turn and made for Piscine, the bay unfurled to her left, crowded with yachts that flashed brilliantly beneath the sun. *Alix*. Alix would help to keep her calm yet honest, wouldn't she? Alix had seen her at her worst but had been willing to forgive.

Thalia turned into the pit lane and pulled up before her garage, shifting the engine into neutral as the mechanics covered the car's tires and pushed her inside. She leapt out as soon as the car was stationary.

Instantly, Alistair and her team of engineers converged on her position, trepidation evident on their faces.

"You're confirmed at P5," Carl said.

"The race stewards know you were on track for a better time," Alistair added. "They're going to investigate Terrence's actions."

"They won't find him guilty." Thalia wrestled off her HANS and looked between them. "I get it. You're afraid I'm going to do something crazy, like in Italy."

"In a word: yes." Alistair never minded standing up to her.

"I'm not planning on it. I've learned my lesson."

Alistair didn't seem convinced. "I know the media will want to speak with you, but I'd prefer to issue a statement that you're waiting on the stewards' decision."

Thalia had promised to play nicely, but she wasn't going to let them take her voice away. "Compromise: I'll be available briefly to the media to say exactly that. And no more." She met Alistair's eyes, trying to project an aura of competence despite being amped up on anger and adrenaline.

Alistair held her gaze for a long moment. "Fine," he said quietly. "But don't fuck this up." His matter-of-fact tone was far more effective as a threat than blustering or shouting would have been.

"How did Peter do?" she asked into the silence.

"P2," he said from behind her.

She turned to find him mopping his face with a towel. He tossed it over his shoulder and gave her a one-armed hug, but didn't say anything. She loved that about Peter. He didn't sugarcoat things or rattle off meaningless platitudes. He was just *there*, solid and sympathetic and consistently excellent on the track.

"Congratulations," she said, hoping he could hear her sincerity.

He moved off, and she paid a quick visit to the restroom in an attempt to tidy up her appearance. She braced herself against the small sink to stretch the aching muscles of her neck. Resentment churned sluggishly in her chest, and beneath it, the anger she had to find a way of containing. She didn't want to be obsessed with Terrence's actions. She didn't want to care that the stewards were going to rule this, too, a "racing incident."

Thinking back to Monza reminded her of Alix, and the lecture she had delivered—in a nightclub, of all places. Thalia had been so infuriated by her then, but also, if she were being honest, intrigued. And now she had the memories of Alix's kisses to supplement that lecture. The press would try to rile her up, but if she kept Alix in mind, she might be able to remember why it was so important not to rise to their bait. Qualifying was over. At this point, focusing on anything other than tomorrow would be a mistake.

She closed her eyes and tried to visualize how it must feel to win the Monaco Grand Prix, with hordes of fans spilling out into the streets to offer their congratulations. It was the crown jewel of Formula One—the race everyone wanted most. She wasn't out of contention. Anything could happen tomorrow. Barring some major catastrophe, the show would go on. And she needed to move on with it.

When she emerged, one of their interns guided her to the front of the garage where a few members of the press corps were interviewing Peter. He was laughing with them as she approached, and she soon learned why: he was trying to conduct the session in French. As she watched him endure the reporters' good-natured teasing about his grammar, Thalia couldn't help but be jealous of his rapport with them. Was it too late to build that kind of relationship with the media? Had she been too antagonistic for too long?

They caught sight of her then, and the tenor of the conversation changed. As she took her place beside Peter, their inquiries turned to the incident involving Terrence at Mirabeau. She stayed true to her word, answering each question tersely with variations on the same theme: she was waiting for the race stewards to sort it out. But just as she had expected, the more she toed the party line, the more incendiary the reporters' questions became.

"Do you think Terrence is singling you out?"

"How did you feel when you saw the yellow flag after making such good time in the first sector?"

"Do you believe Terrence is a misogynist?"

As she stalwartly stuck to her guns, she caught sight of Alix standing off to the side, Claude just behind her. When their eyes met, Alix raised one hand in acknowledgment. Thalia wondered what she was trying to communicate. A simple hello? Or a warning not to say or do something she would regret?

Her mind sought momentary refuge from the tension of the moment by flashing back to the way Alix had responded to her kisses.

Her unfeigned eagerness had made their time together one of the most arousing experiences of her life. She didn't want to be here, pretending to be rational and patient. She wanted to return to the moment they had shared beneath the sunset, when Alix had relaxed in her arms. The memory alone made her ache with wanting.

"If you could speak with the stewards right now, what would you say?" a reporter called, shattering her pleasant thoughts.

Once she had delivered yet another non-answer, the team's PR head mercifully intervened, informing the media that the drivers needed to get their rest. Thalia tried to make light conversation with Peter on their way back inside by asking him about Courtney and Bryce. As she had known it would, that sent him into an exuberant narrative about their trip to Monaco's Oceanographic Museum, which included a world-renowned aquarium.

During the debriefing session with Alistair and the engineers that followed, Thalia could barely concentrate. She always felt restless after qualifying, but this was more than adrenaline and anticipation. The longer she thought about Terrence's maneuver, the more convinced she was that it had been completely intentional. By the time Alistair delivered his parting words, she felt as though her brain was on fire.

She had to find a way to gain some measure of calm, or she wouldn't be able to sleep tonight, and that would be disastrous. Spending time with Alix was the first thought that leapt into her head, but that was a bad idea. She knew herself well enough to recognize that in her present state, she was far too volatile. It had been easy to take things slowly earlier in the week, but she had no reserves of patience to fall back on today.

❖

Alix found Thalia in the Meridien's gym, dancing around a heavy punching bag. She wore only a black sports bra and mesh shorts, and the skin of her midriff glistened with sweat under the neon lights. The onslaught of Alix's visceral response forced her to brace one hand against the wall. She wanted to dip her tongue into the troughs between Thalia's abdominal muscles—to taste her skin and be rewarded by the low moan she hadn't heard for two interminable days.

It should have been easy for Alix to question her own line of thinking. It should at the very least have been *possible* to listen to the nagging, parental voices in her head and walk away from a relationship conceived by and in "sin." But it wasn't possible. Alix didn't want to question her instincts, and she certainly didn't believe in "sin" the way Christianity defined it. Homosexuality occurred naturally in the animal world, and human beings were animals like any other.

Of course, her parents would probably find a way to turn that logic on its head. Religion preferred to think of humanity as special—created pure and sacrosanct in the image of a divine entity. Whereas Alix preferred to think of humanity as a product of evolution, in which case they shared plenty of traits with the rest of the animal kingdom.

"Hi," she called, mostly to distract herself from her swirling thoughts. Or so she justified it.

Thalia took a long step back from the swinging bag and met her gaze. "Alix."

"I may not understand all the racing details," Alix said carefully, "but I know enough to understand that what happened today was unfair."

Thalia's eyes closed briefly before she reached out to steady the bag. "Yeah. It was."

"Do you want to explain it to me?" Alix thought that maybe if Thalia talked about what had happened, she would be able to start to work through her frustration.

"No." Thalia swiftly crossed the space between them. "I don't."

And then Thalia was kissing her, both hands on her hips as she pushed Alix slowly backward until the wall was there to support her. The kiss was confident and possessive and thorough, and Alix instinctually threaded her arms around Thalia's neck. One of Thalia's hands trailed up along her side in a caress that made her shiver and press even closer.

"You feel incredible," Thalia whispered, shifting her focus to Alix's neck. Her lips were as gentle as a butterfly's wings, and Alix felt her body begin to melt. The way Thalia touched her—at once reverently and hungrily—was intoxicating in a way she had already begun to crave. Never had she experienced desire so acutely, and with such urgency.

This was too dangerous, Alix thought dimly, even as Thalia pressed gentle kisses across her collarbone. Anyone might walk in at any moment, and Claude would have to enter with them.

"What's wrong?" Thalia whispered. "You just got really tense."

"I'm worried about getting interrupted." She hated to admit it.

With a groan, Thalia pulled away, bracing herself against the wall with her hands on either side of Alix's head. "I'm sorry. I got carried away."

"I don't want you to be sorry." Now that they were no longer touching, Alix felt bereft.

"No?" Thalia leaned in closer, testing the assertion.

"No. I love when—" She caught herself. "I very much enjoy how you touch me."

Thalia kissed one corner of her mouth. "I want to invite you to my room," she whispered.

"You want to?" It was a battle for Alix to keep her voice steady. "Or you are inviting me?"

"I'm down here beating up a punching bag because I'm angry and frustrated and can't sit still." Her voice was low and intense. "I've never had much patience to begin with, but when I'm like this, I have next to none."

Realization dawned. "And you're afraid you'll lose control if we're really alone?"

She nodded. "I'm afraid I'll push you too hard, too fast."

"Will you stop if I ask you to?"

"Of course," Thalia said quickly. "But what happens if, in the moment, I can make you not want to stop?"

"Arrogant, aren't you?" Alix fired back in an effort to disguise the effect Thalia was having on her. That Thalia wanted her enough to fear losing control was a heady proposition, but it also gave her pause. "We don't have much time before the dinner tonight, but I would like to spend it with you. So what if we institute some rules of engagement?"

A smile tugged at the corners of Thalia's mouth. "Like…no touching below the belt?"

Alix laughed. "That's perfect, actually. Because I'd like to give you a neck and shoulder massage to help you relax."

"That sounds heavenly." Seeming more relaxed already, she stepped back so Alix was no longer pressed against the wall. "In that case, would you like to come up to my room?"

"Yes," Alix said, and accepted her outstretched hand.

Thalia parted from her at the door to the gym before she had to initiate the separation herself. When she faced Claude, she couldn't tell whether he had seen anything, nor was she any closer to deciding whether he could be trusted.

"I will be going up to Ms. d'Angelis's room," she informed him in as flat a voice as she could manage.

"Yes, ma'am." He fell in behind them as they moved toward the elevator.

The ride was interminable, but when they reached Thalia's door, Alix prepared herself for more waiting. Claude would have to check the room before they could be alone in it.

Thalia went straight to the minibar. "Would you like something to drink?"

"No, thank you." She wanted to add that Thalia ought not to drink either, but then she pulled out a bottle of Perrier and the protest died on Alix's lips.

As Thalia poured it into a tumbler, the bubbles frothed and churned, trying to overspill their bounds before retreating below the surface. Alix didn't believe in signs or omens—they were products of the human brain creating patterns where none existed, and nothing more—but in that moment she found herself tempted to read the water as symbolic of her own desire. Tonight, however, she could not let it overspill its bounds.

"All clear, ma'am," Claude said. "I'll be outside."

"Thank you, Claude." When the door locked automatically behind him, she released her breath slowly, feeling at once relieved and self-conscious. Not wanting to betray the latter to Thalia, she walked to the window and looked out at the Mediterranean.

"You're very polite with your staff," Thalia said from behind her.

"I can't help but feel guilty when it comes to them." Her every nerve was on high alert as she sensed Thalia moving closer. "They sacrifice so much to follow us around the globe."

"But they get to *see* the globe." Thalia halted beside her but did not touch. Perhaps it was fanciful, but Alix felt as though she could sense the restless energy crackling around her. "Their job does have some perks."

"I suppose." Refusing to allow her nerves to sabotage the evening's potential, Alix turned to face her. "It isn't the life I would have chosen, but I'm grateful they did."

Thalia drained her glass and set it on a nearby end table. "What life would you have chosen?"

Alix had imagined a different life so often that she had no trouble answering. "I would still be a doctor," she said, "but in a small practice, somewhere I could truly make a difference."

"Husband? Two-point-five kids?"

The question was intrusive, bordering on insulting. A husband? Did Thalia think she was playing a game or going through a phase? She didn't have to respond, of course. She could walk out of this room right now and put an end to this fledgling relationship, if it could even be called that.

But just as she was about to launch into a diatribe, logic prevailed. She had been necessarily candid (she still believed that) about her lack of experience. Perhaps Thalia wasn't trying to insult her, but rather to do the opposite? Alix had yet to claim a label for herself. Had Thalia been offering her a way out of the box, at least for now?

"I didn't think beyond my career," she finally said. Wanting to be out of the limelight, she turned the tables. "And you? What life would you have chosen?"

"This is it for me. I'm doing exactly what I always dreamed of." And then she grinned. "If I had to do it over again, though, I would've asked you out back at Sasha's wedding."

The declaration dissolved Alix's tension, and she had to laugh. "I would have declined."

"Sure about that?" Thalia held out one hand. Beneath her devil-may-care expression hid a softer and stronger emotion—something that made Alix feel truly wanted rather than preyed upon.

But she didn't dare to take Thalia's hand.

"Yes," she said, softening the rejection with a smile. "And I am not letting you lead me to that bed." She sat in the nearest chair and prayed she could keep her composure. "Take off your shirt and sit on the floor with your back me."

She expected Thalia to have some kind of ready quip, but after a moment of what appeared to be frozen disbelief, she hurried to obey. Alix's mouth went dry as her breasts were revealed. They suited her body perfectly, and she allowed her gaze to roam over the pale golden curves, imagining their softness.

"The way you're looking at me right now," Thalia said hoarsely, "makes me want to rethink our rule."

Alix shivered. How could she not? No one had ever wanted her so fiercely. Her fingertips ached with the desire to stroke Thalia's breasts. But she shook her head firmly.

"There will be no rule breaking. Come here."

"Bossy, aren't you?" Thalia said, smiling.

When she was settled, Alix tentatively rested her hands on Thalia's shoulders. Her skin was hot and silky, and as she smoothed her palms along Thalia's upper back, Alix felt the play of powerful muscles beneath. Experimentally, she increased the pressure and was pleased to feel Thalia relax into her touch.

"That feels so good," Thalia murmured.

"Shhh," Alix said. "You don't need to praise me. I'm enjoying this too. Just relax."

She increased the pressure, focusing on the tight, knotted muscles where her neck met her shoulders. This was where she bore the brunt of the g-forces on each turn, as she struggled to keep her heavy head still. When Thalia moaned at her touch, the sensuality of the sound only increased Alix's desire. Daring to intersperse her kneading movements with the occasional caress, she concentrated for several minutes on the muscles around Thalia's shoulder blades. Once they had loosened up, she slowly began to work her way down Thalia's spine.

She watched her hands move nearer and nearer to the gentle swell of Thalia's breasts, their curves just barely visible from this angle. Tentatively, breathlessly, she dared to extend one fingertip to lightly stroke the tantalizing skin. Thalia shuddered and groaned her name. But when she would have turned her head, Alix rested her free hand on the nape of Thalia's neck to hold her in place.

"Stay just like that," Alix whispered. If their eyes met, she might lose her confidence. A thought occurred to her. "Unless…you don't like this?"

"Like it?" Thalia's voice hitched. "Please. More."

Alix had never felt so powerful. She leaned in to plant a gentle kiss behind Thalia's ear before repeating the motion. Her skin was even softer than she had imagined. For one perilous instant, Alix nearly gave in to the impulse to cradle Thalia's breasts in her palms. She wanted to map their contours and test their weight and feel the pleasure her touch would bring.

But she couldn't. Indulging this wish might not violate their rules of engagement, but she would be crossing a different kind of line. And as much as she wanted to push her own boundaries, tonight was not the right time.

She leaned forward to kiss the nape of Thalia's neck, hoping the simple gesture would convey everything she couldn't find the words to say.

CHAPTER SIXTEEN

Thalia slid into position five, fixed her gaze on the lights, and preset her left clutch paddle while fully engaging the right. She took a quick sip of her energy drink and tried to picture the same sequence of events she'd been visualizing since yesterday: a quick start that culminated in her passing Hugo to take fourth position. When her fingertips trembled against the paddles, she tried to downplay the clear sign of nerves. Of course she was nervous. This was the Monaco Grand Prix. The Abu Dhabi Grand Prix might be worth double points, but nothing could compare to this race.

The roar of her engine drowned out whatever noise the crowd was making, but she could still feel their energy. Hundreds of thousands of spectators lined the streets and the harbors and the yacht decks, swelling the population of Monaco to nearly four times its usual size. Her mind flashed to the yacht deck where she and Alix had shared their first kiss, and then to the too-brief interlude they had shared yesterday. She would be nearby, in the grandstand overlooking the start/finish line. As close as that was, Thalia wished she had asked for a token, a talisman—something to remind her of Alix during the grueling odyssey she was about to commence.

The first LED flared red, and Thalia's heart nearly jumped out of her chest. Every muscle in her body drew taut as a bowstring, ready to release. Her fingers flexed on the paddles and her toes twitched inside her flameproof boots. Another light illuminated, and then another. They were her conductor, counting down to the start of the symphony. When the fifth LED came on, Thalia sucked in a deep breath and prepared to battle gravity. They winked out, and she pressed down hard on the throttle while releasing the left clutch paddle.

Her car surged forward as though it were alive. Terrence had made a good start, but Hugo was slow off the grid, and she managed to quickly swerve around him without losing much of her acceleration. But there was no time to celebrate having jumped up to P4 already. The St. Devote turn on the first lap was the prime overtaking opportunity, and she had to play defense long enough to establish her position.

After a very close call with whoever had fallen in behind her, Thalia was finally able to gain good ground on the brief straightaway. Terrence was only a second ahead, and she settled down to working out how to pass him. Patience was crucial here, as she tried to drive as efficiently as possible in order to maximize the longevity of her tires. That meant not going on the offensive, but staying consistently on his tail.

He pitted just under halfway through the race, and for a while, Alix enjoyed her view of the track from third place. Peter was still in first, and she worked hard to gain ground on Lucas. But a few laps later, it was her turn to pit. Her team did an extraordinary job of matching their best ever time, but even so, she slid back into the race just behind Terrence. Now she had to begin attacking him with more purpose, harrying him in hopes that he would make a mistake. But she also had to be cautious not to eat up too much of her tires through aggressive maneuvering.

For lap after lap, she remained in his wake, hoping to lull him into a false sense of security. Every time he deviated—even slightly—from the ideal racing line, she wanted to make her move. And every time, she forced herself to be patient. The moment had to be perfect. This course was unforgiving.

It finally came at the beginning of the sixty-eighth lap, when Terrence swung slightly too wide on St. Devote. If it had been any other turn, Thalia wouldn't have tried to slip through. But this might be her last good chance.

The world telescoped until all she could see was the narrow strip of daylight between Terrence's front tire and the barricade. She *would* push through and take the place she deserved. Slamming down on the throttle, she sucked in a deep breath just before gravity closed down on her chest like a vise. Her car responded beautifully, leaping forward as though it were alive. For one agonizing moment, the shadow to her right threatened to knock her out of the race...and then she was in the clear.

"Brilliant!" Carl exclaimed in her ear. "Now, fend him off. Tight as you possibly can on every corner."

For one lap, she held Terrence back. Then another. And another. The temperature in the cockpit continued to rise, and her shoulders screamed in protest on every turn but she couldn't afford even the most minor lapse in concentration. She had to stay sharp.

On the penultimate lap, she began to pull away. By the time the last lap began, she was five seconds ahead.

"Just keep it clean." Carl was almost begging. "Just keep it clean and you'll be standing on that podium."

It took roughly one minute and twenty seconds to complete a lap of the course at Monaco, but one minute and twenty seconds had never felt so long. The anticipation was so strong that she had to force herself to take the slow, deliberate breaths that would keep oxygen flowing to her brain.

When she was finally shown the checkered flag, her earpiece erupted with the sounds of celebration.

"Thalia!" Carl shouted. "You did it! Well fucking done!" Several other engineers were hollering in the background, but Thalia couldn't make them out. And then Alistair's cool monotone pierced through the chaos.

"Brilliant work, Thalia. Well deserved." For him, that was tantamount to screaming in delight like a teenager.

Belatedly, she swerved back and forth across the track, arm raised above the cockpit, fist clenched in a gesture of triumph. The victory lap was surreal, and she kept trying to freeze it in place—the sensation of having broken yet another record, and of getting to the podium on the most famous racetrack in the sport. But even at slower speeds, the course slid by too quickly.

In the tunnel, her thoughts turned to Alix. Certainly, she would be happy, but was she truly impressed at her accomplishment? By now, Thalia thought she had some appreciation for the sport. But what would really impress Alix was if she were able to convert this success into something bigger—something meaningful beyond the world of Formula One.

And then she was passing the pit lane, which had been the end of every other race. Not this time. This time, she crossed the finish line again and pulled into the spaces reserved for the top three finishers. Peter and Lucas were already there, and she hurried to shut down her car. As soon as her engine quieted, she leapt out of the cockpit and raised her arms to the crowd. It roared back in thunderous approval.

She could feel the city—and beyond it, the world—watching as she dropped to one knee and kissed the chassis to honor her car. When she rose, she saw Alix standing along the barricade with the rest of her family. If only it could be so easy to cross the space and kiss *her*. She raised one hand instead.

"Thalia!" Peter roared from behind her. "You beast!"

And then they were embracing, helmets colliding as they slapped one another on the back.

"I knew you could do it!" he said fiercely. "Just you wait—you'll be stealing the top step from me before long!"

She pulled away, laughing. "I'm happy for you to have it. For now, anyway."

One of the race marshals sidled up to them. "Congratulations, Mr. Taggart, Ms. d'Angelis," he said. "But if you could please follow me to be weighed—"

"Of course," Peter said. He gestured for Thalia to precede him. "The sooner we jump on the scales, the sooner we can get to our champagne!"

❖

The Onyx Salon was held on a yacht of the same name owned by Formula One. Alix stood with her family on the lowest deck at the terminus of the red carpet-covered ramp, welcoming film stars and billionaire entrepreneurs and professional athletes. And, of course, her fellow royals.

Sebastian arrived with a professional tennis player on his arm and greeted her coolly. She accepted his vaguely pitying cheek-kisses while trying not to laugh. His body language suggested that she should gaze upon his girlfriend and feel insecure, but all she really felt was relief.

Thankfully, the royal house of England arrived shortly thereafter.

Ashleigh was six months pregnant now and wore a flowing golden dress that by turns revealed and concealed her baby bump.

"You look absolutely stunning," Alix told her, offering a careful embrace.

"Likewise," Ashleigh said with a warm smile. "And the logo for Rising Sun is just perfect." She gestured to the banner that festooned the deck railing. "I'm so glad—and impressed—that you were able to finalize everything in time to make it the featured charity."

"I couldn't have done it without you," Alix told her before they moved on into the belly of the boat.

She turned to greet Sasha and Kerry, still glowing with newlywed affection. As they embraced and chatted about the race and Rising Sun, Alix couldn't help but wonder whether they could somehow sense the change in her. "Gaydar"—wasn't that what it was called? But if they did pick up on any subtle shift in her identity, they gave no indication.

The constant stream of people was a drain on her energy, especially after such an extroverted weekend, but her fatigue disappeared when Thalia finally arrived. She moved like a jungle cat, striding quickly but gracefully up the ramp as though she owned the yacht, acknowledging the applause of the crowd with a broad smile and raised hand. Beautiful in her triumph, she radiated charisma in palpable waves. Alix experienced a sudden rush of insecurity. Thalia was devastatingly attractive to most people, regardless of gender. But no. She wasn't going to indulge in this kind of self-deprecation. For the briefest of moments, she allowed herself to flash back to last night, when Thalia had actually *begged* for her touch. Schooling her features into an expression of polite interest had never been so difficult.

When her father stepped forward to greet Thalia, Alix watched with some trepidation. He might not "approve" of Thalia, per se, but neither could he discount her strong performance on the racecourse. After a brief chat, Prince Raphael indicated the rest of his family with a sweeping gesture.

"And I know you have met my middle daughter, Pommelina," he said, "in her role as our liaison to the events committee."

"Your Serene Highness," Thalia said, bowing her head briefly over Alix's hand. "It's good to see you again."

Her touch set off sparks beneath Alix's skin, and for one perilous moment, it was impossible to speak. When she glanced up, she saw the humor sparkling in Thalia's eyes. And behind the humor, desire. Directed at *her*.

"Congratulations on your success," she said, before reluctantly letting go of her hand and turning to the next driver.

The party was a whirlwind after that. Once all of the drivers were on board the yacht, her father formally initiated the event with a speech. Each of the top three finishers was able to say a few more words, and Alix watched as Thalia held the crowd in the palm of her hand, inviting them to share in her triumph.

Then it was Alix's turn to take the stage and speak briefly about Rising Sun. Formula One had agreed to give ten percent of its earnings from the after party to the charity, and she acknowledged their generosity while also requesting donations. When she surrendered the microphone to the DJ, she retreated to the stern of the boat where a promotional table had been set up and was being minded by a member of her secretary's staff. When she offered to spell the young woman for a while so that she could enjoy some of the party, her impassioned response was nearly comical. Alix might have offered the crown jewels—such was the level of her enthusiasm.

The night was warm and clear, with a half moon hanging above them like a pendant. A few people stopped by to chat about the charity, but for the most part, everyone was enjoying the dance floor that had been established amidships. Alix leaned against the railing and looked out over the marina, where dozens of other, less exclusive parties were happening on yachts throughout the harbor. All of Monaco was united in celebration. Formula One might be the epitome of excess, but it did bring people together all across this fractured globe. And if a good cause could benefit as a result, so much the better.

When a cheer rose up from the dance floor, Alix experienced an unfamiliar pang. Usually, she wanted nothing to do with noisy, jostling crowds, but she had no doubt that Thalia would be at its heart. There would be fascination and flirting on the part of her fans, and some of them might even attempt to take other liberties. How did Thalia feel about that, now? They had yet to discuss anything like exclusivity, and was it even part of the equation in a relationship with no strings attached? Was Thalia thinking of her at all, or was she simply enjoying the moment?

"You look deep in thought, Your Serene Highness."

And just like that, Alix had her answer. She whirled to find Thalia standing before the table with a grin on her face that grew broader when she saw Alix's expression.

"What are you doing here?" Alix blurted.

"Oh?" Thalia raised an eyebrow. "Would you rather I go back to the bumping and grinding?" She jerked her finger in the direction of the dance floor.

"No!" The syllable came out rather more forcefully than Alix had intended. She tried to compose herself. "It's just that I didn't...that is, I—"

"You didn't expect me to want to be here when I could be there." Thalia braced her arms on the table. They both knew she couldn't come any closer in public.

"Perhaps." But as Thalia stood looking at her, she knew she had to own the truth. "Yes. I'm sorry."

"I do enjoy dancing," Thalia said softly. "But it wasn't much fun without you."

The declaration made her feel warm inside. "Though your toes are probably safer."

Thalia laughed. "The bruises were a small price to pay."

A couple passed by, then—a footballer and his model girlfriend—and paused to congratulate Thalia. Once they had gone, she turned back to Alix and moved closer, picking up one of the brochures.

"I want you to come back to my hotel room," she said, her voice soft and intense. "And this time, I don't want any rules about touching."

Alix felt her heart stutter, then begin to pound. Thalia was giving her a choice, but it was one she realized she had already made. "Yes."

"It's what you want?"

Alix moistened her dry lips and nodded. She felt a little dizzy. "Yes. It's what I want."

"I wish we could go now," Thalia said, and the forlorn note in her voice dissolved the mounting intensity between them, allowing Alix to smile.

"Me too," she said. "But we're both stuck here, aren't we?"

"Maybe by midnight, everyone will be too drunk to notice if we slip away."

"It's worth a try," Alix said. They were going to slip away. They were going to slip away and return to Thalia's hotel room and have sex. "Make love," as Thalia liked to call it. Anticipation rose like a storm, gusty and tinged with fire.

"I'm not going to drink anything else for the rest of the night," Thalia said. "I want to remember everything."

"Oh." Alix didn't know what else to say. That Thalia, who unapologetically loved her liquor, would restrain herself on the night of her first podium finish ever out of a desire to have the most vivid possible experience later meant that she regarded what would happen tonight as more meaningful than her usual encounters.

A rowdy group of partygoers interrupted the moment, and Thalia took a step back. "I'll see you later," she murmured before slipping away in the opposite direction.

Alix prepared herself for the unfamiliar experience of being recognized—she had been up on stage earlier tonight, after all—but the group was already inebriated enough not to notice her. They passed her by, leaving her alone on the deck, counting the hours until midnight.

CHAPTER SEVENTEEN

Alix followed Thalia into her hotel room, clutching her hand tightly. Moonlight streamed through the windows, illuminating the chair from which she had dared to touch Thalia so intimately last night. But that had been a massage in preparation for the race. This…this was a celebration, and anything could happen.

Thalia turned as if she had heard the thought, and cupped Alix's face in her hands before kissing her gently. "Nothing will happen tonight that you don't want," she murmured.

"I want you to kiss me again," Alix said, because it was the truth.

Thalia obliged, and this kiss was an inferno. Lost in the heat of her mouth, Alix didn't realize she had closed her eyes until they flashed open when the backs of her legs hit the bed. Thalia stared down at her, hands on her hips squeezing rhythmically, her face a study in need.

"I want to make love with you more than I've ever wanted anything," she said hoarsely. "Including that trophy."

"I believe you," Alix whispered, because she couldn't fill her lungs enough to speak normally.

Thalia released her and took a step back. Without her support, Alix's knees buckled and she sat down hard on the bed. Her stomach somersaulted as she realized that she might have just sabotaged the entire evening. If she had simply kissed Thalia instead of giving in to her insecurities, they would be undressing each other right now instead of having a face-off.

"That's the second time you've said that without meaning it." Thalia's arms were crossed over her chest and her tone was accusatory.

"I preferred your response the first time," Alix said, remembering how Thalia had shut her up by kissing her beneath the setting sun on the deck of the *Priceless Pearl*.

Her jaw clenched. "There's nothing I'd like better than to be kissing you right now. But we have to clear the air. I have *never* lied to you. Not even once. I am not lying when I tell you that I find you attractive, and I am not lying when I tell you how much I want us to make love tonight. Why do you keep assuming I'm not sincere when it comes to you?"

Alix wanted to apologize quickly and get on with what they had been doing. Even now, in the middle of a heated conversation she didn't want to be having, her desire for Thalia was a drum roll beneath her skin, urging her on. But for whatever reason, Thalia was insistent on having this out. Alix braced both hands on the bed and forced herself to meet Thalia's gaze.

"I'm well aware that I'm not as attractive as most of the women you've been with. When I compare myself with them, I fall short. And then I fall into the trap of questioning whether you're being sincere."

The more she spoke, the more momentum she built. When Thalia opened her mouth to reply, Alix held up one hand to stave her off. "So when you say that you want to 'make love,' I find that confusing. What does that mean to you?"

"Would you rather I tell you that I want to fuck you?" Thalia's temper was flaring.

"If that's the truth," Alix shot back, hoping Thalia hadn't seen her tremble.

"It is. And it isn't." Thalia's fists clenched. "I *want* you, Alix. But you're not some grid girl I just met who wants a one-night stand, or a movie star interested in a quick fling. I would fuck them. It would be fun and meaningless. But I care about you. When I fuck you—if that's what you want—it will be about more than sex. We have a relationship, you and me. We can't pretend we don't."

Thalia's answer had neatly skirted around the word "love," but Alix didn't mind. She seemed to use "make love" as a synonym for "have meaningful sex," and that was at once reassuring and frightening. Was she really prepared for this to mean something? For the repercussions of what happened next to extend beyond tonight?

"Alix." Thalia's voice, low and intense, mercifully halted her spiraling thoughts. "I want you. I'm going to keep saying it until you believe it. I want to look at you and touch you and taste you. I want to give you so much pleasure. As a doctor, you're aware of the body's capacity for sensation. I want you to know it from experience."

Alix shivered, and this time she could tell that Thalia noticed: she took one eager step forward before reining herself in. The knowledge that she could still exert some self-control, despite the professed magnitude of her desire, was a comfort.

"But I'm not going to come any closer until you tell me what you want. If you're having second thoughts, that's fine. I'll go."

Sensing an opportunity to change the tone of the conversation, Alix cocked her head. "This is your room."

Thalia didn't blink. "I'll get another."

"They're sold out. I heard someone say so in the lobby." Alix scooted back until she was reclining against the headboard.

"Peter has a suite. I'll sleep on his couch."

"I saw the way he was looking at his wife earlier," Alix said as she arranged the pillows behind her. Thalia's eyes tracked her every movement. Being the focal point of her attention was exhilarating, and Alix decided to tease her for a little while longer. "And didn't I see his mother planning to take the baby for the night? I don't think he'll appreciate the interruption."

"What do you suggest, then?"

Alix pretended to stretch and closed her eyes, reclining back against the pillows. "I suppose you'll just have to stay here with me."

In the next instant, the mattress dipped, heralding Thalia's arrival. Alix kept her eyes closed, even as eddies in the air currents announced Thalia's approach. Alix's heart pounded against her ribs, but she lay still, wanting to know what Thalia would do next.

Her first touch was a lingering kiss to one corner of Alix's mouth that became a trail of the same along her jawline and down the column of her neck. By the time she pulled away, Alix's hips were shifting involuntarily. When she realized how her body was reacting, Alix froze in a paroxysm of shame.

"Hey, now." Thalia's whisper was accompanied by a light flick of her tongue to Alix's earlobe. "Relax. I love the way you move when I'm kissing you."

No longer content to remain passive, Alix opened her eyes to find

Thalia regarding her with a hungry expression. Cupping the nape of her neck, Alix drew her down. Their tongues tangled slowly, almost lazily, belying the urgency Alix felt and, she was now sure, Thalia shared. When she suddenly pulled away, Thalia drew back in alarm, but Alix shook her head and smiled.

"I want you to take off my shirt."

"Your wish is so absolutely my command," Thalia said, and began to undo the buttons with an enthusiasm that made Alix laugh.

But her laughter turned to a sharp exhale when Thalia's knuckles brushed against her breast, igniting a shower of sparks beneath her skin. Thalia paused, and her eyes grew visibly darker.

"Okay?"

"Oh, yes." Alix hoped she didn't sound too eager, then realized she shouldn't care.

Without looking away, Thalia deliberately cupped one breast, rubbing her thumb back and forth along the underside. Even through her bra, it felt absolutely incredible, and Alix couldn't hold back a low moan.

"That is such a beautiful sound." When Thalia moved her hand away to undo the remaining buttons, Alix whimpered unintentionally, then cringed and lowered her gaze.

"Don't you dare be ashamed," Thalia murmured fiercely. "Look at me, Alix. Look at me."

Face flaming, Alix raised her eyes, fearing to find humor or even perhaps pity for the poor, inexperienced virgin in Thalia's expression. Instead, she found nothing but desire and tenderness.

"Don't hold back with me. Not now, not ever. Your body's reactions are a kind of communication." Thalia parted her shirt and eased it down her arms. "I need to know how you're feeling. So don't censor yourself. Okay?"

Alix saw an opening to reassert herself and took it. Sitting up against the pillows, she let her shirt pool behind her and reached out for Thalia's top button. "Only if you promise the same."

She had briefly seen Thalia topless last night, but now she could savor the experience. Kissing each freshly bared inch of skin, Alix teased Thalia to the best of her ability while divesting her of her shirt and bra. When Alix peeled away the fabric to reveal Thalia's breasts, she was overwhelmed once again by the desire to cradle them in her palms.

"I want to touch you," she said, trying not to regret the tremble in her voice.

"Touch me," Thalia said. "Any way you want."

Alix cupped one breast, weighing its softness as she fanned her thumb across the taut nipple. When Thalia's lips parted on a gasp, Alix repeated the motion. She leaned forward to kiss where her fingers had been and dared to indulge her need to taste Thalia's skin. Soft—her breast was so incredibly soft.

When Thalia gently touched the back of her head, Alix looked up. "Okay?"

"Okay?" Her laugh was strangled. "Please don't ever stop."

The confirmation that she was bringing Thalia pleasure inspired Alix to indulge in one of her fantasies. She skimmed her hands along Thalia's rib cage, holding her in place as she touched the tip of her tongue to the tight knot of Thalia's nipple. Thalia hissed, one hand tightening on her hair. The pressure of her fingers encouraged Alix to take the nipple into her mouth, where she batted it lightly with her tongue before closing her lips around it and sucking gently. When Thalia quivered beneath her hands, a heady rush of power swept through Alix. Right now, Thalia was holding herself in check as she allowed Alix to explore her, and she wanted to take full advantage. Forcing herself to go slowly, she kissed her way to Thalia's other breast and repeated her actions.

"You're driving me crazy," Thalia finally groaned. "Please, *please* let me touch you."

The rush of anticipation prompted Alix to release her. Guiding Thalia's hands, she silently encouraged her to remove her bra. Thalia kissed her neck as she worked the clasp loose and gently brushed the straps down Alix's arms. When her torso was bare, Thalia sat back on her heels. Alix balled her hands into fists in an effort not to cover herself as instinct demanded.

"You are so beautiful. I know it's hard for you to hear that, but it's the truth." Thalia cupped her jaw and traced her lips with one thumb. "Let me show you."

"Yes," Alix whispered, and lay back against the pillows.

Thalia lowered herself gradually, giving Alix plenty of opportunity to second-guess her decision. But when their breasts touched, Alix felt as though she had found the missing piece to a puzzle decades in the solving. Thalia settled on top of her, elbows framing her face, and kissed her deeply. Grasping Thalia's shoulders, Alix surged against her, unwilling to play the part of a passive recipient. Their tongues tangled, then battled in a duel of give and take until Thalia raised her head, panting for breath.

"Who taught you to kiss like that?" she gasped.

"You did." Alix guided Thalia's mouth to her neck. That may have been a mistake, because Thalia proceeded to torment her—first by covering every inch she could reach with tiny kisses, and then by bringing lips and teeth into play, lightly sucking and nipping until Alix was squirming with need. Desperate with desire, she tugged at Thalia's hair, urging her lower.

"Oh?" Thalia raised her head, and her smile was smug. "Something you'd like?"

The old Alix, prudish and proper, quailed at speaking the sensual truth. But over the past few months, she had outgrown that version of herself. It was time to discard it—to cast it away like the ill-fitting skin it had become.

"I want..." But the words died on her lips.

Somehow sensing her struggle, Thalia's expression softened. "It's okay. Let me help." She moved down the bed until her abdomen was pressed between Alix's thighs, then kissed the center of her sternum. "Am I moving in the right direction?"

"Yes," Alix whispered.

With kiss after kiss, Thalia proved her claim and fulfilled her promise. When she finally closed her lips around the tip of Alix's breast, Alix was already transcendent with need. At the first touch of Thalia's tongue to her nipple, she cried out and surged against her without feeling any self-consciousness at all.

Thalia raised her head, and her eyes were dark pools with only a hint of blue encircling them. "Shhh," she said. "We're nowhere near the finish line. Don't rush it. Just feel."

Alix was about to retort that that was easy for her to say, when Thalia's mouth returned to her breast and banished all rational thought. She tried to relax into the exquisite sensations Thalia was eliciting from her body, but every nerve she possessed was drawing tighter and tighter, humming in anticipation. When Thalia dipped her head to nibble at the skin around her navel, Alix shivered as unfamiliar muscles clenched deep inside.

"Thalia," she said brokenly. "Please. I…I need…"

Thalia looked into her eyes and went very still. "I don't want to frighten you. I've been trying to go so slowly. But all my instincts are screaming at me to get you naked and then make you come with my mouth. If that's not what you want—not what you *need*—then you have to tell me right now."

Alix thought she might spontaneously combust from Thalia's words alone. "That is what I want. But I need for you to be naked too."

A sudden burst of adrenaline drove her to sit up and grasp Thalia's belt buckle. Thalia muttered a curse and looked down at Alix's hands. Alix fumbled as she slid the leather through its metal cage, but her fingers were steadier as she drew down the fly on Thalia's slacks. But when she began to push them over Thalia's hips, Thalia stilled her hands.

"You're sure?"

"I have never been more certain of anything," Alix said, knowing she had also never been so truthful.

When there were finally no longer any physical barriers between them, Alix slid under the covers and held out one hand. "Come here."

Thalia closed the space between their bodies, pressing Alix down into the mattress with a deep kiss. At the sensation of skin against skin, Alix moaned and wrapped both arms around Thalia. The softness and strength and heat of Thalia's body made her head spin, and she clutched desperately at her shoulders in an attempt to anchor herself. Thalia pulled back just enough to capture her gaze before sliding one thigh between Alix's legs. The gentle pressure set off fireworks beneath her skin, and she cried out.

"You are so responsive," Thalia whispered, repeating the motion. This time, Alix surged against her, intensifying the sensation and causing Thalia's eyes to glaze. Thalia bowed her head and began to move in earnest, setting a slow and deliberate rhythm that maximized the contact between their skin. Heat poured down Alix's spine. Aching in anticipation, she clutched at Thalia's shoulder blades, feeling the muscles bunch beneath her palms.

Suddenly, Thalia sat up, putting unwelcome space between them. "Oh God, I'm right on the edge," she panted, her body shuddering. But when Alix tried to join her, Thalia held her hips in place. "No. I want to make love to you the way I promised. Right now."

Alix saw the wildness in Thalia's eyes and wanted to yield to it. She wanted Thalia to be the one to show her the heights of the passion only she had ever inspired. She wanted to know. She wanted to feel.

"Yes," she said deliberately. "That's what I want."

With a shaky sigh, Thalia settled against Alix's side, pillowing her head on one elbow and resting one palm on her stomach. Alix closed the distance between them, initiating the kiss to confirm her words. When Thalia's hand rose to cup each breast, Alix groaned into her mouth, and when that hand slid down her abdomen, down toward the apex of her thighs, Alix opened her legs, offering herself up without hesitation. Thalia broke the kiss but remained poised above her, holding Alix's gaze as her fingers dipped down to stroke her most sensitive skin.

Alix gasped for breath, shivering helplessly at each soft, exploratory stroke. When Thalia returned to circle one especially sensitive spot (the clitoris, her medical brain supplied helpfully), Alix's hips jerked and she cried out at the intense rush of pleasure.

"You're beautiful," Thalia whispered, shifting her hand back to Alix's abdomen, where she rubbed soothing circles against her skin.

"Why did you stop?" Alix knew she sounded pathetic but was beyond caring.

"Because I want to be inside you," Thalia said.

A cautionary note in her voice pierced the haze of Alix's desire, and she thought she understood. She grasped Thalia's wrist and guided her hand between her thighs. She had waited long enough for this.

"Do it," she whispered. "I want you inside me, and I'm not afraid—"

She choked off when Thalia touched her again, first in light circles and then more firmly, until she had rocketed back to the edge of the precipice. Thalia held her gaze as she moved down deliberately, dipping one finger barely inside before returning to the swollen nerves above. Alix shuddered, eyes closing automatically as she surrendered to the sensation.

"Keep them open," Thalia whispered fiercely.

With an effort, Alix obeyed.

When Thalia finally slid inside, electricity arced through Alix at the intimacy of their connection and every muscle in her body tightened like a clock being wound. Thalia paused, breathing heavily. "Are you okay?"

Alix licked dry lips. "Yes. Feels…amazing."

"I'm glad." Thalia flexed her finger gently, and Alix's hips surged. "You're so tight." She kissed Alix's stomach and then moved down, nudging her legs apart to fit her broad shoulders between them. "Try to relax. I want you deeper." She held Alix's hips in place with one hand on her abdomen before pushing further inside with gentle pressure.

Beyond words, Alix could only moan in response. She found Thalia's shoulder and squeezed as Thalia's warm breath streamed across her most sensitive skin. Alix's throat contracted in a sharp cry, and she instinctively tried to shift closer to Thalia's mouth, but the hand that restrained her was effective.

"Do you remember what I promised?" Thalia's voice was low and intense. Alix forced her eyes open and looked down over the expanse of her own torso to where Thalia lay between her thighs. It was a moment she wanted to preserve in her mind forever—the tender ferocity of Thalia's expression as she slowly eased her finger in and out in a slow, sensual rhythm. "I promised to make you come with my mouth," Thalia continued. "Is that what you want?"

Unable to speak over the knot of anticipation in her throat, Alix nodded frantically.

"Good," Thalia said, and leaned forward to keep her word.

Softness and heat enveloped her, like warm silk…but all comparisons failed as Thalia moved against her and inside her, sparking currents of pleasure so sharp as to be unbearable. Her back arched and her breaths came in gasps, and when the ecstasy finally consumed her, she cried out in triumph and relief.

She shivered with aftershocks for a long time, and Thalia patiently drew them out, kissing and stroking her until she lay quiescent. Afterward, Thalia moved up to cover Alix's body, smoothing the hair away from her damp forehead before leaning down for a kiss. The realization that she was tasting herself on Thalia's lips made Alix pull her closer in a renewed surge of wanting.

Thalia finally broke away, hands framing Alix's face. "How do you feel?" she asked breathlessly.

"Extraordinary." Alix ran her hands up and down Thalia's back, savoring the play of her muscles beneath the skin. "Nothing could have prepared me for that."

Thalia's smile was incandescent. "You let yourself feel everything, and it was so, so beautiful."

Inspired by the hoarseness in Thalia's voice, Alix shifted onto her own side to face her. She reached out to stroke her face, mapping the contours of Thalia's cheekbones, the ridge of her nose, the plush of her lips. "And you? Will you let yourself feel everything?"

Thalia caught her hand. "I don't want to pressure you," she said, but the words trembled.

"I'm not feeling any pressure at all," Alix said, linking their fingers and pushing down on Thalia's hand until it rested on the pillow beside her head. "Lie back, now." When Thalia obeyed, the desire in her expression inspired Alix to be bold. She sat up and gently pushed Thalia's legs apart before kneeling between them. When she rested both hands on Thalia's abdomen, her hips jerked.

"I'm so ready for you," Thalia confessed.

Alix had never experienced this kind of power, and it sluiced through her now in a heady rush. But when she thought of how many lovers Thalia had had, and how experienced they all undoubtedly must have been, her self-confidence evaporated as quickly as it had arrived.

"Will you tell me what you like?" she asked, hating the insecurity in her voice.

"I like your hands on me." Thalia's eyes blazed up at her. "I want you to explore me however you want. Touch me however you want. Please, Alix."

"And you'll tell me if there's something I'm doing...wrong?"

"There are no right ways and wrong ways to make love," Thalia said. "There's just our way. The way we discover together."

Discover. Alix flexed her fingers experimentally, fanning them out across the ridges of Thalia's stomach muscles. Thalia was giving her permission to do exactly what she had craved—to experiment. Dizzy with anticipation, she lowered herself so that her own abdomen was cradled in the vee of Thalia's thighs, before reaching up to cup her breasts. Thalia's low whimper of encouragement banished her lingering self-doubt.

"You do remember that I'm a scientist," she said. "Trained in the art of data collection. Highly detail-oriented." Thalia watched her hands avidly as Alix reached up to grasp both nipples between her thumbs and index fingers. "For example," she continued, relishing the expectation on Thalia's features, "I wonder what will happen when I do this?" She pinched lightly.

Thalia closed her eyes and groaned. When Alix did it again, this time rubbing her thumbs back and forth, Thalia's hips jerked beneath her. At once delighted and in awe, Alix carried on, first settling into a rhythm that made Thalia's breath hiss in her throat, and then varying the rhythm so she didn't know what to expect.

"You can do it harder," she gasped.

The words sent a jolt through Alix, and she was about to oblige when she remembered that this was her opportunity to explore. She would file away that intriguing detail for future reference. "I'm glad to know that," she said. "But I'd prefer to try something else instead."

When she dipped her head to kiss the tip of one breast, then the other, Thalia threw one hand over her eyes and muttered an unintelligible curse. Settling into a more comfortable position, Alix braced herself on one arm, continuing to tease, but now with both mouth and fingers. Every sound Thalia made increased not only her confidence, but her own arousal.

Thalia's head thrashed against the pillow as her moans began to resolve into a single word: *Please*. Glorying in the sensual power she wielded, Alix dared to smooth her hand down, down across Thalia's ribs, down to rest in the shallow indentation of her inner thigh. She raised her head from Thalia's breast.

"Is this what you want?"

"Oh please," Thalia rasped, raising one hand to cup Alix's face. "Touch me, please. I'm begging you. I'll go out of my mind if you don't."

Alix caught her hand and kissed the palm. "I will."

Thalia's eyes suddenly cleared of haze. "It's what *you* want?"

The vulnerability with which she asked the question made Alix's chest constrict. Even now, trembling with a need that Alix had fired and stoked, Thalia was considerate enough to prioritize Alix's comfort.

"You are what I want," she whispered, holding Thalia's gaze as she slid her fingers down.

At the first touch, Thalia's eyes closed and her back arched. She was warm and wet and slick, and Alix gently traced the contours of her folds with questing fingers. They soon found their target, and she pressed lightly against the swollen bundle of nerves, testing how Thalia liked to be touch.

"Oh my God." Thalia's hips jerked.

Alix circled the spot gently before pressing again, feeling the rapid pulse beneath her touch. At Thalia's strangled cry, she felt as though she had discovered the existence of some mythical country and been proclaimed its savior.

"Al-Alix. I'm going to—"

Not wanting this to be over yet, Alix quickly moved her hand away. When Thalia protested that she was going to perish, Alix demurred and kissed her dry lips. "Shhh. Trust me."

She coated her fingertips with Thalia's wetness, and slid two inside. The sensation of being enveloped by her body was like nothing Alix had ever experienced, and she craved more. Slowly and carefully, she worked her way deeper, before pausing to flutter her fingers. When Thalia's internal muscles flickered in response, she had to do it again.

"Alix." Thalia's voice broke on the syllables, and her eyes were two pools of darkness. "I'm so close."

Triumphant yet tender, Alix shifted her hand to swirl the pad of her thumb across Thalia's most sensitive skin. "Let go," she urged her, holding her breath.

Thalia shouted her name as she found her release, her hips lifting as her body clamped down hard around Alix's fingers. Alix drank in the moment as Thalia trembled in her arms. She had never seen or heard anything more beautifully intimate than the sensation of Thalia finding ecstasy, and she wanted to make it happen all over again. But when she began to thrust lightly, Thalia reached for her wrist.

"Good instincts," she said in a low, gritty voice. "Normally, I'd want more right away. But that was so intense."

All evidence to the contrary, Alix couldn't help but worry that Thalia didn't want her to continue touching her because she had been terrible at it. "Okay," she said softly, easing her fingers from the grip of Thalia's body.

Thalia trapped her hand before she could pull it away entirely. "That was incredible," she said, gazing up intently at Alix. "*You* are an amazing lover. Stop second-guessing yourself."

"You're a good teacher," Alix said, wanting to deflect the attention.

"Maybe," Thalia conceded, "but all I taught you tonight was that you should feel free to surrender to passion. Once you stopped being afraid of it and let instinct take over..." When she shivered at the memory, Alix finally believed she was telling the truth. "Wow."

"Wow?" Alix gave her a skeptical look. "You Americans use that word too much."

"*You Americans*, huh?" Thalia surged up, catching Alix off guard, and rolled them until she was on top. "I'm half British, you know." Settling one thigh between Alix's legs, Thalia looked all too smug as she discovered the physical evidence of Alix's renewed arousal. "Hmm," she said, thrusting lightly. "What have we here? Someone *is* ready for second helpings." Alix felt herself blush, which was utterly ridiculous after everything they had just shared.

Thalia's smile gentled. "Don't be embarrassed," she whispered against Alix's ear, batting the lobe with her tongue. "Your desire is beautiful. *You* are beautiful. And I'm going to prove it to you all over again."

As Thalia pressed a line of burning kisses down her neck, Alix melted into the mattress, surrendering to the maelstrom.

CHAPTER EIGHTEEN

A lix watched the waiter refill her champagne flute and tried in vain not to worry about Thalia. The London skyline lay spread out at her feet like the Lego towns Florestan had enjoyed building as a boy. She had never been permitted to help him, but had admired his civic-minded handiwork from a distance. Now, at the apex of the London Eye in a private capsule rented by the Duke of Suffolk, Lord Brandis, she had a much more profound appreciation for the vision that went into city planning. Immaculate bridges crisscrossed the winding Thames, iridescent under the sun, while buildings old and new formed orderly rows punctuated by the green slashes and dots of parks. Civilization.

But the price of civilization seemed to be that its denizens—who missed, in some atavistic way according to Thalia's argument, the thrill of the hunt encoded into their DNA—found an outlet for those unfulfilled instincts in sanctioned risky behaviors. The military. Skydiving. Motorsport.

Glancing surreptitiously at her watch, Alix mentally calculated the countdown to the Belgian Grand Prix. Just under two hours to go. Thalia would be suited up and getting ready to drive a few practice laps. There had been a few problems with the gearbox during Thursday's practice sessions, and she hoped it was no longer an issue. Thalia had qualified at P3—her best yet—and Alix hoped she made it to the very top of the podium. But mostly, she hoped Thalia would be safe, especially because the forecast was calling for rain.

Since their night together in Monaco, Alix's worries about Thalia's well-being had become sharper and more well-defined. One afternoon, while she should have been making revisions to her business plan to discuss with her lawyer, Alix had instead found herself researching Formula One injuries. For a dark time during its history, the sport had been among the deadliest imaginable, claiming the life of multiple drivers every year. At times, more than one driver had been killed in a single race.

Now, thanks to improvements in the engineering of the cars and construction of the tracks, as well as new rules and regulations about everything from driver helmets to the flame-retardant fabric of their jumpsuits, a driver hadn't been killed in a Grand Prix for over twenty years. But that didn't change the fact that in just under two hours, Thalia would be accelerating to speeds upward of three hundred kilometers per hour while jockeying for position with everyone else on the course.

But now was not a time to indulge in worry. She had business to conduct and social graces to uphold. Fortunately, there was a familiar and friendly face in the small enclosure: Ashleigh, Princess of Wales, still radiant in her third trimester of pregnancy. They hadn't been able to do more than exchange greetings and some small talk earlier, but now, as Lord Brandis paused the conversation about London architecture to consult with the waiter, Ashleigh leaned across the table.

"Thank you for bringing us this Monegasque weather, Alix. It's been an exceptionally rainy spring, and we're all appreciative."

Alix laughed. "I wish I could claim the credit."

"I had intended to write to you after the party but lost track of the time. It was a lovely event."

"I'm so glad you enjoyed it." Remembering that night made her think of Thalia, and she could only hope her face wasn't betraying her. "I owe at least part of my recent good fortune to you, I think," she said. "It was at Sasha's wedding that I met Thalia d'Angelis, and she first introduced me to Lord and Lady Rufford."

"Then you owe your good fortune to Sasha and Kerry," Ashleigh said with a smile.

"True," Alix said, quickly deciding that it would be best not to divulge that the prospect of meeting Ashleigh to discuss not-for-profits had been a significant part of her motivation to attend the royal wedding. "And how are they finding married life? They looked well in Monaco, but I didn't have the chance to speak with them much."

Ashleigh's smile broadened. "It agrees with them immensely. I honestly don't believe I've ever seen either happier. They're an exceptional team."

An exceptional team. That sounded like such an appealing kind of relationship. She and Thalia had that kind of potential: Thalia was the charismatic public figure, while she worked best behind the scenes, nurturing their shared vision by keeping all the details organized.

Then Alix caught herself. Their shared vision? Their career goals couldn't be more different. And was she honestly comparing her relationship with Thalia to Sasha and Kerry's marriage? Thankfully, logic interceded before she could make herself panic. She wasn't falling in love with Thalia, of course—that would be folly, given her reputation—but Alix did care about her. And she supposed it was natural to compare their relationship to the only other lesbians she knew, especially since they were also a royal, high-profile couple.

As she was trying to determine how best to reply to Ashleigh, Lord Brandis took control of the conversation. "Now that we all have our champagne, I would like to propose a toast." He raised his flute to catch the light. "To the excellent work being done in Africa by Her Royal Highness the Princess of Wales, and to the exciting new project initiated by Her Serene Highness Pommelina of Monaco. Brandis Enterprises celebrates your advocacy on behalf of those less fortunate."

Alix tried not to wince at his rhetoric. Who was to say that the Karamoja were less fortunate? By some metrics, certainly. But by others, they were richer than the people in this tiny chamber rotating high above London. Silently, she pledged to be cautious of how her charity advertised its mission. She wanted to empower the people of rural Uganda—especially the women, since they formed the core of the community while the men herded their cattle across the plains—to care for themselves and each other in healthy and sanitary ways. But she never wanted to imply that their culture or lifestyle was somehow inferior.

"The primary goal of this meeting," Lord Brandis continued, "is to discuss how Brandis Enterprises might become more involved with both organizations—to our mutual benefit, of course. I've had my people draw up a plan…"

Alix bent her head to focus on the fine print, but hoped there wouldn't be too much negotiating ahead. The sooner they could arrive at an agreement, the sooner she could satisfy her apprehension about Thalia.

❖

"Yellow flag, Thalia, yellow flag," Carl said into her ear. "Sector two." The indicator on her steering wheel turned yellow as he spoke. Fortunately, she was just out of sector two and didn't have to slacken her pace.

"What happened?" she asked on the next straightaway. Peter was currently in P1, and she had been in second place since beating Lucas at the start. So far, she had been able to hold him off, but ten minutes ago it had begun to drizzle. While a few of the drivers farther back had pitted for wet tires, Thalia had decided to stay out on her slicks. The conditions on the track weren't so bad as to warrant the wets, and they would just slow her down. But if someone had skidded off, that might be changing.

"Mason hydroplaned and went into the barrier at Les Combes. He walked away from the car."

"Good."

Thalia focused on doing everything in her power to stay right on the limit of what her car could do in these conditions. This lap was slipperier than the one before it had been, but still nothing she couldn't handle. She hugged the inside line as she followed Peter toward the corner where Mason had skidded out, alert to the possibility of debris, equipment, or people on or near the track. As she approached Les Combes, she noticed the flicker of red and white lights, and realized the marshals had deployed the emergency vehicles. She was momentarily thankful that all the safety precautions had once again done their job.

The yellow flag indicated the need for caution, but the rule was murky on what that actually entailed, and Peter hadn't slackened his pace very much. Her instincts were screaming at her to slow down, but instead, she followed his lead. The car shimmied a little—enough to make her heart leap into her throat—but she managed to settle it with a subtle touch on the wheel.

Still, that had been too close.

"Peter is five seconds ahead," Carl said. "Lucas is running quicker than both of you right now, so see if you can tighten the gap a bit to stop him trying an overtake."

"Will do."

But Peter, perhaps having been given similar information about Lucas, was eating up the track as though it were bone dry. By the time she returned to sector two, she had only made up a few hundredths of a second. This time, in deference to the increasing slickness of track, Thalia touched her brakes much sooner than she would have on a dry day. As she fought through the gravity, she watched Peter barrel into the apex of the corner and readied herself for the minor disturbance she would feel in the aerodynamics of her own car as he made his turn.

But he never did. Instead of gripping the surface as they were supposed to, his tires hydroplaned, sending him in a wide arc off the track, straight toward Mason's car, which had not yet been extricated from the barrier.

Horror and panic exploded in her brain as his spinning car smashed into the wreck. But even as she screamed, instinct took over. Braking heavily, she half drove, half hydroplaned into the escape road. As soon as she was clear of the track, she stopped, cut her engine, and leapt out of the cockpit. The drivers behind her had followed suit, and she barely avoided being hit by a Ferrari.

She didn't care. She didn't care about anything except Peter. The barricades were designed to cushion an impact, and no one had died from hitting one for decades. But Mason's car was solid metal and filled with fuel and—

"Peter!" The cry was ripped from her throat as she got her first glimpse of the crash. His car, barely recognizable now, had pierced the rear of Mason's chassis before flipping onto its side. Smoke billowed from the wreckage, dark and furious, incongruous against the brilliant blue backdrop. She couldn't see any flames, but the air stank of fuel. A siren wailed mournfully, but it sounded so far away. If Peter's car had punctured Mason's fuel tank, they had only seconds to get him out of there.

"Help me!" she screamed, cursing the weight of her helmet and the fatigue in her legs. The heat buffeted her fiercely, but her suit was flameproof. She could survive in there for a few seconds. Enough to drag him away. It would have to be enough.

And then the earth rose up against her with a deafening roar, knocking her back like a massive hand swatting an insignificant fly and holding her down as darkness swallowed the sky.

CHAPTER NINETEEN

By the time Alix returned to her suite at the Savoy Hotel, the race was half an hour old. She hurried through the lobby, Claude at her heels, and for once headed straight to the bar. The race would be on there. She had to know where Thalia stood—and most importantly, whether she was okay. As she rounded the corner, she sought out a television screen…and froze.

BREAKING NEWS: PETROL MACEDONIA CAR CRASHES AND EXPLODES.

In shock, Alix staggered forward to brace herself against an unoccupied table. Claude was immediately at her side, pulling out a chair.

"Sit down, please, ma'am," he said urgently. "You're white as a ghost."

"Who is it?" she asked numbly, pointing to the screen with a trembling finger. A chill had settled in her chest. She was so cold. *Shock*, her medical brain supplied through the icy fog clouding her mind.

"I don't know."

"Find out." Her teeth were chattering. "Please. Find out."

She stared at the banner on the screen. The words, highlighted in red, underscored footage of the smoking wreckage of the crash. Somehow, two cars had collided and gone up in flames. With all the new safety regulations, that wasn't supposed to be possible anymore, but somehow, it had happened. Shivering as a chill settled in her chest, she realized that Claude was no longer at her side. Instead, he was leaning over the bar, speaking with the bartender. Seconds later, the music died to be replaced by the sounds of the commentators. When he returned, he brought with him a shot of golden liquor and a glass of water.

"What is it?" she asked dully.

"Scotch. Drink. Please."

The glass shook in her hand, but she managed to throw back the liquid. It burned in her throat and down, down into her stomach, filling her with a fire that pierced the insidious chill, expanding until it cracked and melted the ice inside her.

No. She would not be numb. She would think. She would act.

A Petrol Macedonia car had crashed and exploded after smashing into another car caught in the barrier—that was all the news announcers on television knew. Everyone in the bar was remaining far too calm, but to them it was a distant tragedy, not a personal one. Alix wanted to scream at all of them. It wasn't Thalia. It couldn't be. Thalia suffering, burned and maimed by the blast and the fire, or worse...

But of course it could be. There was a fifty percent chance that Thalia's car was the one in flames.

Worst of all, she couldn't give voice or expression to the magnitude of her panic. As far as the public was concerned, Thalia was her business associate and acquaintance. But Alix was reacting as Thalia's lover. She wanted to tell someone, anyone—the perfect stranger nursing a beer in the corner or the couple sharing a romantic drink in the booth—that she was afraid for the life of the woman she cared for. But she couldn't. For one insane moment, she considered confiding in Claude. He must at least suspect her affair with Thalia, but he had never said anything about it to her.

"We have an update on the identity of the driver whose car exploded," said a disembodied voice from the speakers.

Please, Alix prayed aimlessly. It was the only word her mind could latch onto. *Please*. Only when the screen blurred did she realize that tears were trickling down her cheeks. She didn't care.

"Peter Taggart skidded off the track on the same turn where Mason Chadworth crashed into the barricade. Taggart's car crashed into Chadworth's abandoned vehicle before officials could remove it. Chadworth's fuel tank was punctured, causing an explosion. Taggart was pronounced dead on the scene."

For one precarious moment, as gasps filled the air, Alix thought she might faint. Bowing her head, she trembled as relief tore through her, followed swiftly by guilt. Peter was dead. Kind and gentle Peter, who had been such a role model and mentor to Thalia, and such a devoted father to his young son. But Thalia was alive. What she was thinking and feeling right now, Alix could only begin to guess. But she was *alive*.

"The red flag has been shown," the voice continued. "The race will not be restarted. Thalia d'Angelis was in first place at the time of the crash and has been declared the winner. However, there will be no podium ceremony as she has been taken to the hospital with what are being reported as minor injuries from the blast."

Alix's relief gave way to a fresh surge of alarm. Thalia had been caught in the blast somehow? Hearing "minor injuries" might be enough of a reassurance for everyone else, but not for her. She wasn't going to be content until she got to the hospital and examined Thalia herself.

"We're going," Alix told Claude. "Immediately."

"Your Serene Highness—"

"Nonnegotiable. We are going now." She slid out of the chair, grasping the table until she was certain her legs wouldn't give out. "I can't imagine being in danger in a hospital, but if you'd like to arrange for additional security once we've arrived, be my guest."

"Yes, ma'am," he said and began to issue orders into his wrist mic as she moved toward the door. As they left the bar, one of the television announcers was discussing Formula One's safety record: "This is the first fatality at a Formula One Grand Prix in over twenty years, since Ayrton Senna's death in 1994."

She hoped Peter Taggart's wife wasn't listening to this. No statistics mattered when the person you loved was the exception to the rule.

❖

"I'm telling you, I'm fine!" Thalia sat on the edge of the lumpy hospital bed in nothing but one of those paper-thin gowns that barely covered the tops of her thighs. Despite the painful throbbing in her chest, she wanted to lash out at the doctor standing in front of her even more than she had wanted to hit Terrence back in Italy. Back when Peter had been alive.

"You are not fine, Ms. d'Angelis," he said in crisp, barely accented English. "You have vomited twice since you arrived, and your pupils are dilated. You may have a concussion. A PET scan will determine the extent of your injuries."

Thalia clenched the edge of the bed to stop herself from jumping up and grabbing him by the collar. "My friend and colleague—my teammate—*died* today. He died in front of me before I could help him. Of course I'm sick! Of course my goddamn fucking pupils are dilated! Now let me go! I have to get back to my team!"

The doctor's expression morphed from frustrated to sympathetic, but Thalia didn't want his sympathy. She wanted to see Courtney and Bryce and offer them whatever support she could. She wanted to mourn with Alistair and the engineers and mechanics. And she wanted to weep in Alix's arms.

"Ms. d'Angelis, I am very sorry for your loss. This day has been extremely difficult for you, and I understand—"

The door opened, mercifully cutting short his misguided attempt at empathy. When Alix stepped inside, Thalia cried out her name before she could clamp her lips together. She felt herself start to crumble inside and desperately blinked back tears. She could not fall apart in front of this ridiculous physician, no matter what he thought he understood.

"Dr. Messier," Alix said, "I am Dr. Pommelina Alix Louise Canella, Princess of Monaco and a friend of Ms. d'Angelis. I would like to speak with her for a few minutes in private, if you don't mind."

Two rebellious tears leaked out of Thalia's eyes before she could stop them. Alix was her knight in shining armor. Dr. Messier's eyes popped and he stammered, "Of course, Your Serene Highness," before hastily leaving the room. Once the door had shut, Alix raced across the room before Thalia could do more than put one foot on the floor.

"Don't get up," Alix said, cupping her face. "Please. Not yet. Just let me look at you."

As Alix searched her eyes, she gently fanned her thumbs across Thalia's cheeks. That tenderness was her undoing. The dam burst under the pressure, and she reached out blindly to clasp Alix's waist as her lungs constricted in a long sob.

"Thalia," Alix murmured into her hair. "Let it go. I'm right here."

She wept for a long time, and Alix held her gently but fiercely through it all—the hitching breaths that burned her chest, the rivers carving out tracks in the soot on her cheeks, the snot that dripped from her nose. Never once did Alix tell her that she would be okay, for which Thalia was grateful. She wasn't okay. She wouldn't be. But Alix reminded her that she was cared for and not alone.

When she was finally able to pull herself together, her chest burned with every breath, even worse than it had before. "Think I might've bruised a rib," she said thickly. When Alix immediately released her, Thalia shook her head. "No, don't. Please. You're not hurting me. It just…it aches. And sometimes when I inhale, the pain is sharper."

Alix rubbed Thalia's back in slow circles. "I need you to let me examine you," she said softly. "For your sake and mine."

"Okay."

"Lie back on the bed." Alix's voice and hands were gentle as she guided Thalia down. "Close your eyes and try to breathe as deeply as you can without hurting your chest."

But when Thalia closed her swollen eyes, all she saw was the ball of fire, engulfing Peter's car. She started up, winced, and braced herself on one elbow. Immediately, Alix was there, supporting her neck with one hand and stroking her face with the other.

"Sweetheart?" Alix combed the hair back from her forehead. "What just happened?"

"When I closed my eyes, I saw the explosion," she managed.

"All right." Alix leaned down to press a light kiss to her lips. "Keep them open, then. Focus on me. And when I'm finished, I'd like you to tell me what happened."

Thalia watched as Alix bent over her, first palpating her neck and then the contours of her collarbone. Her touch might not be sensual, but Thalia could sense the tenderness behind every movement. Nothing hurt until Alix reached the right side of her rib cage.

"There," Thalia hissed through teeth clenched at the sudden spike of pain.

"I'm sorry." Alix, seeming troubled that she'd had to hurt her, leaned down to gently kiss the spot before continuing her exam.

By the time she was finished, Thalia's adrenaline had been replaced by a bone-deep fatigue. She wanted to sleep for a week, but there was so much that had to be done. And how could she sleep at all when simply closing her eyes brought back the horror of the afternoon?

Alix slid onto the bed beside her and guided Thalia onto her left side before mirroring her position. In all her relationships and assignations, Thalia had never once been the little spoon, and it was surprisingly comforting. And then a thought occurred to her.

"Aren't you worried someone will come in?"

"The hospital staff have my credentials, and Claude is outside. He'll call me if anyone insists on entering. But I don't think they will."

"I need to get out of here. I have to see Courtney and Alistair."

Alix's hand came to rest on her hip, warm and reassuring. "I know. But you also need an x-ray of your rib cage. And I don't think you have a concussion, but I agree with Dr. Messier about the PET scan, just in case."

"Alix—" But when Thalia tried to turn, Alix held her in place.

"You've been through a terrible ordeal today," Alix said softly, her mouth close to Thalia's ear. "You're injured, and it's public knowledge that you're in the hospital. Courtney is being cared for by the team and the FIA. You'll see her soon, but when you do, you'll need to be strong. Let the hospital take care of you for tonight. They can find out the extent of your injuries and give you medication if necessary." She moved closer, until her stomach was pressed against Thalia's back. "Please trust me."

Thalia felt as though she had been given permission to feel the magnitude of her own pain and fatigue, both physical and emotional. But before she could agree, she needed to spell out her expectations. "I do trust you. And I'll stay here for the night, as long as I can call Alistair after the tests and get out tomorrow morning."

"Getting out tomorrow depends on the test results," Alix said. But when Thalia tensed to argue, Alix slipped one hand beneath the flimsy gown to caress her stomach. "Shhh. Let me finish. Based on my exam, I can't see any reason why they would hold you."

"Then we have a deal," Thalia whispered, comforted by the warm pressure of Alix's palm. The world was in chaos, but Alix's touch anchored her.

"You're a formidable negotiator." Alix kissed the nape of her neck. "Now, before I call back the doctor, will you tell me what happened today?"

Part of Thalia wanted to refuse, even as another, more logical part knew that she needed to process it. "I will. But just…just stay like you are, okay?" She swallowed down a fresh surge of bile. "It helps."

"I'll stay just like this," Alix said, smoothing her palm in circles against Thalia's abdomen.

Secure in her embrace, Thalia dared to close her eyes and let the memories take her.

CHAPTER TWENTY

Thalia sat in the same chair as she had six months ago when Alistair Campbell and Lord Rufford had offered her the chance of a lifetime. But today, the magnificent view from his office window was obscured by the creeping mist that had accompanied a drizzling rain coming in from the Irish Sea. Bad weather wasn't out of character for this part of the country, but today, it felt like the world was weeping.

Across from her, Roderick Mathelay lounged in his chair, long legs crossed at the ankles, looking bored. Thalia hated him already. She had lobbied for Alistair to choose one of Petrol Macedonia's test drivers to replace the irreplaceable Peter, but he had instead brought in a disgraced hotshot whose Superlicense had only recently been cleared of suspension. Last year, Mathelay had shown incredible promise in the first half of the season while driving for McLaren, only to fall from grace when a random blood test revealed his use of performance enhancing drugs. But he was eligible again now, and Alistair apparently saw something in him beyond his arrogance and disdain for regulations.

At the head of the table, Lord Rufford sighed through his mustache. He had delivered an eloquent eulogy for Peter two days previously. Mathelay hadn't shown up, and Thalia held it against him. Peter had been a legend in the sport—reason enough to attend. But when you were the one picked to fill, in some small way, the hole he had left on his team, why not make the effort to see him buried?

"We have found ourselves in both a tragic and unfortunate situation," Rufford began. "Peter was one of the greatest racers ever to have graced the sport, and we must find a way to soldier on without him." He looked between them, then to Alistair. "I trust you will work together to make the rest of this season as successful as possible, in order to honor him."

"Of course," Thalia said. Alistair nodded, and after a moment, Roderick did too.

"I must step into a meeting," Rufford continued, "but I leave it to you three to hammer out your strategy."

As soon as the door closed behind him, Roderick opened his mouth. "Given Thalia's inconsistent performance, it makes the most sense to regard me as the number one driver."

Thalia was on her feet without consciously intending to be. "Are you fucking kidding me?"

"Sit *down*." Alistair's voice was a whip, and she reluctantly obeyed. But when Roderick smirked at her, she was gratified to see Alistair turn his attention to him.

"And you. You just got here. Try to show some respect—not only for your teammate, but also for the dead. Or so help me God, I will drop you as fast as I picked you up."

Judging from the shocked expression on Roderick's face, he had never been spoken to before in such a manner. Thalia almost smiled, but found she couldn't quite manage it. She would smile again, she knew, someday—that was the way of life. But for now, it was just too soon.

❖

The tone of Franz Mueller's box was uncharacteristically somber. Death had not touched Formula One for a long time, but its specter was haunting the Russian Grand Prix. Seated at a small table on the balcony overlooking the grid, Alix felt the heaviness in the air as each driver stood by their car, watching as the flags snapping in a light breeze were lowered to half-mast. She watched Thalia bow her head as the marshal announced a moment of silence in memory of Peter Taggart.

The past two weeks had put a strain on them both. Thalia was struggling with grief in all its stages while also trying to recover physically. Her injuries might be minor, but they were still holding her back. Going through the motions of normal, everyday life with bruised ribs was one thing. Enduring the pain of forces five times that of gravity pushing repeatedly against those bruised ribs for two hours on end—that was something else entirely. She hadn't done as well in qualifying as expected, and would have to start from P6.

But the psychological and emotional toll of Peter's death dramatically overshadowed the physical. Thalia's patience had all but disappeared, and her temper flared often and unexpectedly. Under the pretext of business meetings, Alix had been able to join her in Russia for several days, but not a single night passed that she didn't wake from the same nightmare, gasping for breath and drenched in sweat. Alix had tried to cajole her into seeing a professional, but Thalia remained insistent that she didn't need to talk. She had asked for a prescription for sleeping pills, but Alix had refused to oblige until Thalia spoke with someone. Alix had stopped pushing in the days leading up to the race, but once it was over, she planned to present Thalia with a list of London-based therapists specializing in PTSD.

The roar of the engines drowned out her introspection. As Thalia's car sped off for her reconnaissance lap, Alix found herself wishing she believed in some kind of deity—someone or something she could appeal to other than Chance. Thalia was highly skilled, of course, but anything could happen. The commentators kept referring to Peter's accident as a "perfect storm" and a "fluke," but that only underscored the stakes of the uncertainty in this sport.

Once the race was under way, she returned to the box in order to reap the full benefit of the announcers' perspectives on the race. Thalia had made a decent start but was still in P6. Almost immediately, however, she began to fight for a higher position. As the race unfolded, Alix got the sense that Thalia was running even more aggressively than usual, and pushing the envelope in ways that opened her up to additional risk.

The more she heard, the more frustrated Alix became. Why, if your mentor and teammate had just been killed, would you respond that way? Wasn't it logical to be more cautious, not less? Thalia was sad and angry and grieving—she understood that. But to hear the announcers talk, her driving was borderline self-destructive, and it frightened Alix more than she wanted to admit. Should she insist that Thalia see a professional? If she continued to refuse—what then? Was it time for some kind of ultimatum?

And if so, did Thalia care enough about their relationship to make an ultimatum effective?

CHAPTER TWENTY-ONE

Thalia pulled into P2 for the formation lap of the Hungarian Grand Prix, preset her clutch paddles, looked up at the lights…and froze. There was nothing in front of her but the track, snaking away into the distance, framed by the low hills of Budapest.

"I could get used to this," she said, trying to freeze the moment in her mind. When the race was over, she would ask Peter whether he had ever—

Grief crashed down like a wave, threatening to suffocate her.

Deep breaths, sweetheart. She heard Alix's voice in her mind and automatically obeyed. Furiously blinking away the tears that now obscured her view, she tried to regain her focus. She couldn't allow grief to distract her. He would be the first one to demand she get her head on straight and think only of winning.

The lights counted down, and when Lucas pulled out to lead the lap, she slid into place behind him. Between bouts of swerving back and forth across the track to heat up her tires, Thalia watched Lucas and visualized overtaking him—if not on the first corner, then perhaps on the hairpin farther down the track. The day was warmer than had originally been expected, and Alistair had been uncharacteristically uncertain about whether they would need one pit stop or two.

"We'll assume two and start on the conservative side," he had told them at their meeting this morning, "and reevaluate after a few laps." Neither she nor Roderick had been happy to hear that, and she suspected they were both planning to push the envelope more than Alistair would like.

As Thalia crossed the finish line, she was already visualizing—as she had a thousand times since yesterday—a strong start that would allow her to pull in front of Lucas immediately. But when she put the car into neutral, her engine suddenly died.

Panic struck like a rattlesnake, but her instincts were stronger. This had happened before and she knew what to try first. With a practiced motion, she initiated the restart sequence.

Nothing.

Fear and rage began to take hold. She jammed her finger against the mic button. "What the fuck is going on?"

"Seems to be electrical issues," Carl's syllables vibrated with tensions.

The first light went out.

"No," she muttered. "No, no, no, no!"

"Try again!" Carl said.

Nothing. Still nothing. The second light went out.

"You have to signal them, Thalia," Alistair's voice, too calm, flooded her ears. The third light went out.

Gritting her teeth, she raised her arms above her head and waved. The fourth light went out, but a heartbeat later, the marshal waved the yellow flag wildly and the LEDs illuminated in the red pattern that signaled an aborted start.

"They've called for an extra formation lap," Carl said a moment later—unnecessarily, since she could see the goddamn board herself. "We'll come and get you."

Seething, Thalia watched as the field of cars pulled around her to flash off into the distance. As soon as they were gone, her engineers descended en masse, rolling the car into the pit lane and finally backing it into the garage. Hunching her shoulders, she vibrated with rage as they hooked the car back into the computer system and swarmed around it. If they could fix the problem before the start of the race, she would be allowed to join it from the pit lane. The motherfucking pit lane, when she had been P2!

One minute had already passed. By the end of the second minute, she knew it was hopeless. She was out of this race. From second place with a strong chance of capturing first, to DNF. As the cars roared off the grid for the start, her engineers stopped their frenetic activity.

"I'm so sorry, Thalia," Carl said, unable to meet her eyes.

She wanted to scream at him. At all of them. She wanted to curse how unfair it was that Roderick, whose sniping she had tried to endure without retaliation, was now flying around the track despite his inferior start, while she was confined to the garage. She wanted to weep for the lost points and for Peter's death and for how exhausting it was to have to prove yourself at every turn just because you had been born female. She wanted to lie down and sleep without dreams of fire. She wanted Alix's soothing touch and calming words.

But Thalia knew herself. If she didn't get away from other people this instant—Alix included—she would explode just as surely as Peter's car had done. She took off her HANS, laid it on the table, and walked toward the rear exit of their garage.

"Thalia?" Carl called after her. "Where are you—"

"Let her go," she heard Alistair say, before the door shut behind her.

❖

Alix found her, as expected, alone in the gym. This time, instead of pounding against a punching bag, she was pounding out miles on a treadmill. Alix paused inside the door to watch her run—arms pumping in perfect synchronicity with her strides, skin gleaming golden under the harsh fluorescent lights. Desire welled up, swift and powerful like a flash flood. But in the balance hung fear: fear of Thalia's chosen profession, fear for her life, fear of an anger so powerful it had driven her from showing solidarity with her team. Fear of her own feelings, and fear of what would happen if she fully surrendered to them.

When she stepped into Thalia's line of sight, the obvious clench to her jaw was a clear indicator that her workout had not yet been sufficient to boil off her rage. In a moment of doubt, Alix wondered if she had made the wrong decision.

Thalia slowed the machine to a walking speed. "I'm not in a good head space right now," she said.

"Okay," Alix said, feeling like she was tiptoeing through a minefield. "What can I do to help?"

Thalia stared at her for a moment before shaking her head. She stopped the treadmill and reached for the towel hanging on its frame. The dismissiveness of her behavior stung, but Alix wasn't about to give up that easily.

"Does that mean you don't think I can help? Or that you don't want me to?"

Thalia slung the towel around her neck. "I don't know. *I don't know*, okay? All I do know is that it feels like my skin is…is peeling off, I'm so fucking *angry*." She stepped down from the treadmill. "I left the garage to make this feeling go away and now it's even worse!"

Alix crossed her arms beneath her breasts, recognizing the defensiveness of the posture even as she adopted it. Coming here had been a mistake, she realized. But if she couldn't help Thalia when she felt this way, then what did that say about their relationship?

"What?" Thalia asked belligerently.

Alix shook her head. "Nothing."

"No, there's something. Just say it, okay? Clear the damn air."

Her tone was accusatory. Thalia was trying to bully her, and she wasn't going to stand for that.

"I hate it when you're like this." The words tumbled out in a rush. "Being angry and frustrated and disappointed about what happened today—that's understandable. But right now, you're completely irrational, and it's terrifying."

"Terrifying?"

"I have no idea what you might do. In this state, you're capable of actions that would normally be inconceivable. Like punching another driver in the face."

Thalia rounded on her. "You're always going to hold that against me, aren't you?"

Looming over her, Thalia was menacing in her anger, but Alix refused to back down. "I'm not holding it against you. I'm holding it up as an example of what you're capable of."

"What I'm capable of? You make me sound like some kind of psycho! Or a criminal!"

Alix could recognize baiting when she heard it, and so she kept her mouth shut. But she wasn't willing to stay and endure this kind of treatment, especially since she didn't deserve it. Sympathy had gotten her nowhere. She had an early flight in the morning to make it to an important meeting with a potential investor in Germany, and she wasn't about to spend the rest of the night in an argument. Thalia would have to sort out her issues alone.

"What are you doing?" Thalia demanded when Alix began to move toward the door.

"Going to my room."

"Why?"

"Because you want to have a fight, but I need a good night's sleep."

"I want to have a fight?" Thalia's voice rose an octave. "Do you think I wanted my car not to start? Do you think I wanted not to finish?"

"I'm glad you didn't have to race!" Alix fired back, instantly regretting it. All day, she had tried so hard to keep her calm. Thalia had every right to be upset, but she didn't have any right at all to take it out on her. Except now, despite her efforts at equanimity, Alix had sunk to Thalia's level.

"Excuse me?"

En route to the door, Alix paused. Fine. If Thalia wanted to have this out now, then she would play along. "Every time you leave for a race, I have to accept the fact that you might not return. I have to ignore the instincts that scream at me to run after you and beg you not to get in your car. Do you have any idea how exhausting that is?" Alix could tell by Thalia's narrowed eyes that her words weren't having any kind of positive effect, but she had to finish. "You've been suffering since Peter's death but refuse to get help. And you've been driving like you want to join him in the grave. So, yes. I was happy when your car wouldn't start, because that meant you wouldn't have to put your life on the line today. Okay?"

"No." Thalia shook her head vehemently. "Not okay. I can be in a relationship with someone who worries about me—the same way I would worry about you if you were to visit Uganda. But I can't be in a relationship with someone who wants to change me." She balled her hands into fists. "I'm a racecar driver. My job is dangerous. That's always going to be true. So if you can't accept that, leave now and don't come back."

Alix couldn't believe what she was hearing. "That's your solution? I tell you that I'm worried about your *life*, and you give me an ultimatum about our relationship?"

Thalia crossed her arms over her chest. "I am what I am, and I meant what I said."

Alix felt as though the earth was shifting beneath her feet, pain spilling out from the cracks like magma. "You're an adrenaline addict and a bully," she said. "That's what you are."

Forcing herself not to look back, she left the gym. Claude was waiting outside, of course. How much had he heard? Probably every word. She didn't dare meet his eyes, in case censure or judgment was waiting. Or worse: pity.

A chasm was opening inside her mind, threatening to engulf her with despair. All the hours she had spent worrying about Thalia's well-being crashed down on her. All the research, all the lost sleep, all the frantic hours spent watching her drive and praying she would make it through each race unscathed. She should have delivered her own ultimatum before Thalia could beat her to the punch.

"Will you be returning to your suite, ma'am?" Thankfully, Claude's tone was entirely professional.

Alix had booked a room in the same hotel patronized by Formula One to keep up appearances, but she had spent every night of her stay in Thalia's bed. Now, she was thankful to have her own space. But it wasn't enough—she could easily run into Thalia in the hall or the lobby. Her mind leapt to how awful it would be to glimpse Thalia with another woman, someone who cared only about Thalia's fame and wanted only her body. Someone who wouldn't call her out when she was being self-destructive.

The urge to flee and lick her wounds in private was all-consuming. A choking sense of claustrophobia rose in her throat, and she braced herself against the wall to combat a wave of dizziness.

"Ma'am?" Claude, who had never touched her, rested one hand briefly on her shoulder. "I'd like to escort you to your room. Please."

At his solicitous tone, Alix had to bite her lip to hold herself together. She still couldn't look at him, but after a hard swallow and deep, shuddering breath, she forced herself to speak.

"That's fine." The words were steady. So far, so good. "And I'd like to leave tonight. Would you mind calling the airfield?"

"I'll do so immediately."

After another deep breath, she pushed off the wall and walked with measured steps toward the elevator. The effort required all her concentration. While she might be able to escape Thalia, she couldn't give her own emotions the slip. The pressure built behind her eyes like a storm front, and Alix knew that once she was alone, she would no longer be able to contain it. For the first time since she had been a small child, she was going to break down and weep. It was going to be messy and protracted and melodramatic and useless. Turning into a blubbering mess wouldn't help her process what had happened with Thalia. It wouldn't make her a better person. It certainly wouldn't help her prepare for tomorrow's meeting.

If this was the price of falling in love with someone, she never wanted to pay it again.

CHAPTER TWENTY-TWO

A lix sat in the barber's chair at Camille's favorite salon and watched as the hairdresser took up her scissors. She approached with obvious trepidation.

"Are you certain, Your Serene Highness?" she asked. "This is a significant change to make all at once. Perhaps you would like to do it in stages, just to be sure?"

Alix knew the woman was trying to be helpful, and to avoid risking royal ire, but she didn't appreciate being second-guessed. "I'm certain," she said, hoping she sounded confident and not testy.

Since her breakup with Thalia, she had found herself prone to irrational fits of temper. Even the smallest slight or inconvenience—like convincing her hairdresser that yes, she really did want a pixie cut—set her on edge. Had she absorbed some of Thalia's impatience during their time together? If so, she needed to expunge it and become herself again, as soon as possible.

But as she watched the long, auburn strands fall to the floor, Alix knew she could never go back to the person she had been. That person hadn't known how it felt to dance with Thalia in Buckingham Palace, or to watch her encourage a young child with cancer, or to make love with her to the sound of the Mediterranean's lapping waves. That person had only seen the waste of Formula One, and not the good it could do through charity and sponsorship. She wasn't that person anymore. She couldn't go back. But moving on was proving to be just as impossible.

She was stuck.

Despite the finality of their parting, it had proven impossible for her to cut Thalia out of her life. She couldn't help but continue to follow Thalia's career: third place in Brazil, third in Canada, second in the United States. Finally, she was having a run of successful races. But it hurt not to be able to share in her victories. Every day, she wondered whether Thalia had found someone else, or whether she was back to her old philandering habits. In moments of weakness, she searched for news of her on the Internet. But uncharacteristically, photos of Thalia partying with grid girls didn't rise to the surface. What did that mean? And why couldn't she stop caring?

This weekend, Formula One returned to Europe. The German Grand Prix would be followed by the British Grand Prix, before the circuit moved to the final race in Abu Dhabi, which counted for double points. The Alps might separate Monaco from Germany, but it still seemed too close. When the vast expanse of the Atlantic had separated them, Alix had been resigned to Thalia's distance. But now that they were back on the same continent, her nerves felt raw and exposed. She had purposefully scheduled this appointment to coincide with the beginning of the race in order to distract herself from it. Not that the plan was working very well.

Slowly, her face emerged from the curtain of hair that had framed it for years. It was a strong face—too distinctive to be called "beautiful" according to the current standard, but not, she reflected dispassionately, displeasing. There would be other women who would find her attractive enough. Or men.

Alix narrowed her eyes at her reflection. Was she bisexual? A lesbian? How could she tell, when the only person she wanted was Thalia?

When grief washed over her, she reminded herself to stay angry. Thalia had dumped her as unceremoniously as she might one of her flings. One argument, and they were over. That wasn't the kind of relationship she wanted. The ease with which Thalia had broken it off spoke volumes about her level of commitment in the first place.

Commitment. Alix barely managed to keep herself from startling the hairdresser with ironical laughter. Thalia had never wanted more than the most superficial commitment. That was blatantly obvious in hindsight, and over the past several weeks, Alix had chastised herself more than once for being such a fool. Everyone went through something like this when they were inexperienced, she reminded herself. Her foolishness was just happening much later than normal.

The hairdresser (why could Alix not remember her name?) stepped back and smiled nervously into the mirror. "There you are, Your Serene Highness. What do you think?"

Alix inspected her new reflection. For once, her hair lay flat against her head, instead of frizzing and wisping in disobedience. True, the style emphasized the angularity of her jawline, but it also lent her a fresh, clean-cut look. Unburdened of her unruly tresses, she felt light and sharp and powerful.

"It's perfect," she said.

The relief on the woman's face was out of proportion to both her task and Alix's sentiment. "I'm so glad," she enthused, the words tripping over themselves in her obvious relief.

Alix tipped her handsomely before stepping outside with Claude at her heels. As she paused to take stock, the sun emerged from behind a bank of dark clouds. The streets and buildings gleamed wetly, seeming clean and new after their impromptu shower. Unexpectedly, she felt a buoying sense of hope. Thalia had wounded her, but the wound would heal. It was all a matter of time, and she had that now. Her obligations to Formula One had ended, and she wouldn't have to see Thalia again this season. And next season, Florestan would almost certainly want to reprise his role as the family's F1 liaison.

Thankfully, she had her work. Over the next few months, Rising Sun would demand all the attention she could offer. And if some other person ever inspired the passion Thalia had awakened—well then, she would cross that bridge when it appeared.

But her resolve disappeared as they passed a pub advertising the German Grand Prix. Alix slowed, hating herself for her weakness. She only needed a moment—just a moment to see where Thalia stood. To ensure she was okay. If it had rained here, it might also be raining in Germany. And the last time it had rained...

She shook her head to disperse the ominous thought. "I'd like to stop here briefly," she told Claude. "Just to watch the race for a few minutes."

"Very well, ma'am." He spoke softly into his wrist mic before leading the way inside.

It was a fairly upscale establishment, as it would have to be in this neighborhood—packed with what appeared to be a mix of young professionals and tourists. After Claude carved out a space for her along one wall, she turned her attention to the nearest television, where the race was just returning after a commercial break. An overhead camera showed the cars snaking along the course, and Alix squinted, trying to make out the leaders. Fortunately, the announcers chimed in with an update.

"During the break, Thalia d'Angelis continued to close the gap separating her from Lucas Mountjoy. With only five laps remaining, she'll need to make her move soon to claim her first victory."

Alix wanted to protest. Technically, that wasn't true. Thalia had been declared the winner of the race in which Peter was killed. But no one, least of all Thalia herself, regarded that as a true victory. Wishing she had the strength to turn and walk out of the pub—to leave both Thalia and Formula One behind forever—Alix instead kept her gaze fixed to the screen. She didn't know whether to hope Thalia tried to pass Lucas, or settled for what appeared to be a safe second place.

But Thalia wanted to win, and any place below first was a loss.

"There she goes!" the announcer enthused. "D'Angelis is making a move to catch Mountjoy for the lead!"

A chorus of groans greeted this news, reminding Alix that her own preferences were not shared by the majority of diehard Formula One fans. By and large, they wanted the sport to remain as it always had: ruled by men both on the track and off. But as she watched Thalia accelerate in order to pass Lucas on the outside, Alix felt her anger and resentment burn away in a rush of adrenaline. *Pass him*, she silently urged. *Show these people just how good you are.*

Lucas took the turn tightly, and Thalia went wide…but instead of curving back toward the inside of the track, her car kept moving on its original line. Alix's jaw dropped in a silent scream as Thalia hurtled toward the barrier, crashing into it in a spray of water. Pieces of her car went flying like shrapnel. The announcers erupted in sounds of distress and attempts at explanation, but Alix couldn't hear through the sudden ringing in her ears.

"Ma'am? Ma'am?" Claude was gripping her arm. Alix stared at him numbly. Thalia had crashed at the height of her acceleration. She had probably been driving in excess of three hundred kilometers per hour when she hit the barricade. She turned to Claude and tried to focus despite the blurriness of her vision. Why couldn't she see properly?

With his free hand, he proffered a handkerchief. "Use this, ma'am. Please. It's clean."

"Thank you," she tried to say. Her lips felt numb.

"Would you like to go to Germany? I can make the arrangements."

Alix looked between him and the screen, where ambulances were converging on Thalia's car. Alix wanted to shout at them through the television—to admonish them to move her carefully, without jostling her spinal cord. But they were professionals. They knew.

And then she realized it didn't matter what they knew. *She* needed to know. It didn't matter that she and Thalia had broken up. She cared for her still. She needed to be there.

❖

Thalia couldn't get comfortable enough to sleep. The medication had helped her slip into a shallow doze, but the dosage wasn't strong enough to put her out completely. If she twitched or shifted or breathed in too deeply, a spike of pain shattered her fragile rest.

She didn't want to be awake. She didn't want to replay the crash to the metronome of her heart monitor. She didn't want to be trapped in this fragile body in this sterile room while the world turned outside and the clock continued ticking until the British Grand Prix.

"Absolutely out of the question," her doctor had informed her when she had asked about her chances of racing. "Perhaps, if you remain very quiet and follow your rehabilitation program to the letter, you will be able to race at Abu Dhabi in one month's time."

The British Grand Prix, on her home turf, would be another DNF. Another opportunity for points, wasted. All her hard work in the Americas to close the gap between herself and Lucas would be for naught. Roderick had been racing well enough to keep them in contention for the Constructors' Cup, but if she couldn't do her part, it would slip through their fingers. She would be yet another disappointment to one more person.

Alistair and Carl had visited earlier in the day, bringing dark chocolate and telemetry data. Carl had initially been terrified to enter her presence, believing she held him accountable for the failure of her braking system that had caused her crash. And while the thought had occurred to her, Thalia had also had plenty of time to reflect on the nature of her sport: its sensitivity, its unreliability, its fickleness. In the service of her quest to catch Lucas, her engineers had made certain modifications to the car that involved tweaks to the brake-by-wire system. But because she had been driving in Lucas's "bad air" for much of the race, the temperature of her brakes had risen beyond the point where the brake-by-wire would work automatically. Naturally, it had failed at the most critical moment.

She hated seeing Carl so cowed, so hangdog. *She* had put that fear in his mind, that expression on his face. He would have been apologetic and disappointed no matter what, but her patterns of volatility had led him to expect either verbal abuse or the cold shoulder. Never had she hated herself more than in the moment of that revelation. And he wasn't the only one she had bullied.

The last time she had been in the hospital, Alix had come to her rescue. Now, Thalia had only her team members who felt obliged to stop in and check on her. Even her father hadn't done more than call. She reached for her phone, thinking to send Alix a text. *I'm sorry*, it would say. Or perhaps more specific was better: *I was cruel to you and I'm sorry.* Or perhaps instead: *I've thought of you every day since Sochi, but I confused apologizing for being cruel with apologizing for who I am.* That was halfway decent…

A sound in the doorway interrupted her recrimination. She looked up expecting to see a nurse and ready to request a higher dose of pain meds, but instead found herself face-to-face with Alix. Thalia's heart flip-flopped, and she felt her mouth open, then close.

Alix had cut her hair very short, and it suited her. She didn't move into the room, but stood regarding Thalia with an impassivity she found frightening. But if Alix truly felt nothing, then why had she come?

"I'm so glad to see you," she said brokenly.

"Are you?"

Discomfited by the monotone of her voice, Thalia hurried to explain. To apologize. To beg forgiveness. "Yes. I've missed you and—"

"You have an awfully strange way of showing it." Alix entered as far as the foot of her bed and picked up her chart. "Two fractured ribs, a dislocated shoulder, and a concussion."

Thalia knew she should remain apologetic, but the vague accusation in Alix's tone raised her hackles. "Sustained because my brake system failed, not because of my driving skill."

Alix returned her chart to its hook. "I never accused you of being a poor driver."

"Everyone else has," Thalia said bitterly. "Are you here to say 'I told you so'? Because you would be well within your rights to do so."

"No." Alix took the seat next to her bedside. "I'm here to help you recover for Abu Dhabi."

CHAPTER TWENTY-THREE

Thalia sat on the patio of Villa Canella and watched the sun turn Lake Como to fire. The pain in her ribs had woken her before sunrise, but the chance to witness it offered some consolation. As she had slowly shuffled toward the French doors, one of Alix's staff had offered assistance, but she had politely declined. This much, she could do herself.

It hadn't been easy to make the lawn chair recline with only one good arm, but she had managed. It had been impossible to lower herself into the chair without her ribs screaming, but she had ignored their protests. Now, with a blanket tucked around her body, she breathed as deeply as she could, willing the pain to subside so she could enjoy the unparalleled view.

The mansion sat on the western edge of Lake Como and commanded one of the best possible perspectives. Thalia watched as the scintillating light played across the sheer rock faces that dropped precipitously into the water the color of aquamarine. Farther off, the border of the lake gentled into green slopes dotted with homes, their terracotta roofs still plunged in shadow. Turning her face toward the dawn, she surrendered to the haze of fatigue and the seductive pull of her pain pill.

She woke with the sun in her eyes. Overheated, she reached for the blanket only to gasp in pain at the sudden movement. Muttering a curse, she forced herself to move more deliberately. After ineffectually patting the collar of her shirt, she cursed again. She had forgotten her sunglasses and would have to return inside.

"Good morning." As she spoke, Alix stepped into her field of vision. She was dressed simply in jeans and a white Oxford shirt, and the sun backlit her hair, making it glow red. She was stunning. Thalia wanted to kiss her, but thanks to her own stupidity, that was no longer an option.

"Hi," she said, her voice gritty from sleep. She wanted nothing more than to apologize properly, but they hadn't been alone together since that brief interlude in the hospital. Someone—a security officer, the butler, a member of the villa's housekeeping corps—was always hovering nearby, and Alix never asked them to leave. Thalia wasn't about to speak honestly in front of a third party, and she suspected Alix was deliberately using her people as a shield.

Her suspicion was confirmed when Alix's gaze shifted to something behind her. She spoke a string of Italian, presumably to a member of the staff, before moving to one side so Thalia wouldn't have to blind herself.

"I would ask how you slept, but the evidence suggests not well," Alix said. Her voice was carefully modulated, as it had been since they had left the hospital. All trace of the emotion she had betrayed in Thalia's presence on the evening of her accident had utterly disappeared and had yet to return. But it was there, simmering below the surface, bound fast by mental lock and key until Alix could trust her again. Thalia had to believe that.

"The pain woke me again," she said. "But at least I got to see the sunrise." When Alix seemed somewhat impressed at her positive attitude, Thalia felt proud of herself. "And you?" she asked, not wanting to lose this tenuous connection.

But a shutter fell over Alix's eyes, concealing their expressiveness. "I slept fine."

The dark smudges beneath her eyes told a different story. Thalia wanted to stand up and pull her close and insist she tell the truth, but standing up would take minutes to accomplish, and besides, who was she to make demands of Her Serene Highness? *Stop pushing me away*, Thalia wanted to tell her. *Let me back into your life. We'll both sleep better*. Alix wouldn't have brought her here if she hadn't still felt something, would she?

The sound of footsteps on the flagstones stopped Thalia from making any kind of declaration. When a woman in House Canella livery came into view, holding her sunglasses, Thalia looked to Alix.

"It seemed as though you might need them," was all she said.

"Thank you." Thalia put them on, and the world dimmed just enough to be bearable. When the woman moved off to tend to the plants on the far side of the terrace, Thalia saw the opportunity for them to have a real conversation. "Would you like to sit?" She felt absurd asking Alix to take a seat on her own terrace, but she seemed on the verge of leaving as quickly as she had arrived, and Thalia wanted to make the most of this chance.

"I will, for a while," Alix said, seeming almost surprised by her own words.

She took the chair next to Thalia's. They were separated by only a few feet—the width of a small table—the closest they had been since Alix had held her hand in the hospital. The hairs on the nape of Thalia's neck prickled as she tried to keep calm at Alix's proximity. But if she remained too calm, would Alix get the wrong idea?

"So," she said, trying to sound nonchalant, "what are your plans for the day?"

"I have a luncheon at the Villa d'Este this afternoon with a potential investor from Milan." Alix's eyes were closed as she soaked up the sun's rays, affording Thalia the opportunity to observe her silently. Short hair suited her, as did the subtle shift she had made in her wardrobe. Collared shirts had replaced her scoop-neck tops, lending her a more androgynous air. Had the change been deliberate, or instinctual?

"I hope it goes well," was all she said aloud. She was letting the seconds tick past. She had to say something, to start somewhere, but she couldn't stop looking at Alix. The triangle of pale white skin exposed by the top two undone buttons begged for the worshipful touch of her lips. She wanted to remove Alix's shirt slowly, kissing every inch as she went. She wanted to nibble at the edge of her navel, then down until she reached the apex of her thighs. Desire rose like a tsunami, drowning her logic and reason, washing away all the carefully crafted apologies she had committed to memory.

"Alix," she said hoarsely. "I want you."

Alix's head snapped around, but her expression was impossible to read through the dark shell of her sunglasses. "I don't know how to respond to that," she finally said.

If not for the slight quaver in her voice, Thalia might have thought her words had made no impact on Alix whatsoever. But Alix wasn't unaffected—she was trying not to betray weakness. Thalia could recognize the impulse from a mile away.

Confronted by Alix's clear discomfort, she realized her error. Honesty was a virtue, but it could also be used as a weapon. Their romantic relationship was over because *she* had ended it. Alix had given her sanctuary and hospitality despite the awkwardness, because for whatever reason, she still cared about Thalia's well-being. And Thalia had just repaid those gifts by going on the offensive and putting her on the spot. To tell Alix she wanted her, out of the blue, after being the one to end their intimacy…how self-centered could she get? Alix must be so confused.

Awash in self-loathing, Thalia's only clear imperative was to fall back on the apology she should have delivered in the first place.

"That was very selfish of me," she said, wishing she could see Alix's eyes. "And unfair. I was thinking of myself—of what I feel and what I want. I didn't think about how that would make you feel." The words were pouring out of her in a rush. "I'm not going to apologize for what I said, because I meant it. I mean it." She took a deep breath. "I made a mistake when I told you to go, back in Russia. I was being selfish then too. I want you, Alix. That's the truth. But I should never have put you in a situation where you feel uncomfortable in your own home."

Alix sat up and swiveled in Thalia's direction, gripping the edge of her chair. "Did you just say that you think breaking off our relationship was a mistake?"

She sounded angry. She had every right to be. "Yes. Please…can you take off your sunglasses? I need to see your face. Please."

When Alix didn't react for a moment, Thalia thought she might refuse. Finally, she pulled them off, revealing too-bright, green-flecked eyes.

"I want you to know how I feel, but I don't want to push you. And by just blurting it out, that's exactly what I did. Let me take back the pressure. But not the words themselves."

Alix cleared her throat. "I may not have any practice at…this." She gestured into the space between them. "But I know enough to be sure I don't deserve to be bullied or manipulated. You bullied me out the door last month, and what you just said seems designed precisely to manipulate my feelings."

"I know." Thalia felt sick. "I know that's what it seems like. And I know there's nothing I can do to convince you otherwise. But for what it's worth, I'm telling the truth." She swallowed hard. The nausea she was experiencing felt almost identical to her sickness before a race. "You said you don't have practice at 'this.' Well, I don't, either."

"Excuse me?" Alix leaned forward, her features sharp in disbelief. "You've been with how many women, exactly?"

Thalia winced at her accusatory tone. "Okay, yes, I've been with a lot of women. But not *like this*. That's what I mean." When Alix's frown deepened, she hurried to explain. "I've never been interested in a real relationship. In monogamy. In commitment." Words that had once frightened her now rolled easily off her tongue. All because of Alix. "You make me want those things. You're not just some…some roll in the hay. You're not a fling. I want to be with you, Alix. Exclusively."

When a tear slipped from Alix's left eye to trail down her cheek, Thalia's heart broke. She wanted to kiss it away, but knew she couldn't. She had said what she needed to, and promised not to be manipulative. What happened to them next was no longer up to her.

Blinking furiously, Alix swiped the droplet away. "I still don't know what to say. I need…I need some time to process this. It's difficult to trust you."

The words were a knife, but one she deserved. Biting her lower lip, she fought back her own swell of emotion and nodded. "I understand," she whispered.

Alix returned her sunglasses to her face. "I'll check in on you tonight," she said. And then she was gone.

Thalia wanted to turn and watch her go, but that would be too painful, and not just on her ribs. As she stared unseeing at the lake instead, she let the tears roll down her cheeks. She was so tired—as battered emotionally as she was physically—and the only person she had to blame was herself. Alix had accused her of issuing ultimatums and not being willing to have authentic conversations. Both were true, but now that she was finally trying to change her ways, was it too late? She had to confront the possibility that she had hurt Alix too deeply for the wound to heal. Nauseous and aching, she cautiously turned onto her good shoulder and curled in on herself, searching for some trace of comfort. Exhausted again, she closed her eyes. Patience had never been her strong suit, but now, it was all she had to give.

❖

By the third day, Thalia was feeling stronger. Alix watched from the window of her bedroom as she slowly picked her way down the stone stairs leading to the quay that stretched out into Lake Como. Alix leaned forward enough to rest her forehead against the cool glass pane. She had managed to get some work done over the last few days, but only through sheer force of will. Having Thalia under her roof was beyond distracting. Alix could only keep her at arm's length for so long. Eventually, she would have to make a decision: to bridge the space between them or walk away. The status quo was not an option.

I want to be with you, Alix. Exclusively.

The words were an inescapable echo in her mind. She heard them everywhere—whether she was trying to sleep or trying to concentrate or trying to relax. What if she had done what she wanted in that moment— to get on her knees before Thalia's battered body and confess that the desire was still mutual? Did she have the mental and emotional resolve necessary to open herself to Thalia again?

Hindsight told her that their initial relationship had always been doomed to fail. Now that she had tried "no strings attached," she realized she didn't want that. For her, the strings were necessary. The stakes needed to be high. She wanted to invest in her significant other, and she wanted that person to be invested in her right back.

Thalia had spoken of monogamy. Of commitment. Never in a million years had Alix expected to hear those words leave her mouth, but they had. And a significant part of Alix wanted nothing more than to nurture the fragile emotional connection they had been slowly in the process of forging before its sudden unraveling. As she thought about it, she realized that Peter's death had been the catalyst for everything falling apart. Thalia's anger and grief had contributed to her recklessness on the track, and if Alix were being honest with herself, the specter of Peter's horrible accident had shaken her deeply. Could their relationship really go anywhere? Thalia wasn't going to stop putting herself in danger. If they rekindled their romance, Alix would have to stand by and watch her race. She would have to patch her up whenever required. What kind of life was that?

A life plenty of people manage to live, her rational mind whispered.

The partners of police officers and firefighters and military servicemen and women—all of them lived with the burden of knowing their loved one might return from their work hurt, or not at all. And they were only the tip of the iceberg. Plenty of athletes had died in service to their sport: skiers, rock climbers, equestrians. And while one could argue that fighting fires was certainly more necessary to the continuance of the human race than jumping horses, both kinds of vocations were valued by society.

Besides, death wasn't unique to dangerous jobs. During her brief stint in emergency medicine, she had seen young, healthy people suffer heart attacks. And anyone could be struck by a car while crossing the street. Death was certain. Life was uncertain.

Which meant it should be cherished. Celebrated. Enjoyed.

But even so, that didn't mean she was *obliged* to throw herself into a relationship with someone who engaged in risky behavior as a matter of vocation. In this respect, at least, she was the mistress of her own destiny. No matter what she might feel now, if she distanced herself from Thalia, she would eventually get over those feelings. Wouldn't she?

Blinking, she pulled back and focused not on the lake but on her dim reflection in the window. If she had truly wanted to distance herself from Thalia, why on earth had she invited her here? Why was she having this internal debate right now?

Unwilling to plumb the depths of her own motivations any further, Alix turned away and began to prepare herself for dinner. This would be the first night that Thalia felt well enough to join her for the evening meal, and Alix would need every ounce of poise at her command.

❖

On the evening of the fifth day since their arrival, Thalia decided she'd had quite enough of Alix avoiding her. They weren't going to make any progress so long as they barely spoke to one another, and if Alix wasn't going to initiate more contact, she would find a way that wouldn't seem manipulative. She had thought they might be able to talk during dinners, but the presence of the waiters dissuaded her from bringing up any personal topic. The last thing she wanted was to do something to further compromise Alix's trust in her. This was the twenty-first century, not the sixteenth: one of the villa staff could easily record their conversation on their phone and then sell it to the tabloids.

As desperate as she was to speak with Alix, Thalia had resolved to hold off until they could be truly alone. And since showing up at her room might be conveyed as too pushy, Thalia was forced to wait and watch and content herself with discussing the weather over their perfectly prepared meals while she schemed up ways to put Alix in a position where honest dialogue would be possible. Ironically, she needed to get Alix away from Villa Canella. In frustration, she finally turned to the Internet, which informed her that the marina outside Villa d'Este included sailboats that could be chartered for a two-hour tour. That was perfect. Trapped on a boat in Lake Como, Alix would have to listen to her. Now, all she had to do was successfully pitch the excursion.

"I was thinking," she said as the salad course arrived—a tower of lettuce artfully adorned with tomatoes and bleu cheese, festooned with ribbons of vinaigrette, "of chartering a boat to tour the lake tomorrow. And I was wondering if you'd like to come."

Alix had picked up her fork, but now she put it down. "Are you certain you feel well enough?"

Thalia considered the question and her possible answers. She didn't want to offend Alix's hospitality by confessing to her cabin fever, especially since the "cabin" was practically a chateau, and very much in the lap of luxury. But she was used to exercising for a significant portion of every day, and now that her ribs weren't quite so tender as they had been, the inaction was unfamiliar and unwelcome. It would have been a different story had she and Alix been a couple, of course—they could have spent hours watching silly movies, or taking slow walks along the lakeshore, or best of all, holed up cuddling in bed. But as it was, all the frustration—physical and emotional—was conspiring to drive her insane.

"I'm sure," she said, hoping she sounded reasonable and not desperate. "I'd like to see the view from the water."

When Alix's gaze strayed to the lake, visible from the floor-to-ceiling windows on the eastern side of the room, Thalia held her breath and prayed. When she turned back, her gaze was measuring. Had she seen through the premise?

"It is beautiful," she said finally. "And the weather tomorrow should be perfect for a sail."

The weather, again. But this time, it was blowing in her favor. "Does that mean you'll join me?" She held her breath.

"Yes," Alix said, before concentrating on her entrée.

The rush of exhilaration reminded her of stepping onto the third-place podium in Monaco. Thalia smiled triumphantly down at her plate. She could celebrate this victory, but she still had a long way to go.

CHAPTER TWENTY-FOUR

The roar of the speedboats was vaguely reminiscent of the sound of racecars at a Grand Prix. It was fitting, she supposed—the team was flying to England today for a week's preparation before the race. This morning, she had called Alistair to wish them a safe trip. She had spoken with their top test driver, James, who would be taking her place. She had tried to joke with him about taking care of her car, but her joke had fallen as flat as a tire on glass shards.

For the second race in a row, she would earn no points. If Lucas won, he would pull far enough ahead that there was virtually no chance of Petrol Macedonia regaining the lead in the battle for the Constructors' Cup. At the thought, twin pangs of grief and anger brought tears to Thalia's eyes. When she passed them off with a yawn, Alix frowned.

"You're tired."

"I'm okay." She forced a smile, and then forced thoughts of racing out of her mind. There was no use in brooding over lost opportunities, especially since the fastest way to make it back to the track was to focus on healing. Besides, this afternoon's excursion had nothing to do with her professional life, and everything to do with her personal one. "I'm really looking forward to this."

They were waiting on the quay for their captain to finish inspecting his boat. It was a beauty: forty-five feet long with an immaculately polished deck and elegant green sails. When making the reservation, Thalia had requested that once they were under way, the captain and his crewman give them as much privacy as possible. She had thrown in an obscenely generous tip to ensure their cooperation.

The captain—a middle-aged man with a salt-and-pepper beard—

emerged from the hold and stepped off the boat to greet them. He introduced them to his crew, a younger version of himself. If either of them recognized her or Alix, they gave no indication. So far, so good. Privacy was a precious commodity, and she didn't mind paying up for it.

The only part of the experience Thalia couldn't control was Claude, and she waited anxiously as he cleared the vessel. Upon his return, he stationed himself near the lifeboat mounted on the stern. Thalia was relieved when the captain guided them to a slightly recessed space in front of the main sail where two chaise lounges flanked a small table on which a bottle of champagne sat on ice. When Thalia picked it up, Alix shot her a look.

"Do you know how to open one of those without spraying it everywhere?"

Thalia had to laugh. "Trust me," she said, referring to more than the champagne. She twisted the cork gently, feeling Alix's gaze on the movement of her hands, and it slid out with only a gentle pop.

"Maybe I should," Alix murmured when Thalia handed her a brimming flute.

Hope rushed into the empty, aching space in her chest that had nothing to do with her injury, but she didn't want to pounce on the words and make a big deal. Contenting herself for the moment with an answering smile, she raised her glass.

"Alix," she began, hoping the fine tremor of her hand wasn't obvious. It was critical that she get this right. "Your generosity is your defining attribute, and those who have been touched by it are changed for the better. The people of Uganda. The children in that hospital in Graz. The Ruffords and Petrol Macedonia. Me." Alix dropped her gaze, clearly self-conscious. "Your example makes me want to give back. To pay your kindness and compassion forward. Thank you."

"That was a generous toast," she said.

But Thalia shook her head. "It was only the truth."

As they sipped, the boat got under way. Thalia stretched out her legs and turned up her face into the breeze. "This has to be one of the most beautiful places in the world," she said.

Alix began to speak, then, sharing what she knew of the history of the lake and the villages along its shores. At times, she pointed out various homes and other landmarks, weaving their tales into her narrative. Thalia listened eagerly, loving how Alix paused sometimes as she translated a thought between languages, and the way her hands sliced through the air when she became especially passionate about her topic. In preparation for this stolen afternoon, she had rehearsed so many talking points in her head, but now they all went out the window. She wanted Alix to feel how good it was to be able to let down her guard; how easy it was to spend time together. Any future relationship worth its salt would be built on who they were together when no one was watching, and for now, this was as close as they could get.

"You've really made a study of this place," Thalia said during a lull.

Alix smiled—the most carefree smile Thalia had seen from her all week. "That's what happens when you prefer reading to practicing makeovers with your sisters."

At first, Thalia laughed, but then she realized Alix had given her an opening. "I've been trying to give myself a makeover, recently. Not physically—emotionally."

Alix tensed, but she didn't close down. That was progress. "What do you mean?"

Thalia prayed for eloquence. "I meant what I said a few days ago, about never having been in a relationship like this before. I've always held myself at a distance from my lovers, because they were never going to be around very long. Most of them did the same." She glanced at Alix, but found no judgment—only attentiveness.

"You and I have always been more than casual. But whenever something became difficult in my professional life, I pushed you away, just like I would have done with any of my…"

"Flings? Conquests?"

Thalia winced, but she felt a little better when she saw a small smile curving Alix's lips. "Can we call them dates?"

"Since I'm feeling so generous."

"Ha ha." Thalia turned to face her. "I think what I'm trying to say is that for all of my adult life, I've been closed off emotionally. On purpose. Because I'm gay, because I'm a woman in a man's sport…it's easier to put up a shield so everything bounces off. Except that I want to let you in."

Alix was looking at her intently. "You've been terrible at that."

"I have. I know. But now *that* I know…I want to fix it. I want to change. I'm trying to change. And maybe it's too late and I've lost you, and—"

Alix reached across the space between them to touch her arm. "You know that's not true."

"I do?"

"Why would I have come to you in the hospital, if it was too late?" Alix's eyes were bright and her voice trembled and her words were the most beautiful sounds Thalia had ever heard. "Why would I have brought you here, if it was too late? I've never been able to listen to my head, when it comes to you, and that terrifies me. But I've also never felt so...so alive. So present. So wanted."

Needing to eliminate the space between them, Thalia started to get up, but Alix beat her to it. "No, you stay still." She moved around the table to perch on the arm of Thalia's chair.

"I do want you," Thalia murmured, entwining their fingers together. "But it's gone beyond that. I need you, Alix. I've fallen in love with you. With your generous heart and your scientific mind and your sarcastic wit. I've fallen in love with the way your body moves against mine when we're together—with the way you feel and the way you taste. I've fallen in love with your independence and your strength."

She brought Alix's hand to her mouth and kissed each knuckle in turn. "I love you." Tugging her closer, she murmured it again. "I love you." And just before their lips met, one more time.

"I love you."

❖

Alix lay awake, listening to the cool breeze stir the leaves outside her bedroom window. It was past midnight, and she should have been tired, but every nerve in her body was humming in the kind of anticipation she had not felt in months.

Thalia loves me.

The smile stretched her cheeks, reminding her of the truth: that while they still had plenty to work out, she had been unhappy without Thalia in her life. They should take these next few weeks to focus on laying a strong foundation for their relationship as Thalia continued to heal physically. There would have to be more discussion of the past, but not at the expense of future plans.

She touched one index finger to her lips. They were a little bruised. Thalia's kisses had, for the most part, been gentle. Outside the door to her bedroom, she had ended up with her back to the wall while Thalia braced herself with her good arm and claimed Alix's mouth with a tenderness that belied her hunger. But the hunger had soon gained sway, and Thalia had unbuttoned her shirt most of the way before realizing what she had done.

"Sorry," she had gasped, while frantically doing up the buttons. "Didn't mean for that to happen."

"Don't you dare apologize," Alix had said. And then she had done something rather uncharacteristic, by cupping the back of Thalia's head and kissing her fiercely. She had wanted so very badly to invite Thalia into her room, but on the boat, they had agreed to take this second chance slowly. Pressing their foreheads together as she tried to catch her breath, Alix had traced Thalia's cheekbones with her thumbs.

"Thank you for today," she had said. "Sleep well. Good night." And before she could change her mind, she had slipped into her room.

Was Thalia also lying awake, she wondered. Was she also reliving the day? Was she smiling? Turning onto her side, she watched the moonlight that bathed her floor in silver, filtered by the latticework of her curtains into a pattern that resembled a fine mesh net. Its brilliance wavered as clouds scudded across the sky. The moon was nearly full, and she thought of all the myths and legends and old wives' tales that had to do with the full moon…and then she thought of how these nights were always busiest in the ER, and that perhaps there was some kernel of truth to the idea that it pulled at the blood as it pulled at the tides, the lack of scientific verification notwithstanding.

Her own blood was on fire. She smoothed one hand down her stomach, but was unwilling to go further. She didn't want a release of her own making. She wanted to make love with Thalia—to yield to her touch and feel her surrender in return. She wanted to consummate the reunion they had begun this afternoon.

Skin hot with desire, Alix threw back the covers and stared up into the dark corners of the ceiling. Why was she holding back? Were there any good, legitimate reasons not to put on her robe and slip down the staircase, down the hall, and into Thalia's room, when that was what she wanted? Life was so short and so fragile. Why erect artificial barriers to happiness when there were already so many real ones? As they began to forge a new future together, they would need to talk in more depth about what had happened in the past. But why couldn't those discussions be supplemented by the more intimate conversations they were clearly both craving? That closeness was just as important to their emotional connection.

Suddenly decided, she slipped from the bed, turned on the light, and went to her chest of drawers. There was a pair of silk pajamas somewhere inside it. Her fingers trembled in anticipation as the cool fabric slid against her heated skin. The thought of Thalia easing the silk off her shoulders made her face warm, and a quick glance in the mirror confirmed her blush. She took a step back to survey herself with a critical eye and was pleased with what she saw—the way her short hair feathered across her forehead; the barest hint of her breasts revealed by the V-neck top; the contrast between the dark green silk and her tan skin. Thalia had always told her she was beautiful, and she thought she might actually be starting to believe it.

As she stepped out into the corridor, Alix glanced up at the nearby security camera. It would have caught footage of her passionate embrace with Thalia earlier in the evening. A twinge of anxiety dampened her anticipation as she wondered what the guard on duty had thought then, and what he—or she—must be thinking now. But she couldn't live in fear of her own staff, especially when she wasn't doing anything wrong. She had to remember that. Her relationship with Thalia might appear scandalous to some people, but she couldn't internalize their values and remain sane. Holding her head high, she walked briskly down the hall, determined not to skulk about when she had nothing to be ashamed of.

As she descended the staircase, Alix remembered why Thalia's bedroom was on the bottom floor. She couldn't allow herself to forget Thalia's injury in a moment of passion. She would have to be careful with her ribs and her shoulder, but without seeming to be. She would have to keep Thalia still, but without calling attention to her fragile body. She would have to be in charge of this dance, directing it in subtle ways. Alix smiled tightly at the quick blur of her reflection in a mirror. The promise of such a challenge was more alluring than she had expected.

She knocked lightly on Thalia's door, and then called, "It's Alix," hoping Thalia would give her permission to enter without getting up.

When she heard a faint, "It's open," in reply, she moved quickly inside.

Thalia was half sitting up, half reclining, the blanket clutched to her neck. "Is everything all right?" she asked, clearly worried.

"Yes." Alix sat on the bed and reached out to smooth her fingertips across the ridges of Thalia's cheekbones. "Everything is much better than all right."

She leaned down to claim Thalia's mouth in a firm, purposeful kiss meant to leave no doubt about her intentions.

"Alix?" Thalia asked breathlessly when it finally ended. "What happened to going slowly?"

Alix leaned down until her lips were a mere fraction of a hair's breadth from Thalia's. "I reconsidered," she whispered, and kissed her. Certain that Thalia would be nude beneath the blankets, Alix began to peel them back, but Thalia trapped her hand in place.

"Talk to me," she said, her eyes wide and dark and pleading in the light of her bedside lamp. "Please."

In a moment of clarity, Alix knew exactly what to say. "I love you."

Thalia's breath hitched and her eyes filled. "You…could you say that again?"

Alix's exhilaration fled, to be replaced by an aching tenderness. "I love you, Thalia. I love you. And I will tell you as often as you need."

Thalia smiled tremulously. "I might need you to tell me a lot," she said, her voice thick with unshed tears.

Alix kissed Thalia's forehead. "I love you." She kissed Thalia's lips. "I love you." And then she tugged at the coverlet. "And now, I want to show you."

The barrier fell away to reveal Thalia's wounded body. Mottled bruises spread across her shoulder and torso, fading from purple to green at the edges.

"I'm a mess," Thalia said, watching her reaction.

Alix leaned in to brush the lightest of feathery kisses across each separate mark. "You're beautiful."

"I know you wish I would stop racing—"

"No." Alix shook her head for emphasis. "I'll always be afraid for you, and I'll always want you to take every precaution you can. But racing is your vocation. I love you for your calling, not in spite of it."

When Thalia appeared to be at a loss for words, Alix knew it was the right time for a different kind of communication. Carefully, she settled herself along Thalia's uninjured side and then rested her palm against Thalia's abdomen, delighting in the flicker of muscles that welcomed her touch. "I want you to lie perfectly still, now," she murmured, "or I'm afraid I'll have to stop."

Thalia swallowed noisily and her eyes grew even darker.

"Do you understand?"

"Yes." The word was barely audible.

Alix bent her head but paused when her mouth was an inch above Thalia's. Slowly, she slid her fingers down until they encountered the wet warmth of Thalia's desire.

"I'm going to make love to you now," she whispered. "For the first time." And as she gently slid into the embrace of Thalia's body, Alix sealed the promise with a kiss.

CHAPTER TWENTY-FIVE

All too soon, reality intruded. Thalia wanted to be a visible, supportive presence at the British Grand Prix, as well she should, and she departed from Villa Canella in time to join her team for the practice sessions that preceded qualifying. Still, their first night apart was torturous, and it got Alix thinking about the necessary limits to any relationship that was secret. The secrecy was her own doing, of course, and the facts were clear: if she wanted the right to accompany Thalia to certain events and places, their relationship had to become public.

There was only one person who could truly empathize with her situation—and so it was that Alix found herself requesting a meeting from Princess Sasha to discuss a sensitive personal matter. They could talk over a meal, Alix said. She would buy.

"Oh, well in that case," Sasha teased her, "I'm in."

"You're always welcome in Monaco," Alix said, relieved that Sasha had accepted her invitation. "Or I'm happy to come to you in London."

"Let's split the difference," Sasha said after a moment's consideration. "I know a place in Paris with great food and better privacy."

"Oh?"

"It's called *Oubliette*." Sasha gave her the address. "Dress casual. I'll take care of the reservation. Are you free tonight?"

"Tonight is perfect," Alix said, knowing she would be grateful for the distraction.

After disconnecting, she called her secretary, who would make the necessary travel arrangements. He seemed surprised by Alix's request but didn't hesitate to do her bidding. Camille and Florestan had done these sorts of things before, of course—haring off to Prague or Paris or Reykjavik without any notice, usually to patronize some chic nightclub. But this was the first time Alix had ever flexed her royal muscle in such a way.

When her driver pulled up to the restaurant's address, Alix thought Sasha must have made a mistake. They were in a small backstreet just below Montmartre on a block shared by a Laundromat, a dry cleaner, and an adult video store. Claude bristled and insisted she stay in the car while he investigated. As he got out, Alix peered at the gray door crowned by the right number: 222. It was unmarked except for a small stenciled "O" just beneath the peephole. Perhaps they had the right place after all.

Alix saw Claude's mouth moving and realized he was somehow having a conversation with the people inside. After a few moments, he returned to open her door. "Stay close, please, ma'am," he said, as he shepherded her through the door, holding aside the thick black curtain that obscured its entrance.

Once inside, a bald, clean-shaven man materialized before them with a low bow. When she greeted him, he bowed again but did not speak. He was dressed entirely in white, from his collared shirt to his slacks to his belt to his shoes. Silently, he led them down a short corridor and down a small flight of stairs into a small, recessed chamber with one table in the center. Sasha must have reserved the entire room in order to arrange for a quiet place to talk where their privacy could be maintained.

Alix sat in the chair facing the doorway and examined her surroundings. From her perspective, she was able to witness the comings and goings of the staff, presumably back and forth between the kitchen. All wore white. None of them were speaking. Were they mute by nature or necessity?

An *oubliette*, a forgotten place, was historically a deep and narrow prison cell with sheer walls, its only entrance a hatch at the top of the cell. The ancestor of solitary confinement, it was a place designed to make its captives lose hope. But the atmosphere of the restaurant was mysterious rather than sinister. Tapestries covered most of the walls, depicting abstract patterns woven in muted, earthy colors. A low fountain trickled into a stone basin in one corner, and neatly trimmed bonsai trees filled the other three. Soft electronica played from hidden speakers, providing a rhythm for her thoughts. Protected from the prying eyes of the outside world, attended to by silent staff, she felt safe and contemplative. *Oubliette* wasn't a dungeon, but a space where you could forget external pressures. It was the perfect venue for the conversation she was about to have.

When a blond woman wearing black cargo pants and a gray crewneck top entered the room and moved directly toward her with a smile of recognition, Alix was momentarily taken aback—first by a bolt of attraction and then by panic. Who was this person? But as the woman drew closer, Alix realized with surprise that it was, in fact, Princess Sasha. She stood, and Sasha came around the side of the table to embrace her.

"I should have warned you about the wig," she said by way of greeting.

"It's an effective disguise." Until now, Alix had never felt a visceral response to any woman other than Thalia, and she was disconcerted by her reaction. What did it mean? Shoving the question aside, she took her seat and fell back on politeness, asking Sasha how her travel had been.

"The Chunnel makes everything easy." She smiled. "Kerry decided to come with me—we've both been working like mad and needed a brief escape."

"She's welcome to join us—" Alix began, but Sasha cut her off.

"She's dining with one of her mates from the Rhodes. Besides, I suspect it might be most helpful to keep this particular conversation royal-to-royal."

"You may be right," Alix said, steeling herself for what she was about to say.

But Sasha reached across the table to squeeze her elbow. "You look as though you're preparing to go to war. I'm a friend, and everything you say tonight will be held in confidence." She picked up her menu. "But before either of us speaks another serious syllable, let's order, shall we?"

Relieved that her secret would have a brief stay of execution, Alix focused on her own menu. Sasha was able to recommend several items but sang the praises of the oysters in particular, proclaiming them "as effective as they were delicious" with an accompanying wink. Alix wasn't as naïve as she used to be, and when a quick retort leapt to mind, she decided not to rein it in.

"Would Kerry agree?"

Sasha laughed heartily even as a light blush covered her cheeks. "You're sharp! I'd better watch my step."

After they had ordered, Alix asked her for the latest news from the British court, which Sasha was more than willing to share so long as Alix reciprocated about her own siblings and cousins. When the conversation fell into a lull, Alix took a sip of her cocktail and forced herself to meet Sasha's gaze. This was the moment when she would first come out to another human being. Her hands were shaking, and she folded them in her lap.

"On a more serious note," she began, "I imagine you may have put the puzzle pieces together that the personal matter I wanted to discuss has to do with sexual orientation. Recently, I've been struggling to understand my own." Her mouth was already dry, and she paused to take another sip. "The truth is that for the past several months, I've been in a relationship with Thalia d'Angelis."

"That's fantastic!" Sasha's response was immediate and her delight unfeigned, as far as Alix could tell. "Thalia is wonderful. Insane, but wonderful."

Alix felt her smile mirror Sasha's. "That's her exactly."

Sasha reached across to take her hand. "I'm so very happy for you, Alix. And for her."

It was such a simple declaration—the obvious and correct response to a friend telling you about her new relationship—but Alix didn't take it for granted. Her own family would be shocked and disappointed when she told them, and much of the public would likely mirror that response. Tears pricked Alix's eyes and she blinked quickly in an effort to banish them. As much as she thought Sasha would understand, she would much prefer not to break down.

"Thank you," she managed to say.

"Just because it's wonderful doesn't mean it isn't also stressful. How are you holding up?"

"I'm…" Alix stopped herself from saying that she was fine. "I honestly don't know how I am."

Sasha's expression was empathetic. "And how is Thalia feeling?"

Alix brushed her fingertips across the metal outline of her phone in her pocket. It felt like a talisman, connecting her to Thalia. The last message had been several hours ago—that she had landed safely and was en route to her hotel. The long flight had made her stiff, and she had scheduled a massage. Alix knew massages were part of the routine for any professional athlete, but even so, the thought of someone else's hands roaming all over Thalia's body lit a wholly irrational fire in her brain.

"She's still in some pain," Alix said, not wanting to betray too much, even to Sasha, "but healing steadily and determined to race in Abu Dhabi."

"I'm glad to hear the latter," Sasha said. "And in terms of your relationship?"

Alix remembered the intensity that had shaken Thalia's voice when she had spoken so eloquently of all the ways in which she had fallen in love with her. "We went through a difficult patch earlier this summer. But—and this might sound terrible—when she was injured, everything became much more clear for both of us."

"That doesn't sound terrible. Just human."

They were interrupted by the arrival of their meal, but as soon as the waiter left, Alix picked up the thread of their conversation. "I'm finding it difficult to stomach the cloak-and-dagger antics required to keep this a secret. It's exhausting to live in fear, and I'm starting to seriously consider making some kind of announcement."

A pained look crossed Sasha's face, and Alix wondered whether she was reliving the chaotic time that had followed the world's discovery of her relationship with Kerry. "It's a good idea to be proactive and try to control the narrative at the beginning," Sasha said slowly. "But it will slip out of your hands almost immediately."

Alix didn't like the sound of that, but she knew it was the truth. No matter how she decided to come out—the staging, the media outlet, the clothing, the words—she would have no decision about how their message was received. And the will of the public was capricious. No one knew that better than Sasha. But the public was comprised of strangers who didn't know her. Their disapproval didn't matter the way her own family's would.

"I'm concerned about the public's reaction," Alix said, "but I'm more worried about my family's. There's a reason why Monaco hasn't followed France's example in passing a gay marriage bill. There's a reason why I was the one to attend your wedding, instead of Florestan or Camille."

Sasha's laugh was sharp enough to cut and devoid of humor. "How ironic, since it's where you met Thalia."

"That hasn't escaped me." But Alix couldn't seem to smile. "I've not offended you, have I?"

"Offended me?" Sasha put down her fork and leaned in close. "I'm so glad you were there. I know you're a woman of science and you probably don't believe in coincidence, but I do. The universe put you at our wedding as a deliberate move in whatever chess game it's playing."

"We'll have to agree to disagree there," Alix said lightly, "but I am in your debt for introducing us."

Sasha dismissed that claim with a wave of her hand. "Back to your family. What do you think will be their primary objection?"

Alix had considered this very question repeatedly. "My parents remain devout and conservative Roman Catholics who believe this pope is too liberal, so I think they will object on religious grounds. But more pressing than that, I think, are the objections about scandal and besmirching the family name."

Sasha's eyes narrowed. "Florestan and Camille have both been through scandals, haven't they? I distinctly recall photos of her sunbathing topless on a yacht somewhere. And it's an open secret that he and Monique had a shotgun wedding."

"Ironically, they were angrier about the photos of Camille."

"Ah, the double standard." Sasha raised her glass sardonically, as if to toast it.

"And proof that they react poorly to scandals of a sexual nature," Alix added. No longer hungry, she laid down her fork.

"But this *isn't* a scandal," Sasha said, picking up another oyster. "You and Thalia are dating exclusively, correct?"

"Yes." Alix felt an echo of her old insecurity and mentally shoved it aside.

"Then you're one step away from being an old married couple. What's less scandalous than that?" When she grinned, Alix couldn't help but smile in response.

"If only the rest of the world would see it that way." Her smile faded. "I can't even predict how my siblings will react."

Sasha swirled the last remaining sip of her cocktail in the bottom of her glass. "You can never know how *anyone* will react. In my experience, coming out begets surprises, both positive and negative."

She drained her glass, signaled for a waiter, and ordered what Alix recognized as a ridiculously expensive bottle of champagne. "And forget paying for this meal. It's your coming out party, and I'm buying." She raised one hand to forestall Alix's protests. "There's just one thing more I want to say. You will feel alone, sometimes, despite having Thalia. But you aren't alone. Kerry and I will do everything we can to drum up support for you, if you'll let us."

"Yes, of course," Alix said, tears pricking behind her eyes. "Thank you."

As she was attempting to collect herself, the champagne arrived. Once the waiter had poured it and retreated, leaving them alone again, Sasha raised her glass.

"To you and Thalia and new beginnings," she said. "Love conquers all."

"Love conquers all," Alix murmured, missing Thalia more intensely in that moment than she ever had before.

CHAPTER TWENTY-SIX

Alix had barely slept, but all she felt was anticipation. In a few short hours, she would be off to London to attend the British Grand Prix the next day. She had booked a room at the Savoy but that was only for the sake of appearances. Once Thalia had fulfilled her media obligations, they would return to her flat for the evening.

She smiled in the act of raising her coffee to her lips. The days of their separation had been interminable, and she couldn't wait to hold Thalia again, to feel the lithe strength of her body and hear the soft catch of her breath when they kissed. Would these cravings ever disappear? They were distracting and sometimes downright inconvenient, but now that she knew what it was to love and desire with such intensity, she hoped the emotions never faded.

At the sound of the sliding doors, she turned in surprise. It was just past six in the morning—early even by her father's standards. Yet there he stood, dressed in immaculate tennis whites. His expression was grave, and the nape of her neck prickled in sudden anxiety. Had he found out? The question exploded in her mind, consuming every other thought.

"Hello, Pomme."

As he seated himself across the small table, her mental paralysis thawed just enough to allow a trickle of rational thought. Her secret was making her jump to conclusions. She had to act normally. He could be here to discuss anything.

"Good morning, Father." By some miracle, her tone was light.

"I'm glad I caught you before your departure to London."

Caught you. His words seemed sinister, and she struggled to maintain a poker face. "Oh?"

He leaned forward, intent. "I'm concerned about your relationship with Thalia d'Angelis."

The world dimmed as her vision blurred. She had nothing to be ashamed of—she had to remember that, if nothing else. If this was the moment in which she came out to her father, she wanted it to be defined by courage, not by the terror crawling beneath her skin.

"What is it that concerns you?" Pride filtered through her panic at the steadiness of her voice.

Strangely, her father appeared relieved at her question. He sat back in his chair and sighed. "Pomme, you have a good heart. A trusting heart. I know that Thalia has assisted you with your recent philanthropic efforts, but I want you to be wary of her."

He didn't know. It was all she could think. He didn't know.

"Hear me out," he said, misinterpreting her shock. "She has a terrible temper and a deserved reputation for promiscuity. When you consort with her, going so far as to allow her to be a houseguest..." He shifted in his chair, clearly uncomfortable with the direction his thoughts had taken. "You must consider how that will look to the public."

The anger was a drumroll in the back of her head, and as it filtered through the haze of her adrenaline rush, she latched onto it for strength. "I'm not sure I take your meaning." It was her turn to lean forward, propelled by the momentum of her frustration. "As you said, Thalia has been incredibly generous with her time, resources, and connections. When she was injured, it seemed only right to offer her a place to convalesce. What do you suppose the public will criticize?"

He looked as though he had swallowed something distasteful but didn't want to admit it. "Pomme, she is a...a lesbian. If you continue to associate with her, people might believe you are one as well."

Hysteria bubbled up in her chest, and for one fraught second, Alix wanted to laugh. This could be the instant, she realized. Right here, right now, she could throw out her arms and embrace her identity. *I am.* That was all it would take. No more secrets, no more lies.

But if she took the opening he had inadvertently handed her, the aftermath would be entirely unpredictable. She didn't want everything to spiral out of control—not right away. How had Sasha put it? *It's a good idea to be proactive and try to control the narrative at the beginning.* Yes. That was what she wanted. To come out on her own terms, at a time and place of her choosing, in words she had carefully selected and arranged.

No, she would not come out today. But neither would she sit by and listen to him slander the woman she loved. Thalia deserved so much more than that, especially from her.

"I appreciate your concern, Father, but I don't share it." She met his gaze and held it. "Thalia is a talented athlete who has been obliged by rampant sexism to fight hard for a position she has earned many times over. She may be a controversial public figure, but I know her to be a kind and generous person. We, of all people, understand how capricious the media can be. If its portrayals of our family aren't accurate, why would you assume its portrayal of Thalia is? It would be absurd and cowardly for me to renounce her company simply because some tabloids might find scandal where there is none." She made a show of looking at her watch, then drained her cup and stood. "I need to catch the jet. It's a lovely day for tennis. Enjoy it."

"Pomme." She turned to face him, fearing he had seen through her words to the depth of emotion beneath. "Be careful."

Alix could interpret neither his expression nor his tone. Was that a paternal admonition? Or a threat? Either way, she didn't plan to heed it in a way he would approve of.

"Have you ever known me to be otherwise?"

She walked away briskly, tamping down the atavistic part of her that wanted to run. Once inside the palace, she pulled out her phone... and realized her hand was trembling. She desperately wanted to hear Thalia's voice, but at this hour she would almost certainly wake her, and Thalia needed all the rest she could get as she continued to heal. Besides, her father had just made it abundantly clear that it wasn't safe to speak to Thalia under his roof.

Tonight, they would be together. It was enough. It was more than enough—more than she had ever dreamed. She might not have been searching out love, but now that it had found her, she would be damned before she let anyone frighten her away from happiness.

❖

Once she could afford it, Thalia reflected as they slowly ascended to her floor, she was going to purchase a fancy penthouse with its own elevator. The other residents crowding this one made it impossible for her to slide her arms around Alix and ask her what was the matter. Then she caught sight of Claude, jammed into the back corner, and remembered just how rarely Alix was ever alone.

She had been waiting as planned in the lobby, but her smile had been forced and her embrace all too brief. Had the intervening days opened up a space for regrets or second thoughts?

Thalia felt her stomach sink even as the rest of her body rose. She watched the numbers illuminate, one by one, and latched onto their orderly progress in the face of her panic. She was jumping to conclusions. Alix was here, wasn't she? She wouldn't be here if something in her heart or mind had changed. Unless, of course, she had come to break up.

Her ribs twinged as she took a deep breath. She was being neurotic. Alix had nursed her back to health even *when* they'd been broken up. Whatever was wrong, they would work through it together. She had to believe that.

Despite her silent pep talk, nerves made her fumble with her keys before she finally slotted the right one into the lock. "After you," she said lamely, knowing that Claude would have to inspect her apartment before they could be truly alone.

While he poked around, Thalia gave Alix the tour, such as it was. She traveled so much that her flat was barely lived in. At least that had made it easy to clean. The space was unremarkable except for the shelf full of trophies in the living room, and the balcony, which had a view of the Eye.

"I had a meeting there," Alix murmured. "While you were in Belgium."

A spasm of grief made Thalia's throat tighten. But when Alix reached out to quickly squeeze her hand, relief took its place. That comforting, affectionate touch—Alix wouldn't have bestowed it if she were about to break off their relationship. Right?

"All clear, ma'am." Claude said. "This building is quite secure. I will wait in the lobby."

He didn't look at their joined hands, and Alix made no move to pull away. That was new.

"I won't be returning to the hotel tonight," she said. "And I won't be going out. You should take the evening off. I promise to call you well in advance of when I wish to leave here tomorrow."

Thalia felt her jaw drop, and she quickly closed her mouth. Alix intended to spend the night, and had just said as much to her bodyguard. Relief filtered through her shock at Alix's forthrightness. In the past, she had been worried about the trustworthiness of her staff, and now she was no longer making an effort to hide their relationship?

There was a long pause during which Alix and Claude regarded one another silently. Then, he dipped his head. "Very well, ma'am."

"I appreciate your discretion," Alix said.

"Your Serene Highness," he replied quietly. "I hope you know that you can count on every member of your security detail to protect not only your life but also your privacy." He turned slightly to include Thalia in the conversation. "Have a pleasant evening."

Only as the door closed behind him did Thalia realize she had been holding her breath. When she released it on a long exhale, Alix squeezed her hand again. Thalia wanted nothing more than to crush their bodies together, but she forced herself to wait for Alix to come to her.

"Hi," she murmured instead, trying to saturate the syllable with all the longing she had felt in Alix's absence.

"Hello." Alix looked up at her and smiled. It was an unfettered expression, without any premeditation. Alix was happy because they were together. Pure and simple. The weight of Thalia's doubt fell away.

"You're beautiful," she said, praying Alix would believe her. "I've missed you so much."

Alix finally bridged the space between them, embracing Thalia with a fierceness she hadn't anticipated. Something *had* happened, but as concerned as she was, Thalia refused to mount an interrogation. Instead, she rested one hand on the back of Alix's head and curled the other around her waist, holding her in silence until she was ready.

The seconds ticked into minutes. Gradually, Alix's swift breaths slowed to match the steady pace of Thalia's inhales and exhales. When she finally stirred, Thalia loosened her arms enough to allow Alix to lean back and meet her gaze. Her eyes were bright with suppressed tears, and Thalia could no longer keep a lid on her concern.

"What is it?"

Alix shook her head and freed one hand to wipe at her eyes. "I'm being silly. It's nothing serious."

"Let's sit, and you can tell me."

Once they were side by side on the sofa, thighs touching lightly, Alix began to speak. The longer she spoke, the stronger her voice became—as if by reliving the confrontation with her father, she steadily gained power over the memory. Thalia listened in supportive silence, forcing herself not to react even when she felt defensive.

"His hypocrisy is ridiculous," Alix said. "Our family has been through its fair share of scandals, most of which were embellished by the press. Yet there he sat, believing every piece of slander about you." She rested one palm on Thalia's knee and squeezed lightly. "I tried to show him how absurd he was being, but I don't think he got the message."

"Of course not," Thalia said, unable to keep the bitterness from her voice. "Because then he'd have to admit we're not so different, when all he wants is to paint me as a negative influence." Her indignation abruptly gave way to guilt. "Though if I'm being honest, he does have a point about my bad reputation. I've willingly embraced it—even cultivated it over the years."

Alix went very still. "And now?"

Thalia hadn't intended to blow open the lid on Alix's insecurity, but she could see that was exactly what she had done. "Now I'm finally happy. Because of *you*. From this vantage point, I can look back on my past with clarity." She shifted on the couch and reached for Alix's other hand. "I'm not going to apologize for going out and having a good time when I was single. But I let the fame and the parties and the women become more important than they should have been. I got caught up and started acting a part instead of being myself."

She leaned closer, praying her words were the right ones. "I know what I want now, Alix. I want you. A relationship with you. The chance to change the world with you."

When Alix freed her hands, Thalia experienced a rush of pure terror that she had gone and said the wrong thing, after all. But then Alix's palms were cupping her face, and then she was pulling her close for a soft, lingering kiss. The sweetness of it was an affirmation that filled her chest with warmth. When, several stuttering heartbeats later, Alix pulled away, Thalia couldn't suppress the inarticulate whimper of disappointment that left her mouth.

But Alix didn't go far. She continued to cup Thalia's face, sweeping her thumbs back and forth along her cheekbones, smoothing the puffy skin beneath her eyes from nights of restless sleep. Her expression promised passion and tenderness and resolve, all at once.

"I love you, Thalia," Alix said softly. "I love you. And once your season is finished, I want to be honest with both my family and the rest of the world. Is that also what you want, or—"

Thalia didn't let her finish. She leaned forward to capture Alix's mouth, and without breaking the contact, threw one leg over hers to straddle her where she sat. Thalia kissed her as thoroughly as she knew how, running her fingers through Alix's hair while she feasted. Alix's hands came to her waist, fingertips dipping below her shirt to trace patterns against her skin. She shivered and sat back on her heels, breathing heavily.

"The past few days have been torture. Please let me take you to my bed."

Alix stilled her hands. "I want that," she said. "And I want you. But…after tonight, we need to be more cautious."

Thalia did not like the sound of that. Her ribs twinged as she tensed. "What does that mean?"

"It means we shouldn't see each other again until Abu Dhabi," Alix said. "You need to prepare for the race, and the best way for me to protect *us* right now is not to be seen anywhere near you."

Thalia struggled not to react defensively. She might not like Alix's logic, but she had to hear her out. "How can not being together ever be good for us?" she said, wishing the words had emerged less plaintively.

"Because this is a war we're fighting," Alix said, gazing up at her intently. "A war against everyone who wants to keep us apart. Sometimes, you have to let the enemy think they're winning, when in fact you're staking out a better position."

"And that's what we'll be doing?" Thalia hated the insecurity in her voice, but at least Alix would know just how difficult this was for her.

"Oh yes, my love." Alix traced her thumbs across the ridges of Thalia's abdominal muscles in a way that was entirely distracting. "I'm a Monegasque princess, remember? Centuries before our casinos and racecars, we were masters of military strategy."

CHAPTER TWENTY-SEVEN

Alix stood on the terrace of her family's Presidential Suite at the Yas Viceroy Hotel and looked down at the racetrack. Already swarming with activity as the Yas Marina staff made final preparations for the race, it would soon be the stage on which the Constructors' Championship would be decided. Aiglon Motors would claim the trophy unless one of the Petrol Macedonia drivers finished first and the other finished no lower than third. Yesterday, Thalia had managed to qualify on pole position, while Roderick had come in at P4. Alix couldn't have been more proud. It would be a battle until the very end.

A light breeze tugged at her hair, for which she was thankful. The day was already hot despite the fact that it was not yet ten o'clock in the morning. Her family was brunching on their yacht, and she had told them she would be late, citing a business meeting. She had lied. Again. With each falsehood, Alix felt as though she lost a tiny fragment of her integrity. She had to come out to them, and soon. The longer her subterfuge went on, the more likely it was that she would make a mistake, or that luck would turn against her. If she was going to control the narrative, time was not on her side. But there had been no way to make any kind of statement until after the conclusion of the Formula One season, lest the media uproar distract Thalia from racing.

Thalia. Alix turned her face into the sea-scented breeze, remembering the last night they had spent together—an interminable fortnight ago, on the eve of the British Grand Prix. She remembered Thalia's expression of dismay at her suggestion that they keep their distance from one another until Abu Dhabi—made as much for Thalia's sake as for her own. She remembered kissing away that frown, and she remembered all the other kisses that had followed in her attempt to reassure Thalia that their separation would only be temporary. And she remembered what Thalia said later, as they lay entwined in the bed, each holding the other and being held herself: *I need you.*

"I need you." Her whispered words were caught by the wind and blown out across the expanse of the marina.

In the past, Thalia had said "I want you" and "I love you," but never before that night had she spoken of her need. Alix should have been terrified by the prospect of being so important to another person, but exhilaration buoyed her up beyond the grasp of fear. She had instinctually pulled Thalia even closer, inaugurating a second, less frantic round of lovemaking. And as she slowly teased Thalia into abandon, Alix had put her mouth to Thalia's ear and confessed her own truth.

"I need you too."

She wanted to shout that truth to the world, but the logistics of *how* to do it were still tying her brain into knots. Where should she make her declaration? When? In what language, and with what phrasing? Should she call a press conference from the Prince's Palace? Offer the story to a journalist? Take to social media? She wanted to choose her moment and her medium wisely. Her announcement could change the world in a real, material way for many people. That was a terrible responsibility, but also a gift. She could leave the world better than she found it, simply by proclaiming who she was. And then she could take the next step—to use her wealth and status to campaign on behalf of LGBT rights. Sasha had made a similar move, but her efforts thus far had been focused on the United Kingdom. Alix wanted to extend her reach beyond the European Union, and Rising Sun would be the perfect vehicle for her vision.

"That's a beautiful view. I wish I had a camera."

Alix whirled at the sound of Thalia's voice. Claude must have let her in. Dressed to be incognito, she wore jeans, a plain T-shirt, and her Cardinals cap. Her hands were jammed into her pockets, and she rocked back and forth on her heels in a clear display of eagerness. Even so, she stayed put, waiting to be invited closer. Part of Alix wanted to run to her, but another part wanted to savor the anticipation.

"It's quite a striking perspective, isn't it?" she said, certain her face was belying her reserve. She watched the flicker of muscle in Thalia's forearms and wondered just how long she would suffer the distance between them.

"I wasn't talking about what's outside that window. I was talking about you."

The grittiness of her voice destroyed what was left of Alix's desire to tease. "I missed you so much," she confessed. "Please come here."

Thalia crossed the space between them, trapped Alix between her body and the railing, and kissed her. This wasn't a quick peck to bid her a good morning, but a deep, devouring, soul-stirring kiss that conveyed need and craving and passion.

Alix threaded her arms around Thalia's neck, fitting their bodies together. She loved this—the flame that smoldered quietly at the heart of their relationship, only to flare up at intimate moments like these. She wished there was time to channel that fire—to drag Thalia into her bedroom and claim her all over again. But today, Alix had to let her go. As much as Thalia belonged in her arms, she also belonged on that track. Gentling the kiss, she stroked the nape of Thalia's neck before finally pulling away.

"Good morning."

"I want that every morning," Thalia said. It wasn't an offhand remark or joke. She wasn't smiling or laughing—she was staring down at Alix with the kind of intensity that had marked all of their watershed moments. "The past two weeks have been torture. Move in with me. Into the flat I have now, or one we choose together." She swallowed audibly. "Please say yes."

Alix felt her own smile break free, and in a rush of exhilaration, she rose onto her tiptoes to kiss both corners of Thalia's mouth. The prospect of living together in London was appealing on so many levels, not the least of which was its healthy distance from Monaco and its proximity to their allies in the British royal circle. She wasn't about to give in to cowardice when it came to facing her family, but having a safe space that she and Thalia could call their own would make her feel stronger.

"Yes," she whispered, and joined their lips again.

This time, it was Thalia who eventually pulled back. "I have to go soon. For what it's worth, I don't want to."

A stab of fear brought Alix back to earth. Tamping it down, she cupped Thalia's face in her palms and said what she knew Thalia needed to hear. "Yes, you do. You were born to do this. You love to do this. It's part of who you are, and I love who you are."

Thalia stared into her eyes for a long moment before pulling her close. Beneath her cheek, Alix could feel Thalia's heart beating, strong and steady. Silently, she offered up a prayer for safekeeping.

❖

Thalia furiously blinked back tears as she came out of the hairpin and throttled hard to make the most of the straightaway that followed. At the apex of every corner, her ribs felt as though they were being pulverized from the inside out—and the race was only half over.

"Terrence is three seconds behind you and closing in fast," Carl said into her ear. "Box on the next lap."

Thalia grit her teeth. Her father's decision to start the Ferrari cars on the medium tires instead of the softs—which everyone else had chosen—was proving to be the correct one. Terrence had passed Lucas a few laps ago, and now he had his sights set on her. This would have felt like déjà vu, except that today they were battling for first instead of for sixth.

And because now, she could hear Alix's voice in her head: *You were born to do this. It's part of who you are, and I love who you are.*

Thalia hadn't been born to let all hope of the Constructors' Cup slip away because of a memory and a grudge. She wasn't going to let Terrence rattle her into making a mistake. The persistent pain receded slightly as a fresh surge of adrenaline sharpened her vision and reflexes. She drove as aggressively as she knew how, fighting for every second of daylight even as she prepared for the rapid deceleration of the pit lane.

At the apex of the final turn, as her lungs froze and her vision telescoped, her car unexpectedly lurched toward the inner barricade. Every nerve in her back and chest screamed in agony as she fought to wrestle it off the collision course. Juddering, the car responded sluggishly, but it *did* respond. She missed the barrier by a fraction of an inch and swung back out into the center of the track, gasping for breath as the g-forces eased. The red haze of pain clouded her mind, but instinct demanded she open the throttle. Her car surged forward.

"Can you make it in, Thalia?" Alistair's voice was uncharacteristically agitated.

"Think...so." Speaking against the force of her acceleration required a Herculean effort. What—"

"Terrence made contact. He may have damaged your rear wing."

Thalia's disbelief turned to a white-hot fury that was eclipsed only by her need to get to her mechanics as soon as possible. As she continued to accelerate, the car began to shudder more dramatically. Cursing, she eased off the throttle. At least she wouldn't lose too much time. The entrance to the pit lane was just ahead.

The yellow flag indicator on her dashboard lit up at the same moment that Carl's voice vibrated through her headpiece. "Yellow, yellow, yellow. Terrence spun out and went into the barrier after clipping you."

"Serves him right." Mentally leaving her anger in the dust, she focused on thinking through the repercussions of his actions. Lucas would take the lead. Hopefully, whatever was wrong with her car could be fixed quickly and she would find herself in second place. "Get me back out there, boys," she said as she slipped into place before the garage. "Please."

There was the familiar sensation of rising as the jack lifted the car into the air. But instead of falling just as quickly after the customary whirlwind change of tires, Thalia hung suspended while her team troubleshot the damage. Meanwhile, she prayed. In these fraught moments where every thump of her heart measured the time she would have to make up, she had only a wordless, silent plea to offer up to the universe.

And then, miraculously, she was descending. As her wheels touched the ground, Carl gave her a thumbs-up and jumped out of the way. Thalia roared out of the pit, careful to remain just below the lane's speed limit even as she catalogued the car's behavior. So far, so good: everything seemed tight.

"We replaced the rear wing," Carl said breathlessly. "But there doesn't seem to be any damage to the axle."

"Lucas is now five seconds ahead of you," Alistair chimed in. "And Roderick is three seconds behind."

Thalia wanted to tell them they were the princes of engineering, and that she would buy them all a round of very expensive scotch later.

But she had to save her breath. She refused to lose this race. With Roderick in P3, she could make Petrol Macedonia's Cup dreams come true by overtaking Lucas.

When he pitted on the next lap, she hoped for an error from the Aiglon crew that would work in her favor—but she must have used all her available luck in avoiding more serious damage during the collision. Lucas roared out of the lane four seconds ahead, and she settled in for a long duel to the finish. He was protecting the inside line on every corner as though his life depended on it, and she knew she would have to go outside if she wanted to pass. She also knew that he was forcing her to contemplate the same kind of action that had, a few weeks earlier, resulted in her accident. But that time, the track had been slightly slick and her brakes had been faulty. Today, thanks to the heroic efforts of her team, her car remained competitive. She was *not* going to let Lucas Mountjoy get under her skin or into her head. He had already won the title of world champion. She wouldn't let him have the Constructors' Cup as well.

For lap after lap, she observed how he took each corner—in particular the ones where he seemed to leave the most space. Finally, in the penultimate lap, she made her move. As he braked, she slingshotted around him before decelerating. Her chest was on fire as her newly healed ribs took the brunt of the g-force, but she managed to hold on to the turn and speed away with nothing but daylight before her.

Carl hollered congratulations in her ear, but she didn't dare to smile. Not yet. Not until she saw the checkered flag. She could *feel* Lucas behind her, menacing, testing her resolve at every possible overtaking point. Grimly, she held him off.

The last lap was an eternity, and when she finally crossed the line, her first sensation was that of tears trickling down her face. The exultation from the engineers made her smile in joy through her relief, and when the news came in that Roderick had successfully defended P3, she extended her hand to flash a thumbs-up to the crowd as she began her victory lap.

"That was for you, Peter," she whispered, before opening her mic to congratulate the team.

Later, on the podium, she echoed that sentiment in public. "I'd like to dedicate my victory to Peter Taggart," she proclaimed to the crowd, which roared its approval back to her, "one of the finest human beings I know, and one of the most talented drivers in the history of this sport. I miss him every day."

Once, she glimpsed Alix in the crowd below, and the princess dared to blow her a kiss before the sea of people once again blocked her from view. Everything was a whirlwind: the post race interview led directly into the press conference, and then Petrol Macedonia wanted to parade her in front of a few of their most influential sponsors. By the time Thalia had finished with her on-track obligations, it was nearly time to leave for the Onyx Salon.

She ducked back into the garage to collect her personal effects, only to laugh in delight as Alix poked her head out from between the curtains that cordoned off the medical bay and gestured that she should join her. Once inside, Alix stepped into her arms.

"You were brilliant," she said fiercely, enclosing her in a tight embrace.

For one blissful moment of respite, Thalia rested her cheek on Alix's hair. "I love you."

"And I love you." With obvious reluctance, Alix stepped back. "I know it's time to go. But I just wanted to tell you...when we're back in London, I want to find an opportunity to come out publicly as a couple."

"You do?" They had discussed the prospect of being open about their relationship several times, but never with a timetable.

"Yes." Alix cupped her face and kissed her lightly on the mouth. "No more sneaking around. No more lying, even by omission. I want to tell the world who I really am. And I want to tell them I love you."

EPILOGUE

A lix sat on the king-sized bed, waiting for Thalia to finish primping in the bathroom and reflecting on how glad she was to have a reason to make new memories at the Savoy Hotel. Her previous visit here had been on the day of Peter's death. It was fitting, then, that today they would celebrate his life's work and establish one branch of his legacy by officially founding a scholarship to Eton for disadvantaged boys in his name. An extension on the school's gymnasium had also been commissioned with Petrol Macedonia's funding and would be named in his honor. The team principals were all present, and both Lord Rufford and Thalia would be delivering speeches at the luncheon that had been prepared so many flights below where they now stood.

She and Thalia had also decided that this would be their first public event as a couple. They would arrive together, hand in hand, as though their relationship was the most natural and normal thing in the world. Because it was. And when the inevitable barrage of invasive questions was fired, they would refuse to answer. Alix had already lined up an exclusive interview for the next day with a reporter recommended by Sasha. The world—her family included—could stew in its juices for twenty-four hours and reflect on the ethics of their obsession with public figures' private lives. Alix was nervous, certainly, but not paralyzed by anxiety. It would be a relief to stop looking over her shoulder. She did worry that her parents would feel betrayed. All she could hope was that one day, they would come to understand that her sexuality wasn't a scandal, and that she would have been much more forthcoming with them had they given any indication they might be tolerant.

The bathroom door opened and Thalia emerged, banishing Alix's moment of melancholy. She was stunning in the emerald, floor-length gown she had selected for the occasion. Alix had chosen to wear a charcoal pantsuit, and she smiled at the realization that their respective choice in clothing had shifted dramatically from their first meeting at Sasha and Kerry's wedding. When Alix thought of how much more comfortable she felt now in her own skin, she could hardly remember the woman she had been before Thalia.

"You look beautiful," she said.

"Pot, kettle." Thalia held out her hand, and when Alix stood, she pulled her close for a lingering kiss. Finally, she pulled away just enough to press their foreheads together. "Last chance," she said, a note of trepidation in her voice. "It's really fine if you don't want to do this today. You can stay here and I'll rejoin you after the event. It will turn into a madhouse, you know—lots of camera bulbs going off, and plenty of inappropriate questions." Her mouth compressed into a line. "Though I hope they hold back for the sake of Peter's memory."

Alix appreciated the opportunity to change her mind, but she also needed Thalia to know that wasn't going to happen. "The only place I want be is up at the podium, celebrating and supporting this very important moment with you."

Thalia's answering smile was brilliant. "Then shall we?"

Hand in hand, they stepped out into the hall.

About the Author

Nell Stark is an award-winning author of lesbian romance. In 2013, *The Princess Affair* was a Lambda Literary finalist in the romance category, and in 2010, *everafter* (with Trinity Tam) won a Goldie award in the paranormal romance category. In addition to the everafter series, she has published four standalone romances: *Running With the Wind*, *Homecoming*, *The Princess Affair*, and *All In*.

By day, Nell is a professor of English at a college in the SUNY system. With their son and two dogs, she and Trinity live a stone's throw from the historic Stonewall Inn in New York City.

Books Available From Bold Strokes Books

Illicit Artifacts by Stevie Mikayne. Her foster mother's death cracked open a secret world Jil never wanted to see...and now she has to pick up the stolen pieces. (978-1-62639-472-8)

Pathfinder by Gun Brooke. Heading for their new homeworld, Exodus's chief engineer Adina Vantressa and nurse Briar Lindemay carry game-changing secrets that may well cause them to lose everything when disaster strikes. (978-1-62639-444-5)

Prescription for Love by Radclyffe. Dr. Flannery Rivers finds herself attracted to the new ER chief, city girl Abigail Remy, and the incendiary mix of city and country, fire and ice, tradition and change is combustible. (978-1-62639-570-1)

Ready or Not by Melissa Brayden. Uptight Mallory Spencer finds relinquishing control to bartender Hope Sanders too tall an order in fast-paced New York City. (978-1-62639-443-8)

Summer Passion by MJ Williamz. Women loving women is forbidden in 1946 Hollywood, yet Jean and Maggie strive to keep their love alive and away from prying eyes. (978-1-62639-540-4)

The Princess and the Prix by Nell Stark. "Ugly duckling" Princess Alix of Monaco was resigned to loneliness until she met racecar driver Thalia d'Angelis. (978-1-62639-474-2)

Winter's Harbor by Aurora Rey. Lia Brooks isn't looking for love in Provincetown, but when she discovers chocolate croissants and pastry chef Alex McKinnon, her winter retreat quickly starts heating up. (978-1-62639-498-8)

The Time Before Now by Missouri Vaun. Vivian flees a disastrous affair, embarking on an epic, transformative journey to escape her past, until destiny introduces her to Ida, who helps her rediscover trust, love, and hope. (978-1-62639-446-9)

Twisted Whispers by Sheri Lewis Wohl. Betrayal, lies, and secrets— whispers of a friend lost to darkness. Can a reluctant psychic set things right or will an evil soul destroy those she loves? (978-1-62639-439-1)

The Courage to Try by C.A. Popovich. Finding love is worth getting past the fear of trying. (978-1-62639-528-2)

Break Point by Yolanda Wallace. In a world readying for war, can love find a way? (978-1-62639-568-8)

Countdown by Julie Cannon. Can two strong-willed, powerful women overcome their differences to save the lives of seven others and begin a life they never imagined together? (978-1-62639-471-1)

Keep Hold by Michelle Grubb. Claire knew some things should be left alone and some rules should never be broken, but the most forbidden, well, they are the most tempting. (978-1-62639-502-2)

Deadly Medicine by Jaime Maddox. Dr. Ward Thrasher's life is in turmoil. Her partner Jess left her, and her job puts her in the path of a murderous physician who has Jess in his sights. (978-1-62639-424-7)

New Beginnings by KC Richardson. Can the connection and attraction between Jordan Roberts and Kirsten Murphy be enough for Jordan to trust Kirsten with her heart? (978-1-62639-450-6)

Officer Down by Erin Dutton. Can two women who've made careers out of being there for others in crisis find the strength to need each other? (978-1-62639-423-0)

Reasonable Doubt by Carsen Taite. Just when Sarah and Ellery think they've left dangerous careers behind, a new case sets them—and their hearts—on a collision course. (978-1-62639-442-1)

Tarnished Gold by Ann Aptaker. Cantor Gold must outsmart the Law, outrun New York's dockside gangsters, outplay a shady art dealer, his lover, and a beautiful curator, and stay out of a killer's gun sights. (978-1-62639-426-1)

White Horse in Winter by Franci McMahon. Love between two women collides with the inner poison of a closeted horse trainer in the green hills of Vermont. (978-1-62639-429-2)

Autumn Spring by Shelley Thrasher. Can Bree and Linda, two women in the autumn of their lives, put their hearts first and find the love they've never dared seize? (978-1-62639-365-3)

The Renegade by Amy Dunne. Post-apocalyptic survivors Alex and Evelyn secretly find love while held captive by a deranged cult, but when their relationship is discovered, they must fight for their freedom—or die trying. (978-1-62639-427-8)

Thrall by Barbara Ann Wright. Four women in a warrior society must work together to lift an insidious curse while caught between their own desires, the will of their peoples, and an ancient evil. (978-1-62639-437-7)

The Chameleon's Tale by Andrea Bramhall. Two old friends must work through a web of lies and deceit to find themselves again, but in the search they discover far more than they ever went looking for. (978-1-62639-363-9)

Side Effects by VK Powell. Detective Jordan Bishop and Dr. Neela Sahjani must decide if it's easier to trust someone with your heart or your life as they face threatening protestors, corrupt politicians, and their increasing attraction. (978-1-62639-364-6)

Warm November by Kathleen Knowles. What do you do if the one woman you want is the only one you can't have? (978-1-62639-366-0)

In Every Cloud by Tina Michele. When Bree finally leaves her shattered life behind, is she strong enough to salvage the remaining pieces of her heart and find the place where it truly fits? (978-1-62639-413-1)

Rise of the Gorgon by Tanai Walker. When independent Internet journalist Elle Pharell goes to Kuwait to investigate a veteran's mysterious suicide, she hires Cassandra Hunt, an interpreter with a covert agenda. (978-1-62639-367-7)

Crossed by Meredith Doench. Agent Luce Hansen returns home to catch a killer and risks everything to revisit the unsolved murder of her first girlfriend and confront the demons of her youth. (978-1-62639-361-5)

Making a Comeback by Julie Blair. Music and love take center stage when jazz pianist Liz Randall tries to make a comeback with the help of her reclusive, blind neighbor, Jac Winters. (978-1-62639-357-8)

Soul Unique by Gun Brooke. Self-proclaimed cynic Greer Landon falls for Hayden Rowe's paintings and the young woman shortly after, but will Hayden, who lives with Asperger syndrome, trust her and reciprocate her feelings? (978-1-62639-358-5)

The Price of Honor by Radclyffe. Honor and duty are not always black and white—and when self-styled patriots take up arms against the government, the price of honor may be a life. (978-1-62639-359-2)

Mounting Evidence by Karis Walsh. Lieutenant Abigail Hargrove and her mounted police unit need to solve a murder and protect wetland biologist Kira Lovell during the Washington State Fair. (978-1-62639-343-1)

Threads of the Heart by Jeannie Levig. Maggie and Addison Rae-McInnis share a love and a life, but are the threads that bind them together strong enough to withstand Addison's restlessness and the seductive Victoria Fontaine? (978-1-62639-410-0)

Sheltered Love by MJ Williamz. Boone Fairway and Grey Dawson—two women touched by abuse—overcome their pasts to find happiness in each other. (978-1-62639-362-2)

Death's Doorway by Crin Claxton. Helping the dead can be deadly: Tony may be listening to the dead, but she needs to learn to listen to the living. (978-1-62639-354-7)

Searching for Celia by Elizabeth Ridley. As American spy novelist Dayle Salvesen investigates the mysterious disappearance of her ex-lover, Celia, in London, she begins questioning how well she knew Celia—and how well she knows herself. (978-1-62639-356-1).

Hardwired by C.P. Rowlands. Award-winning teacher Clary Stone and Leefe Ellis, manager of the homeless shelter for small children, stand together in a part of Clary's hometown that she never knew existed. (978-1-62639-351-6)

The Muse by Meghan O'Brien. Erotica author Kate McMannis struggles with writer's block until a gorgeous muse entices her into a world of fantasy sex and inadvertent romance. (978-1-62639-223-6)